The Bookbinder's Daughter

Jane Glatt

The Bookbinder's Daughter

Jane Glatt

TYCHE BOOKS LTD.

The Bookbinder's Daughter
Published by Tyche Books Ltd.
www.TycheBooks.com

Copyright © 2016 Jane Glatt
First Tyche Books Ltd Edition 2016

Print ISBN: 978-1-928025-63-4
Ebook ISBN: 978-1-928025-64-1

Cover Art by Niken Anindita
Cover Layout by Lucia Starkey
Interior Layout by Ryah Deines
Editorial by Karley Hauser

Author photograph: Eugene Choi
Echo1 Photography

This book was funded in part by a grant from the Alberta Media Fund.

For the many long discussions – accompanied by wine, of course – thanks to Sandra/Cassandra/Alexandra.

Thanks also to the crew at Tyche Books – especially my editor Karley Hauser and publisher Margaret Curelas.

Chapter One

FAELIN LED THE way down the narrow, steep staircase. Her woollen skirt brushed against the wooden walls as she stepped from the stairs into the low-ceilinged passageway.

"This way," she said as she hurried past the narrow door that led to the binding room—what she thought of as her workroom—to her father's room at the end of the narrow hall.

"Papa," she called. She rapped on the door, the hollow sound muffled in the tight space. "Conjurer Hewitt has come for his book." She waited a minute but there was no sound from the other side of the door, so she knocked again. "Papa!"

She looked behind at her companion, Conjurer Horace Hewitt. "It should be ready," Faelin said. "I know the pages were bound last week. Papa just needed to finish tooling the leather cover."

"Papa!" She pounded on the door. "Are you in there?" She jiggled the handle.

The door was locked, as usual. Over the years, her father had become increasingly guarded about anyone seeing the inside of his workroom, and now he locked the door whether he was inside or not. Faelin couldn't remember the last time she'd been in the room.

"Is there another way in?" Conjurer Hewitt asked. He brushed one oversized hand across his forehead. "Could he have left? Perhaps he has a delivery?"

"No," Fae replied. She was really worried now. Her father was in his workroom—he was *always* in his workroom. "Deliveries come to the book bindery." She pointed to the door they'd passed. "The stairs down to the river are accessed through that room."

"Papa!" Fae wrenched at the door, frantically trying to pull it open. "Papa!" She turned to the conjurer. "Something's wrong!" Her eyes darted to the door. "He's in there, I know it. Could you . . ." She paused, knowing that she had no right to ask this of him, to ask him to use magic to open the door. She stared at his hands, almost twice the size they should be, before her eyes dropped to his feet. The leather of his shoes was already stretched tight. She looked back up and met his eyes.

"Could you open the door?" she asked softly.

Conjurer Hewitt met her gaze and nodded. "I need new shoes anyway," he said. "And it's a small spell, one I know by memory. Stand aside, please."

Anxious, Fae edged past the conjurer, apologizing when she stepped on one of his immense feet. She stood a few paces behind him, fretfully watching his back.

Conjurer Hewitt bowed his head and muttered something under his breath. The door shuddered and the handle rattled. Fae heard the sound of the lock turning, and then Hewitt pushed the door open.

"Master Keetley," the conjurer called. "Lachlan. Are you there? Oh!"

"What is it?" Fae called as she pushed past the conjurer into her father's workroom. The small windows let in enough daylight for Fae to see two books lying side by side on the worktable.

"Papa?" The large table crowded the room, leaving barely enough space to walk around it. Various tools hung on hooks on the far wall and other than the two books, the table was bare. Where was her father?

Hewitt shuffled into the room behind her, forcing Fae to move around the table. She heard a rasping breath and she craned her neck to look. There, under the table!

"Papa!" She crawled over to kneel beside him. His face was red and when he opened his eyes, he looked right past her.

"Fae," her father croaked. "Sorry . . ."

"Papa?" Fae dragged him out from under the table and pulled his head onto her lap. His skin was damp and clammy, and one hand clutched at the fabric of his shirt, right over his heart.

"Should have told . . ." His whisper ended in a gasp for breath.

"Shhh," Fae said, frantic. "Just rest. Don't try to say anything."

"Lachlan?"

Hewitt hovered above her, a worried look on his face.

"Dying . . ." her father whispered. "Need to tell . . ."

"Shhh," Fae crooned. "You're going to be fine. You just need to rest." He had to be fine—he had to. "Conjurer, can you help him?" She looked back at Hewitt. "We'll pay you whatever you want, whatever we have, if you can save him." Her father was dying—he knew it and so did she. Hewitt was her only hope, her only chance. He could do it, couldn't he? Heal? Her father had told her that one conjurer had, years ago. But it was at such a terrible cost.

When he was just a child, her father had seen a Sherston conjurer save a man. An accident on the bridge right outside the Sherston house had left a man from across the sea hurt so badly they all knew he would die. But he was rich—rich enough to pay his weight in gold—except the Sherston had asked for *more* than gold. If he was going to lose his sight, he'd said, the man would have to lose a son. The deal was struck and the man lived. The last thing the Sherston conjurer ever saw was the face of the man he saved, and the son was handed over to him as an apprentice. That boy was the current Sherston conjurer.

"I have a spell that might help," Hewitt said. "But I don't know it by heart, and I don't think there's time for me to go home and get it."

"Is it in your book?" Fae asked. "The new one Papa was working on? It's there, on the table." Her father gasped and Fae cradled his head. "Stay," she whispered. "Don't leave."

"Hmph," Hewitt muttered. "The spell is not in this book." He held out a book with one large hand. "Nor in this one." In his other hand he held another book. Both books had the same grey leather binding.

"How long will it take to get the right book?" Fae asked. Her father was dying. Hewitt had to save him. She looked down at her father. His lips were turning blue and his breathing was shallow, his chest barely rising on each indrawn breath.

"Too long," her father gasped. "I have to tell you . . ."

"It's not too long," Fae said. She felt the warmth of tears as they tracked down her face. She brushed one away before it could fall onto her father's face.

"It is," Hewitt said. When he leaned over her she smelled the onions he'd eaten for lunch.

"It's not!" Fae said. "You just don't want to. You don't want to pay the price." She wiped another tear from her face and met her father's clear-eyed gaze.

"No," her father whispered. "I won't pay his price."

"What do you mean?" Fae asked, but her father had closed his eyes. She turned to Hewitt. "What does he mean?" she demanded.

"It's an old argument," Hewitt said as he straightened. "I've offered any spell your father could wish for, but he's never been willing to agree to my terms." He looked down at her.

"I'll pay," Fae said. "Whatever it is, I'll pay."

"Ah, I finally have an agreement and yet I have nothing to bargain with." He shook his head. "I am sorry. It really *is* too late."

Fae smoothed a hand across her father's clammy forehead. His breathing was ragged when he looked up at her.

"Need to tell you," her father whispered. "Need to tell . . ." His voice trailed off and Fae hugged him to her.

"Papa," she begged. "Don't leave me."

"*Geedcenne deanboc boc*," her father said into her ear. "*Geedcenne deanboc boc*," he repeated.

"What is it?" Fae asked. She loosened her grip on him in order to look into his eyes but they were closed. She felt his body shudder and then he went limp in her arms.

"No!" she cried. "Papa, Papa!" Fae gently set him back down on the floor and put her ear to his chest. No heartbeat! She sprawled over him, sobbing. After a few moments, she felt a hand on her back. Conjurer Hewitt. She straightened up, roughly brushing her tears away.

"I am truly sorry, Faelin," Hewitt said softly. "I will report his death."

"Thank you," Fae said, grateful that she would at least be

spared having to see Conjurer Wailes. He was the oldest of the seven conjurers, and he had used the most magic. His body was so twisted that he could no longer stand, and he had a servant—a simpleton—carry him about. His current servant, Tymm, licked his lips and leered at Fae whenever their paths crossed.

Fae looked back down at her father. In death, his face looked slack and foreign, not like her father at all. She fussed with his clothing and put his hand at his side, straightening his shirt a little.

"Hmph," Hewitt cleared his throat.

Dazed, Fae looked up at him. She'd thought he'd left to inform Conjurer Wailes.

"We must tidy up before others enter this room," Hewitt said.

Fae grabbed the edge of the table and pulled herself to her feet. She glanced around the almost empty workroom before her gaze settled on the two books Hewitt still held. She peered at them more closely.

They were both bound in seal skin, Hewitt's binding. She'd finished binding the book last week before handing it to her father for embossing. But she'd given him one book and now there were two. She reached a hand out and trailed it over the cover of first one and then the other. They were identical. How could that be? There should only be one book. She met Hewitt's gaze.

"How are there two books?" she asked. She wanted to say that she'd only bound one, but couldn't, since binding books was a man's trade.

"The spell," Hewitt said.

"You used a spell?" Fae asked, confused. "To copy the book?" But he'd entered the room after her and she'd clearly seen both books on the table.

"No, your father's spell," Hewitt replied. "The one he told you just before . . ."

"What he said to me—that was a spell?" Fae was shocked. Her father couldn't read. Conjurers never would have let him near their books of spells if they thought he could read. So how did he even know a spell? And why?

"Don't worry," Hewitt said. "I didn't hear it clearly—just enough to know that it's a spell." He hefted the two books. "I believe it creates a duplicate book." He set the books down and opened them both, flipping through pages randomly. "Both books seem to contain all my spells." He let the books fall closed and looked up at her. "We cannot let the others know about this." He glanced around the room. "And I need to know if there are copies of other books. Where would he have kept them?"

"Where would he . . ." Fae trailed off as what Conjurer Hewitt said sank in. Her father had a *spell* that copied books. Hewitt was right, there was no way Lachlan Keetley would have used that spell only this once. Fae looked around her father's workroom. There were no shelves, no doors leading to another room—no place to hide books.

"I don't know," she said to Hewitt. "He spent all of his time in here."

Hewitt shuffled over to the small window and peered out. Fae didn't have to look to know what he saw—it would be identical to the view from her workroom window. It faced south, towards the mouth of the Aberhayle. At this time of day the tide was in: the river would be flowing high along its banks and the marshes would be flooded.

"Who lives on this side of you?" Hewitt gestured to the stone wall that held a few hanging tools.

"That's Pullen the baker," Fae said. "The ovens are behind the wall. In the winter Papa enjoys—enjoyed—the warmth." Her voice caught in her throat. Her father was dead.

"And the bindery," Hewitt said, either ignoring or not noticing her grief. "I'll need to look there as well."

"Of course." With one last, desolate glance at her father's body, Fae led the way out of the room and down the hall.

The book bindery was as tidy as her father's workroom, although there were more tools hanging on the walls and a long low shelf stretched below the window. Stacks of hides lined the shelves, sorted by type—and who they were destined for. The top shelf closest to the door held sealskin for Conjurer Hewitt. Next to it was Conjurer Wailes' sharkskin. Every shelf held a different hide to bind each of the seven conjurers' spell books.

Hewitt trailed a hand along the shelves until he stood at the far wall, in front of the small door that was inset into the stone blocks. He rapped one large knuckle on the door.

"And the stairs are here?"

"Yes. They go down to the river," Fae replied. "They're shared with the fishmonger next door."

"And no other rooms down here?"

"No. There's the kitchen and living room on the main level and two rooms above that where we sleep. I'll show you."

All Fae wanted to do was curl up and grieve the death of her father. Instead, she led Conjurer Hewitt on a tour through her home. It didn't take long; like all houses on the bridge it was small.

On the main level, the same as the workrooms, the windows faced downriver—south—and no room was deeper than ten feet. But upstairs each room had two windows—one facing south and the other facing north, looking across the narrow span of the cobbled street to their neighbour's second level. It wasn't much of a view, but cross breezes were welcome on warm nights.

Hewitt went over every inch of her father's bedroom, tapping the stone walls, looking in the cabinet, even lifting the mattress from the bed frame. He then watched while Fae opened her small cupboard and the trunk that stood at the foot of her bed.

Finally, Conjurer Hewitt seemed to accept that there was no hoard of hidden books to be found anywhere in the small house. He tucked his two identical spell books into his robe, and Fae let him out the front door.

"I'll have someone come over," Hewitt said. "For your father."

"Thank you," Fae replied. She went to close the door but Hewitt held a hand out.

"They're there somewhere," he said. "Don't let anyone else look too hard. I'll come back when I have a chance."

Then he was gone. Fae shut the door and was alone with her grief.

She couldn't face waiting in the dark, cramped lower level with the body of her father. She needed to feel the sun on her face and look out over the river. She ran up the stairs to her room and leaned out of the bridge side window in time to see Hewitt shuffle down the street to his own house. He was probably going to hide his books before contacting Conjurer Wailes about her father. Conjurers always kept their spells from each other—having two identical books wouldn't change that.

Fae stepped away from the window and suppressed a sob. She had to think, clear her head. People would come soon, people who would force her to make decisions.

She crossed the room to the other window and opened the casement as wide as she could. She pulled the trunk over, climbed up on it and stepped onto the window ledge. Grasping the top of the window, she wedged her shoe into the corner where the gently sloping roof met the wood of the window frame. In moments she had climbed up to her perch, her feet jammed against the top of the window. She sighed and closed her eyes, letting the tears track down her face.

Her papa was dead. She sucked in a shaky breath. And no matter how much she wanted to simply mourn him, she couldn't—they wouldn't let her.

She looked out to where the Aberhayle River met the Dark Sea. The tide was going out and the marsh was slowly being exposed. Soon the Rivermen would be out, gathering the fish that would be stranded in the deep trenches that had been dug in the soft mud of the marsh.

Would Aric be there? He'd promised her that the next shark they caught would be hers. She was low on shark skin—there was barely enough to bind a small book if Conjurer Quillan Wailes asked.

Not that it would matter anymore. Without her father there was no bookbindery. As a woman she wasn't allowed to have a trade, nor was she allowed to inherit the home that had been in her family for generations. A wind blew in from the sea and she closed her eyes, feeling the cool damp of tears on her face. What would she do? Where would she go?

For so many years it had just been her and her father. She'd stopped worrying about her place, and that she could never inherit from her father, because he'd promised so many times that there was a way for her to stay, to take up the family trade of bookbinding, to stay in the only home she'd ever known. Now she feared that while her father may have truly believed what he'd said, he'd lost touch with reality.

Because today she knew that there was no way for her to stay. And she had nowhere else to go.

She looked east, to Durnham. Her mother's family lived there, but would they help the child born to their estranged relative? A child they'd only seen once? And did Fae want the life they would offer? She had inherited her dark hair and height from her mother's family but that was all she had in common with them.

Besides, she wanted what she had here—a trade, a home, a friend or two. She wouldn't get that with strangers, though they may share the same blood.

She stared back out towards the sea.

Geedcenne deanboc boc. Her father's words echoed over and over in her mind.

A spell! What was her father doing with a spell? Had one of the conjurers traded it to him for some favour? Fae shook her head. The conjurers guarded their spells so jealously that she couldn't imagine any of them giving one away. And her father couldn't read. The conjurers would never have left their spell books with him if he'd been able to read—they wouldn't have left them if they'd known that *she* could read. So he hadn't simply stumbled across it. And why tell her? Why were her father's last words to her a spell?

Fae sighed and dropped her head onto her chest. She would never know. Her father was dead. The wind gusted, bringing the salty tang of the sea with it. A few gulls screeched as they circled high above the marsh.

Fae took a deep breath and closed her eyes for a moment, trying to soak in the calm. She had to go down. Hewitt would have informed Conjurer Wailes by now. They would come for her father and to sort out her situation. She crawled back down and through the window, pausing at the mirror that hung on her wall to smooth a hand across her dark, shoulder-length hair. She heard the sounds of a cart stopping outside but instead of leaning out the other window to look, she hurried down the stairs. She was waiting at the door by the time the first knock sounded.

FAE TRIED TO keep her eyes on Conjurer Wailes and ignore his servant, Tymm, who licked his lips as he stared at her from the corner he'd been relegated to. Horace Hewitt sat beside Conjurer Wailes.

"Your father's passing is a shock to us all, my dear," Wailes said. He was propped up in a chair, his twisted body perched sideways to allow his head to face her. He held a soft rope in one hand, and the other end had been fastened to a chair leg and looped over the back of the chair. Every few minutes he started to lose his balance and had to tug on the rope to stay upright.

"Yes, Conjurer," Fae replied. They'd removed her father's

body half an hour ago—she'd heard the rattle of the cart as it took him across the road to Conjurers Hall. The day after tomorrow, Quillan Wailes, as Head Conjurer, would conduct the memorial service.

"It's really a shame your father left no male heir," Wailes said. "Now we've no one to bind our spells into books." He frowned at her. "Very irresponsible of him, really. Generations of Keetleys have been binding books on the bridge and now here we are without one." His eyes narrowed. "Who inherits?"

"I don't know," Fae said. "My mother's family, I suppose."

"No, no," Wailes said. "That won't do. The bridge belongs to the Conjurers. We have final say about who lives here." He turned to Hewitt. "We'll need to find another bookbinder. There must be someone in the towns."

"I will search both Durnham and Waglenn Landing tomorrow for the best bookbinder," Hewitt replied.

"Make sure you find one who is unmarried," Wailes said. "We must preserve the tradition."

"Tradition?" Fae asked. "What tradition?"

"The tradition of your family, of course," Wailes replied. "Of Keetley bookbinders."

He smiled at her, but she saw no warmth in his eyes.

"Keetleys have been binding books on this bridge for as far back as our histories go," Wailes continued. "I will not have that tradition broken during my time as Head Conjurer." He paused. "Though it is not common practice, he must take the Keetley name so that a son will be a true Keetley bookbinder."

Fae felt cold all over. "Whose son?" she asked quietly, even though she knew the answer.

"Why yours, of course," Wailes said. "Yours and whatever bookbinder Hewitt finds tomorrow." He nodded at Tymm, who lumbered over to him. At a signal from Wailes, the large man began untying the rope.

Panicked, Fae clenched her hands into fists. She wouldn't marry a stranger, she wouldn't. "Conjurer Wailes," she said. "Conjurer Wailes!" she repeated more loudly.

The conjurer looked at her, and then waved a hand and Tymm backed off a step.

"Yes, Faelin," Wailes said.

"I have a confession," Fae said. She looked down at the floor.

She'd promised her father that she would never tell, especially not a conjurer. But it was the only thing she could think of that could prevent her from being forced to marry a stranger.

"Since I was fifteen I've been doing all the bookbinding." She looked up into the surprised face of Wailes. "My father was only interested in tooling the leather covers. I've bought and cured all of the leathers and skins and bound every single book for over five years. You don't need to find a bookbinder in one of the towns. I have the skills."

After a moment, Wailes smiled widely. "That's even better. I didn't like the idea of moving an outsider onto the bridge. Hewitt," he turned to the other conjurer. "There must be a Bridger who'd be willing to marry Faelin. He wouldn't even have to change trades. She would do all the bindery work, at least until they have a son grown and trained." He turned back to Fae. "It seems your father wasn't quite as irresponsible as I'd accused him of being. That's settled. Tymm!" He tucked his head into his shoulder as his servant reached out and picked him up.

Stunned, Fae sat where she was as Tymm carried Wailes out the door.

Hewitt paused and touched her shoulder. "It will work out, Faelin," he said before he followed the others out.

HEWITT CLOSED THE door and trailed Tymm and Wailes to Conjurers Hall. His shoe stubbed against the lintel as he stepped through the doorway and he sucked in a breath. The spell he'd recited earlier to unlock the door had made his feet tender and swollen. Wailes' sharp eyes peered at him over Tymm's arm and Hewitt ducked his head. It always took him a few days to get used to larger feet. And he really should see about new shoes.

Tymm gently lowered Wailes into a specially built chair and the head conjurer twisted his body into position and swivelled his head around to look at Hewitt.

"I think Shiv has a son," Wailes said. "See if he's available to marry the bookbinder's daughter."

"Yes, Conjurer," Hewitt replied, suppressing a shudder. He found Wailes' pet Bridgers repulsive. They were mean and brutally violent and worse—totally loyal to Wailes. Hewitt was a dozen years younger than Quillan Wailes and had known him all of his life, but he'd never understood the power Wailes had over the Bridgers. Especially Shiv.

Wailes picked a sheaf of paper up off the desk in front of him and Hewitt understood that he'd been dismissed—again. He backed out of the room and headed out onto the bridge. He would have to visit Shiv of course, Wailes would find out if he didn't, but he didn't have to go tonight. There were things he needed to do.

Nothing on the bridge was very far away, and a few moments later Hewitt stepped through his own door. By choice, his quarters were small. As a conjurer he could have chosen a larger house—sometimes he thought he should have—but this one suited him. He'd moved here as soon as the Hewitt who had trained him had died. It had belonged to a Wailes years ago, before a Wailes had become Head Conjurer and moved into the hall.

Some of his fellow conjurers felt that a larger house made them more powerful, but Hewitt didn't. His authority came from being a conjurer, not the size of his home. Not that he could do more than simple tricks, like unlocking doors. Oh, he pretended to have spells that were worth something: just as he'd implied to Faelin that he could save her father. The reality was that he had little magic.

And he did prefer his simple set of rooms—a bedchamber, a tiny kitchen and sitting area, and his large study, where he spent most of his time.

Right now, though, his small house meant he had few places to hide the duplicated books. He didn't expect anyone to visit any time soon but he couldn't allow the others to know Lachlan Keetley's secret.

Hewitt headed upstairs to his bedchamber. It was a small room with a single window that looked upriver, past the docks for the towns and the steep cliffs, to where the river snaked out of view. Though it was unlikely that anyone was watching, he closed the shutters before bending down beside his bed. He pulled the two books out from underneath the wool-filled mattress, where he'd hidden them earlier, and placed them side by side on the bed.

He brushed a large hand across each cover, feeling the ridges and bumps where Lachlan Keetley had tooled the sealskin leather. At least, he'd worked the binding of one of the books— the other had been copied using magic.

"What other secrets did you have, my friend," Hewitt whispered. And Lachlan *had* been a friend. One of the few men Hewitt could say that about, despite refusing his offer so many times. Perhaps Faelin would now be willing to accept his terms?

Hewitt sighed and picked up the two books. He'd put them with the rest, in his bookcase. Books anywhere else would be far too conspicuous if anyone did come into his home. Besides, he had dozens more that looked much the same as these. They even contained the same spells. You would have to open them up and compare each page before you'd be able to tell that they were identical.

Chapter Two

FAE DROPPED HER head into her hands. Horace Hewitt had said that it would all work out, but how? If she did what Wailes wanted she would be able to stay on the bridge and bind books, but she would be forced to marry a Bridger.

They were loud and stupid and violent, and she knew they drank themselves into stupors. Then they would fight—each other, their women, any passing stranger unlucky enough to catch their attention. She wouldn't survive marriage to one of them.

Fae took a deep, shaky breath and sat up straight. She would refuse, that's what she would do. The conjurers wanted her talents; they wouldn't get them if she was unhappy—she shuddered—or dead.

She got up and walked over to the front door. It had been so long since the lock had been used that she had to jiggle it in order to loosen it enough to turn, but eventually she heard it click. She tugged once to make sure the door was locked.

She'd refuse to marry anyone the conjurers selected. They could order her to leave her house—leave the bridge—they had that right. But they *could not* force her to marry someone against her will.

She headed downstairs, her stomach in knots. She hadn't been off the bridge very often and it had mostly been on the river with Aric. How could she survive somewhere else?

Nervously, she walked into her father's workroom. As far as she could see, nothing was out of place, but there was so little in the room to start with.

Avoiding the spot on the floor where her father had died, she skirted the worktable and headed to the far end of the room. Various metal tools for embossing leather hung on the wall. She trailed a finger across them and they clattered against each other as they swung on their hooks.

She placed a hand flat on the wall behind the tools. It was still slightly warm, despite the evening hour. Pullen would have banked the fire in his oven for the night: in a few hours he'd rise to start his early morning baking. She passed her hand across the stones. There were no breaks or cracks that could signify a hidden cabinet or door.

What had her father done with the books he'd copied? There were more, she was sure of it. And they had to be here: in the last few years her father had barely left this room. She stepped away from the wall, surprised by another thought.

When she was nine, her mother died. Since then her father had grown increasingly preoccupied and guarded. Had using the copy spell caused her father's mind to slowly cloud? Is that why he never remarried? Why she never had a sibling?

Growing up, she and the other children of bridge merchants had teased each other with whispered stories about the conjurers. And sometimes a Bridger child would try to impress the rest of them with their knowledge.

Bridgers worked for the conjurers. They collected the tolls for those wanting to cross over and under the bridge. They worked the pulleys that raised and lowered the iron grills that blocked the river passageways between the stone arches of the bridge. They knew conjurers better than anyone else on the bridge.

And one time a Bridger child had claimed that magic made the conjurers unable to father children. It was another consequence of using magic, he'd said, like the deformities they all suffered.

Fae had only heard it mentioned that once, but in the years since, she'd often wondered about it. Conjurers never married— their apprentices were always chosen from amongst the children on the bridge. The apprentices inherited everything from the conjurer. Last name, position, house, spells—*and* the type of deformity caused by using magic.

She sighed. Was using magic the reason why her parents had no other children? Was it why her father had become increasingly reclusive? She would never know. But if he had been using magic all these years, if he had been copying books, he would have kept every single one.

Fae stared at the wall. It was the only one in the room that didn't lead to another part of the house, or to the outside. She shook her head. There was no trace of any opening on the wall. Besides, she'd been to the bakery—she *knew* that the oven was on the other side of the wall. She could feel the heat from it. There was no hidden shelf full of spell books in this wall.

She shrugged and wandered over to the window. A few lights dotted the river and she wondered if Aric was out in his boat tonight. She hadn't seen him for a few weeks—another Riverman had been bringing the catch to sell to the fishmonger. She needed to tell him about her father, talk to him about what she should do. He would have some ideas, he always did.

She stepped back from the window and looked down at the floor—at the place where her father had died. She frowned. What had he been doing on this side of the table?

When she and Horace Hewitt had entered the room, the two books had been on the side of the table closest to the door. She had to assume that's where her father had stood when he'd duplicated the book she'd bound. So why was he on the floor on this side of the table?

Fae bent down and passed a hand across the floor. The wooden planks were worn smooth from years of feet shuffling back and forth. She reached further under the table.

"Ow!" She snatched her hand back. Something had pricked her. She peered at her hand; a small splinter poked out of one finger. She pulled it out and a tiny drop of blood welled up. Wiping the blood on her skirt, she crouched down with her chin on the floor. There! A foot under the table she could see a darkened spot and a small gouge in the wood of the floor. She reached out and feathered her fingers across the floor. The wood was rough and more splinters jabbed at her.

Fae slid further under the table. In the dim light she could see an indented line cutting across the wooden planks, the edge slightly darker than the rest of the floor. She dug her fingernails under the edge and sucked in a breath.

The indent was smooth from use and just deep enough for her to get her fingertips under the edge of it. She tugged upward and a square section of the floor lifted up.

When she'd lifted the section of floorboards up a few inches, she shimmied closer and peered in. Iron steps spiralled down and a well-used lamp sat on the second step, but it was too dark to see anything beyond a few steps.

Fae lifted the section of flooring higher, trying to allow more light into the space, but the wood slipped from her fingers and the floor crashed back into place. She dragged a hand across her brow. She wasn't sure she wanted to see what was down there. Spell books her father had copied, no doubt, but what else?

She checked to make sure the section of floor was back in place and crawled out from under the table. Leaning against the wall below the window, she sat staring at the floor that covered the stairs—just a few inches from where her father had died.

Now she knew what he'd been doing on this side of the table. He'd been opening the trap door so he could hide the copied spell book. Had he struggled to get it closed before he was found? Is that what had caused his death? The effort to close the trap door, to keep this secret?

If she'd walked in with Conjurer Hewitt and found the entrance uncovered there would have been no way to hide it. She hugged her arms to her chest and shivered.

And if she was right, and her father had copies of every spell book he'd ever bound, Hewitt would have helped her keep the secret. Not because he cared for her or her father, but because he would have wanted all the other conjurers' spell books for himself. And she thought he would do just about anything to get them.

Conjurers were always combining the spells they had into new collections—that was why they had to have so many spell books bound. Five or six books each, every year—for seven conjurers and three apprentices. A spell another conjurer was willing to trade could complete a collection, so Hewitt had told her father, and require a new book. It hadn't sounded like they used them much, these spells from other conjurers, but there was always the hope that a new spell would somehow reverse their deformities.

What if Hewitt thought a spell hidden below would make him normal? Or allow him to use magic without increasing his deformities? He would do anything to have—and keep—them for himself. All of the conjurers would do the same if they found out about these books. There would be a war—a conjurer war. They would fight amongst themselves at first, but soon enough they would involve everyone on the bridge. Conjurer Wailes already had the Bridgers working for him—what would he allow them to do in war? No one on the bridge would be safe.

She couldn't tell anyone on the bridge about this—she didn't trust anyone enough. She glanced up at the tools that hung on the wall. Could she permanently seal the trap door? Cover it so that no one could get in? The books would still be there though. She felt a chill. If she didn't marry someone the conjurers approved of, she'd be forced to leave the bridge. Someone new could find the books.

Fae got to her feet. She had to talk to Aric. He would help her decide what to do.

After making sure the door to her father's workroom was locked, she hurried down the hallway. The lamp she carried cast an eerie glow on the bindery as she passed through it. She threw the bolt and tugged open the door to the outside.

She didn't use the stairs at night very often. They were narrow and crumbled in places. The fishmonger had replaced the rope handrail recently and it glowed in the lamplight. She gripped it tightly as she carefully made her way down towards the river.

Halfway down, she paused to look up at the bridge. The stairs were perched on the wall of the centre abutment: the two largest arches of the bridge looped towards shore in both directions. Where she stood, the abutment narrowed to a fifteen foot width. The book bindery was where the abutment was the widest, at almost thirty feet across. The windows of the two workrooms were well above the lower edge of the span, allowing plenty of room for another level. That's where the trap door led. How long ago had the secret room been built? And how many spell books were hidden?

Fae turned to look out over the water. A single light shone—a lone boat was out on the river. The light swung from side to side— once, twice, three times. Fae sighed in relief and swung her own lamp in response. It was Aric. He'd seen her light and was coming to meet her.

She hurried down the steep stairs, her head down as she concentrated on her footing.

In low tide a pier was exposed. Its footing allowed a landing for the fishmonger to unload fish bought from Rivermen like Aric. But the tide was in now and the water lapped at the stone of the abutment. Fae waited on the lowest step above the water, clutching the rope in one hand and her lamp in the other. The other light steadily approached and soon she could see the back of Aric's head as he bent over his oars.

They'd first met years ago on a night much like this. Fae had been ten and Aric a year older. Fae had been daring herself to climb down the steps at night for weeks, scaring herself with tales of sea monsters and sharks that circled the pier at the base of the abutment. Even now she wasn't sure if she had really wanted to see anything.

Instead her lamp had drawn Aric, a young Riverman night fishing alone. Later he'd told her that he'd been curious. He'd come close enough to see her—a girl around his own age, standing on the stairs. He'd been wondering if she was planning on jumping—if she would become one of the bodies the Rivermen found. He'd seen one pulled out of the marsh a few weeks earlier and thought that if he found one himself, he could maybe secure a finder's fee. Instead, he'd found an inquisitive girl who just wanted to see the river at night.

Fae shivered. People travelling across the bridge at night sometimes went missing. Conjurer Wailes said they jumped; although, there were only a few places to jump *from*. Fae was sure others were thrown. The Bridgers kept a tally of everything that crossed the bridge—everything had a cost—and it seemed to her that every year more people than goods failed to reach the other side.

Since it belonged to the conjurers, the laws of Cleebrock did not apply to the bridge. The seven families had created the bridge, according to history, and Wailes didn't care if those not of the bridge lived or died. But if Rivermen could recover the bodies, families could grieve.

Aric said that some finder's fees were more than a man could earn fishing in a year, so there was always a race to recover a body.

"Fae."

At the sound of her name, Fae looked up. Aric was silhouetted by the light of his lamp, which swayed from where it hung off a hook on his boat.

"Jump in," Aric said. He reached out a hand, the webbing between his fingers translucent in the lamplight.

She grabbed his hand and stepped into the stern of the small wooden boat. The odour of fish and seaweed and the sea assaulted her. She sat down quickly, dropping Aric's hand to clutch the worn wood of the seat underneath her. Carefully, she leaned over and secured her lamp on the hook beside Aric's.

"My father is dead." Fae's chest constricted as she spoke.

Aric looked up from the oars in alarm. "Fae, I'm so sorry," he said softly. "When?"

"Today." Had it only been one day? Fae closed her eyes. This morning, just as they'd done on many other mornings, she and her father had shared a warm loaf of bread before he'd headed to his workroom. But not tomorrow. Tomorrow her life would be different—it already *was* different. But tomorrow she'd start to learn exactly how.

Aric shook his head and frowned as he shifted the oars, preparing to row. "I'll just get us away from the bridge," he said.

Fae watched him bend and straighten as he rowed them towards the mouth of the river. Maybe she should just keep going, she thought. Ask Aric to help her find a ship and sail away to another country. Let someone find the spell books, let the conjurers fight over them—let the bridge be destroyed. What did it matter to her? Her whole world had changed. Why shouldn't everyone else's?

Aric pulled the oars into the boat, carefully laying them against the gunwale. "Hang on," he said. "I'm just going to throw the nets so we don't drift so much."

Fae shifted her legs to one side as Aric grabbed the fishing nets and started to feed them over the edge. The current pushed the boat along and the nets trailed behind them. Once the nets were out he wiped his hands on his trousers and sat facing her.

"The nets should keep us here a while," he said. "And we should be far enough from the bridge that our voices won't carry." He reached out and took her hands in his. "Now tell me."

Fae took a shuddering breath in and exhaled slowly. "We found him in his workroom," she started. "Conjurer Hewitt was with me."

As always, when she mentioned a conjurer, Aric frowned. The Rivermen didn't trust the conjurers. Aric wouldn't tell her why, said that it was a secret, so she assumed it was something big, something that affected *all* Rivermen.

"He used magic to unlock the door. Papa was on the floor," Fae said. She closed her eyes and gripped Aric's hands tighter. "Dying. He . . . he whispered something to me before he died." She opened her eyes and looked at Aric. "It was a spell, Hewitt said. My father used his last breath to tell me a spell."

"Sweet Berhalla," Aric swore. "A spell for what?"

"To copy books," Fae said. "There were two on the work table—they were identical. I bound only one and yet there were two. Papa was using magic to copy the conjurers' spell books."

"He was copying books?" Aric asked, and Fae nodded. "Did you find more?"

"No—at least not when Conjurer Hewitt was there." She paused and glanced around. The night was quiet and dark. In the distance she could see the lights of the bridge and the towns on either bank—but there were no other lights on the water. "We looked everywhere and didn't find anything. But I went back," Fae lowered her voice. "Later, after they'd taken Papa—after everyone had gone. I went back to his workroom." She met Aric's clear gaze. "And there's a trap door under the table. I didn't go down, but Aric, my house sits right on top of the widest part of the abutment. If Papa has been copying books all his life, there will be hundreds of them." She didn't say what she was really worried about: that her father's last words were his legacy, and that he was the last in a long line of bookbinders who had copied every spell book they had ever bound.

"Who else knows?" Aric asked.

"About the trap door, just us. About the copied book—Horace Hewitt."

"Will he tell the others?" Aric leaned in closer, his voice barely audible.

"I don't think so," Fae said. "He'll want the books for himself. They'll *all* want the books to themselves."

"You'll have to look," Aric said.

"Can you come with me?" Fae asked. "If you were to attend Papa's final ceremony you could come back to the house and look."

"Of course," Aric said. "I'll tie up at the pier and come up when it's time."

"Thank you," Fae said, relieved. At one time Aric had been a regular visitor to the bookbinder's house; his presence for her father's final ceremony shouldn't raise any eyebrows.

"Conjurer Wailes wants me to wed," Fae blurted.

"What? Who?" Aric's grip tightened painfully on her hands, and Fae looked down to hide her wince.

"Anybody really," Fae said. She looked up and met his eyes. "Once I told him I was the one doing all the binding he really didn't care." She looked away from him to hide her despair. "Hewitt was charged with finding an unmarried Bridger."

"A Bridger! You can't marry a Bridger," Aric said. He dropped her hands and stared past her towards the bridge. "They're sharks, predators."

"I won't marry one," Fae said. Something in her voice must have caused him to look at her. "I'm hoping that they want my bindery skills enough to let me alone, but they could rescind my permission to live on the bridge."

"Would they do that? Your family has been there as long as any of the conjurers."

"I don't know," Fae said. She sighed and reached for one of Aric's hands. She'd once hoped Aric would marry her; would he reconsider now that she had so few choices? With the stairs they could easily manage life on both the water and the bridge.

"I told you before," Aric said quietly. "It's impossible."

"Then I have to hope they let me stay," she continued. "Perhaps I'll be able to convince Conjurer Wailes that I can continue binding until the day I do meet a man I'm partial to." She paused. "It's a risk, but I can't marry a Bridger. I *won't* marry a Bridger."

"That's settled then," Aric said. He gave her hands a squeeze then rose to his feet. "I'll just get these nets in and take you home."

Fae sat quietly while Aric pulled in the nets. A few dozen fish flopped in the bottom of the boat by the time the nets were once again bundled at her feet. Aric slipped the oars into the oarlocks and soon they were at the stairs.

The tide was going out now, and the stair she stepped on was wet and slippery.

"Put a light in the window if you need me," Aric said as he helped her out of the boat. "And expect me before the ceremony." He looked up the abutment. "I'll find out when from the fishmonger."

She nodded, gripped the rope railing, and took the lamp he handed her. After one single backward glance, she carefully climbed the steep stairs to her workroom and her first night alone in the house.

ARIC WATCHED FAE'S lamp bob and flicker as she climbed up to her home. He sucked in a ragged breath and ran a hand over his forehead. Why did he have to let her face this alone? Why couldn't *he* marry her? She didn't have a good option, he knew it, yet he couldn't help her, not if she wanted to stay on the bridge. And from what she'd said, it sounded like Wailes would only let her stay if she married.

He slipped the oars into place and pulled them through the water, sending his boat skimming away from the base of the bridge. He'd marry her if he could—if it was possible—and live with her amongst the Bridgers and Conjurers. He snorted. His mother would never forgive him—all Rivermen hated the Conjurers although she hated them more than the rest—but he would do that for Fae. Except it wasn't possible. The curse made it impossible.

Once he reached the middle of the river, he stopped rowing. The tide was almost out. He should see if the receding water had trapped anything in the marsh, but he had no appetite for more fishing tonight. His mother would be angry at him for his small catch but when had she ever not been? She'd been angry ever since he could remember—since he was born—or maybe since *she* was born.

To the Rivermen, their shaman was a physical representation of Dea Berhalla, the goddess of the river. The goddess gave them everything—food, water, and a place to build their homes. Even though shamans were born into their talents, Aric often wondered at the wisdom of having the angriest person in their village interpreting their history and counselling the elders.

He drifted awhile, staring upriver at the bridge. Lights flickered along it—Bridgers on patrol, no doubt. Fae couldn't marry one of them—he'd *make* her leave before that happened. He'd bring her to the Riverman village, despite his mother's wishes, to protect her.

He'd seen the bodies of those the Bridgers had tossed into the river. Faces beaten bloody and bones and skulls shattered. Bridgers claimed—and Conjurers supported them—that the injuries had been caused by the fall, that despairing men jumped alive and whole, and that heads were cracked by hitting the bridge on the way down, and bones were broken by the impact of the water.

But the bridge didn't slice a man's neck, and the water didn't make his skin bubble and blister. Aric didn't know what the men had done to incur the Bridgers' wrath, but they hurt them. And if Fae married one he might hurt *her*. Aric *would not* let that happen.

He was still no closer to an answer when the sky lightened. He rubbed his eyes and headed towards the mouth of the river. His decision was made for him: it was too late to fish the marshes. He'd head home and get some sleep.

Chapter Three

Despite her late night on the river with Aric, Fae was up early. She sat in her father's bedroom and waited for the day to start, trying not to dwell on her limited options. A knock on the front door startled her. She raked a hand through her hair and smoothed her skirt as she descended to the front door.

"Faelin," Hewitt said when she opened the door. "I apologize for the early hour but I need to talk to you." He stepped inside and she led him into the small living space.

Fae headed for the small stove. A hand on it told her it was stone cold—the fire neglected in her grief yesterday.

"Sorry, I cannot make tea," she said. "Can I get you anything else? Water? Or something to eat?" Too late she realized that she had only stale bread left from yesterday's breakfast—her last meal eaten with her father. She closed her eyes and willed the tears away. She could not afford to be weak, especially in front of a conjurer.

"Thank you, Faelin, but no," Hewitt said. "Please, sit down. We must talk."

Nervously, Fae sat on the small stuffed chair that had always been hers. Hewitt's large hands looked foreign as they clutched the rolled arms of her father's chair.

"You know Conjurer Wailes tasked me with finding a Bridger for you to marry," Hewitt said. "It's not a request I can refuse, though I think it's not what you want."

Fae looked up and met Hewitt's eyes. "I won't marry a Bridger," she said. "And Conjurer Wailes can't make me."

"He *can* ban you from the bridge," Hewitt said.

"That's his right," Fae said. "Unless the rest of you disagree." She didn't expect them to—conjurers always agreed with each other, at least in public. But who knew what went on in Conjurers Hall? "But you will all lose your bookbinder."

"Yes," Hewitt said. "And you'll lose your home."

A cart rattled along the roadway, reminding Fae that life— *ordinary life*—was happening just outside her home. But for her, an ordinary life was in the past.

"Perhaps it's for the best," Fae said. "I can't inherit nor can I ply a trade. With Papa gone, there's nothing for me on the bridge anyway." She hoped he believed her. She desperately wanted to stay on the bridge and live the only life she'd ever known. Would the conjurers be more likely to let her do that if they thought she didn't care? If they thought she had another option?

"I can offer you a life on the bridge," Hewitt said. "One that even Quillan Wailes cannot prohibit. I can make you my apprentice."

"Your apprentice?" Fae was stunned. Never in her life had she thought to become a conjurer. "But I'm a woman!"

"Yes," Hewitt replied. "But you're also *of* the bridge. Your family has been here as long as any of the conjurers have—longer, because your bloodline is intact, while ours . . ." He lifted his oversized hands. "We bear the names of the first conjurers but none of us carry the blood."

"Could you do it? Would the rest of the conjurers allow it?" Conjurers had always been men—everyone of import had always been a man. "That's what my father wouldn't trade, isn't it?" she whispered. "Me as your apprentice for any spell he wanted."

"Yes," Hewitt agreed. "I've been asking him for the past three years." He looked at her with narrowed eyes. "I always assumed it was because he didn't want you to have a trade. If I'd known that you were binding the books I might have pushed him harder."

"You're sure you would be able to choose me as your

apprentice?" Fae asked. It would be a way to stay on the bridge, but at what price? "Would Conjurer Wailes allow it?" And did she want it? She eyed Hewitt's hands and feet. Would a woman suffer the same effects as a man or would some new, worse, deformity strike her?

"Yes," Hewitt said. "The selection of an apprentice is personal and cannot be contested by anyone, even the Head Conjurer." He paused. "There must be complete trust for an apprentice."

"Because as you . . . become more infirm they look after you," Fae said softly. She'd often wondered why some conjurers didn't have an apprentice. But this was someone who could eventually hold your life in their hands. Conjurers had no families—when someone became an apprentice, all ties were cut in case relatives expected spells to help them, spells that caused great harm to the conjurer.

"Yes," Hewitt agreed. "An apprentice becomes much more than a student, they become family."

"And since I now have none, I would be an even better candidate. There would be no possibility of divided loyalties." Fae closed her eyes, wishing her father had talked to her about this. He'd had so many secrets.

"And now that I know about your father, I think you are an even better choice," Hewitt said. "He used magic. We can never know how long ago he started, but I checked his body carefully. There were no physical deformities." He leaned towards her, excited. "I think that you may be the same—fewer deformities would mean you can wield more powerful spells without harm to yourself. You could live twice, maybe three times as many years as any other conjurer."

He smiled and Fae had to stop herself from flinching at the feverish look in his eyes.

"You could eventually become Head Conjurer!" he continued. "Imagine! A woman and a Hewitt—Head Conjurer."

"No!" Even Fae was startled at the vehemence in her voice. "It is not the life my father wanted for me. I'd rather be barred from the bridge than go against my father's last wishes."

"But he would agree now," Hewitt said. "I'm sure he would."

"No." Fae shook her head. "My father knew he was dying and he still said no. So do I."

"Then I cannot help you," Hewitt said. He gripped the arms of the chair as he got up. "Your father's ceremony is tomorrow. Bring something heavy that he owned to Conjurers Hall by the end of the day."

Fae remained seated as Hewitt shuffled out of the room. Without Hewitt's help the conjurers would not side against Wailes. She would have to leave the bridge. She dropped her head into her hands. And go where?

The morning passed quickly. Word of her father's death travelled and neighbours dropped by to give their condolences. By early afternoon the last visitor had left, and an exhausted Fae deposited another fish pie onto the table in the kitchen.

Someone had managed to get the fire in the stove going and there was a pot of tea warming on top. She poured some into a mug and sat down in her father's chair.

She had to see him. Today, before they . . . prepared his body, she had to see him. Papa was in Conjurers Hall, where everyone who died on the bridge was laid out. The only time Fae had been there was when her mother had died. She didn't remember much, only that her mother had looked pale and fragile. The table she'd lain on had been only a few feet from the furnace, and nine-year-old Fae had been horrified that her mother would be burned in there.

Since then she'd come to realize that being reduced to ashes was fitting for those who lived on the bridge. On land the dead were buried, and on the water the Rivermen took their dead out to the open sea, weighted down so they would sink. But those who lived on the bridge were of the land and sea, as well as the sky. Some of their ashes were scattered to the winds, some were sprinkled onto the stones of the square and the rest was bundled with a tool or prized possession and thrown into the river.

Fae finished her tea. She had to find something of her father's to take him down into the river, something that wouldn't let him surface, ever. It should be something from his workroom; something that represented his life's work.

The key to her father's workroom was on the cabinet near the stove. Fae found a piece of twine, looped it through the key and tied the ends together. It was the only key and she couldn't afford to lose it, or have someone else take it. Not with whatever secrets below her father's workroom that the locked door guarded.

Hewitt couldn't force her to become his apprentice any more

than Wailes could force her to marry a Bridger. But why hadn't her father even discussed Hewitt's offer with her? Did he think she would have accepted? Would she have?

Fae stopped in front of the door to her father's workroom. She wouldn't have, not without his approval. That's why she'd turned Hewitt down now. It wasn't what her father had wanted for her. Maybe Papa had been worried that she would talk him into giving in to Hewitt? Or had he simply thought that she had a better choice? She had, at least as long as her father was alive. Did his death change that? No. She was not going to accept Hewitt; although, she would have liked to know her father's reasons for refusing.

She unlocked the door and entered the quiet workroom. After relocking the door, she slipped the twine over her head. The metal of the key felt cool against her skin when she tucked it under her shirt. She went to stand in front of the stamping instruments that hung along the wall.

She picked up the largest tool. Made of iron, it was used to stamp leather and would be heavy enough. She flipped the end up to see what the image was and a sad smile crossed her lips. The bottom of the stamp was shaped like a crescent moon. It was an image the conjurers liked to have on their books—and since her father had been a conjurer of sorts, it was fitting.

Deliberately ignoring the far side of the table and the trap door underneath it, Fae exited the workroom, making certain the door was locked.

She sat in the small living room until the sun had set and she could barely see the unlit lamp. With a sigh, she stood up. She couldn't put it off any longer. It was time to visit her father.

CONJURERS HALL WAS across the road, opposite the fishmonger's, but it was very different from the rest of the buildings on the bridge.

A long, narrow building, the smooth, white marble it was constructed of made the river stone used for the rest of the bridge look dirty and rough in comparison. The mountains that rose above Waglenn Landing had provided the marble, but the huge slabs used to construct the hall had been transported and set in place using magic, so her mother had told her.

The marble glowed in the pale moonlight and the wood of the

door looked black in contrast. Carvings surrounded the door—a repeating wave design with crescent moons placed above. Fae lifted a hand and knocked. A moment later the door opened and Conjurer Sherston blinked out at her.

"Faelin Keetley," he said. "You are expected."

He stepped aside and Fae entered. The hallway was dimly lit by one small lamp that was set high up on the wall. Conjurer Sherston shielded his eyes from the light as he led Fae left, along a narrow hall. He stopped at a whitewashed door and gestured to her. Fae walked past him to the door and started to open it. She turned to ask Sherston a question but he had already retreated down the hallway. When she opened the door, she understood why.

The room was ablaze. Lamps crowded each other on small tables and rows of them lined the walls. After the near-dark of the bridge and the hallway, Fae had to squint against the brightness. Conjurer Sherston—with his sensitivity to light—would find it painful to be in this room.

When her eyes finally adjusted to the light, Fae saw her father.

He had been laid out on a table that ran the length of the room. He was wrapped in white cloth that covered everything except his face. She bent over him and placed the iron stamping tool she'd brought on his chest.

Oh Papa, what am I supposed to do? A tear fell onto her father's shoulder and Fae straightened, roughly wiping at her eyes. A single chair was beside him, and she sat down and leaned her head against the table he rested on.

He hadn't meant to die, she knew that, but part of her couldn't help being angry that he had—and even angrier that he'd left her with mysteries and no options. How could he have done that to her?

She wished he'd never spoken that spell, she wished she hadn't been with Conjurer Hewitt—but mostly she wished Papa hadn't died and left her all alone.

Fae wanted her old life back. Her father had been distracted and had spent most of his time in his workroom, but she'd been safe. Now she wasn't sure she'd ever feel safe again.

Her father should have lived another twenty, even thirty years. She should have had his protection for all those years. Had he planned on telling the conjurers that *Fae* was the bookbinder, that *Fae* was the skilled craftsman? If they'd had years to become accustomed to it would they have allowed her to continue once her father died of old age? Is that what her father had hoped would happen?

Now it was too late. Her father was dead and there was no chance for anyone to get used to a woman bookbinder. She'd told Wailes that she was the one doing the work and all he could think about was how to get a man back into the trade. Why should Fae do all the work and let a man—someone not even of her choosing—reap the rewards? If she married she'd be less than she was now—would have fewer rights than she had at this moment.

She lifted her head off the table and stared into her father's face, trying to find something, anything, that would tell her what she should do.

Fae sighed. She only knew what he *hadn't* wanted her to do. He hadn't wanted her to become Hewitt's apprentice. But would that be so horrible? As his apprentice she would have to do Hewitt's bidding—and Wailes' as well once she became a full conjurer. She wouldn't be allowed to bind books, something that she loved and excelled at. And she would have to practice magic and become disfigured from it.

She'd seen the way the apprentices were used. Their masters forced them to recite spells so that their own deformities didn't worsen. Thorpe Wailes had been used the most cruelly.

Three years ago, when he'd been selected to become Quillan Wailes' apprentice, Thorpe had been a robust young man close to Fae's age. The third son of the baker, he'd been used to steady labour, hefting sacks of flour and grain around the bakery. Now the poor man's twisted legs barely held him. But Quillan Wailes' deformities hadn't changed much in that time—he'd made Thorpe cast all the spells. Spells sold to people with nothing better to do than wish for success, or a few more years of beauty or bad luck for their enemies. Thorpe's life was being used up piece by piece by people with petty wants and the money to buy spells.

If that had been Fae she would have been furious. It was a surprise no apprentice had ever killed their master, if that was the regard they held for them.

No wonder her father hadn't wanted that life for her.

"Faelin."

Fae looked up. Horace Hewitt stood in the doorway.

"It's time to say goodbye," Hewitt said. "We need to prepare him for the ceremony." He took a step closer. "Ah, I see you've brought one of his tools." He picked it up. "This should be heavy enough." He turned the tool over in his hand and glanced at the stamp. A smile flitted across his lips. "And appropriate." He pocketed the tool and turned. "I'll give you a few more minutes."

Hewitt left the room but Fae could sense him out in the hallway, hovering. She didn't need more time anyway. She leaned over her father and kissed his cheek. His skin was cool and papery to the touch, and he smelled slightly of lavender.

"Goodbye, Papa," she whispered.

Fae brushed past Hewitt on her way out and blinked away tears as she left Conjurers Hall and crossed the road to the square.

The square was the only section of the bridge not lined with houses. She leaned against the stone wall and peered upriver. Lights lined the docks on either side of the river and reflected on the water. The Waglenn Landing dock was bigger—the town itself was bigger and had better commerce than Durnham, so said Mistress Charnock, the fishmonger's wife, although Fae had little knowledge of the trade that allowed the towns to survive.

A few lights bobbed upriver; Rivermen fishing, no doubt. Their catch would be sold to the towns, not the bridge, although a few times a year one of them had the skins she needed—eel for Sherston and turtle for Dabel. Not that she'd need those skins again; she wouldn't be binding any more spell books.

The cool wind ruffled her hair and plucked at her skirt; Fae wrapped her arms tight around herself and yawned. She should go to bed. She'd slept little last night and she'd need energy to get through the ceremony tomorrow. She looked back at Conjurers Hall. Had her father already been *prepared*—reduced to ash and placed in a silk sack?

She sighed again and headed home. The sign out front needed new paint—not that anyone on the bridge needed the sign. Only outsiders, people from the towns or sailors and merchants from ships, would need a sign to find the bookbinder.

And no one from across the sea had ever come into the shop. Did they even have bookbinders? Did they allow women to learn and work a trade, or would every place require her to have a man?

She reached her house and quickly unlocked the door and entered. Fae didn't bother with a lamp as she made her way to her bedroom.

HEWITT WATCHED FAELIN pause out on the square before making her way home. He hadn't wanted to press her again, not so soon after she'd refused his offer and not while she stood watch over the body of her dead father, but he would soon be out of time—as would she. Wailes would expect him to confirm a willing Bridger following Lachlan Keetley's ceremony. After that Faelin would have no more time to grieve.

Once Faelin was in her house, Hewitt stepped out onto the bridge. It was time to talk to Shiv.

The book bindery was dark, as was the bakery when he passed it, but a dim light showed from inside the seamstress' shop. A few steps ahead, light spilled out onto the cobbles from the open doorway to the brewery. Hewitt glanced in as he went by. Bridgers were inside keeping the taps busy.

Shouting from the direction he was heading in made Hewitt pause. He muttered a spell just under his breath, not reciting it, but keeping it ready in case he needed it. It wasn't a powerful spell—just a loud noise and a flash of light, but it would startle anyone he used it against.

He was only a few steps from Conjurers Hall but it already felt like a different bridge. The cobble streets were kept in the same repair but the buildings that now lined them were grimy and dilapidated. The houses here were made of wood rather than stone, and light escaped from the gaps around doors and sagging shutters.

"Who's there?"

"Conjurer Hewitt," Hewitt said. "I need to speak with Shiv."

"What if Shiv don't want to speak wit ya?" A man edged out into the street, a wooden club with a hook fixed onto the end of it in his hands. He spat and a clump of spittle landed beside one of Hewitt's oversized shoes.

"Then I'll have to tell Conjurer Wailes that I was unable to fulfill his request." Hewitt stared until his words had registered with the Bridger. The sneer fell from the man's face, and he lowered his club.

"I'll get 'im," he said, taking a step back. "I'll be a minute s'all."

The Bridger hurried towards the stone gatehouse that stood half a block away.

A few minutes later, Shiv stepped out, his eyes shadowed in the dim light. He strolled towards Hewitt, fingering a knife that hung from his belt.

"Hewitt," Shiv said and stopped a few paces away from the conjurer.

"Shiv," Hewitt replied. "Certain . . . events have transpired and Conjurer Wailes would like your help."

"Anythin' for *Conjurer* Wailes," Shiv replied, emphasizing Wailes' title, just as he'd omitted it for Hewitt.

Hewitt stared at the Bridger, his spell ready. He didn't want to cast another spell, not so soon after opening Lachlan's workroom door, but neither could he let this Bridger treat him with such open disdain.

"Well," Shiv said in a bored tone of voice. "Say what Wailes wants."

"*Conjurer* Wailes," Hewitt said. When had the Bridgers become so insolent and disrespectful? Had Wailes made them promises? Promises he hadn't told the other conjurers about?

"Yeah, right, that's what I said. *Conjurer* Wailes," Shiv said. "Tell me what he wants me to do."

"*Conjurer* Hewitt," Hewitt prompted. "Please tell me what Conjurer Wailes requests, *Conjurer* Hewitt." Hewitt was aware of a few people peering through doors and windows at them as he met Shiv's glare calmly. He seemed to think Hewitt had no power. Was that something Wailes had told him? He hoped he didn't have to prove how wrong that was.

Shiv's right hand twitched and Hewitt saw the glint of steel in it.

"Do you really think Conjurer Wailes will allow you to live if you hurt me?" Hewitt asked, his voice pitched low so that only Shiv could hear him. "No matter how useful you are to Wailes, the other conjurers will not allow leniency for the injury or murder of one of their own. I suggest you show me the respect my title demands."

Shiv's eyes narrowed, but he shrugged and the blade disappeared.

"*Conjurer Hewitt*," he sneered. "Please tell me what Head Conjurer Wailes asks of me."

Chapter Eight

"FAE, THIS IS Pax Oldham." Aric gestured and an older man who stood staring at the ray looked over at her. "He's the leader of the Rivermen on this side of the bridge. Pax, this is Faelin Keetley, my friend from the bridge."

"Ah, the bookbinder's daughter," Pax said. "And you helped Rand catch this monster?"

"Yes sir," Fae said. She looked down at her leg. It was still red and swollen but it no longer throbbed. "Rand saved me. The ray had already stung me."

"A fair trade then, if this catch really does bring change with it."

"Pax," Aric cut in. "It will. I have news." He looked at Fae. "*We* have news that you need to hear."

His face serious, Pax looked from Fae to Aric and back again. "I assume this has something to do with why Conjurer Wailes asked the Rivermen to look for the bookbinder's daughter *before* she found her way here?" He looked back at the ray and shook his head. "Come with me."

The crowd parted as Pax led them along the dock. They stepped across two boats that were lashed together and onto another dock. Fae, too tired to really think, simply clutched at

Aric's hand as the two Rivermen led her over and across docks and boats. Finally they stepped onto a larger boat that huddled near the edge of the village.

A few boats beyond this one, the steep bank of the river led up to ward Waglenn Landing. She stopped and let go of Aric's hand. Was Pax going to hand her over to Wailes? She couldn't let that happen. Aric turned to give her a puzzled look.

"I can't go back to the bridge," Fae whispered.

"We won't . . ." He followed her gaze to the riverbank. "Pax isn't going to contact Wailes." He gestured as Pax opened a small door to the cabin and disappeared inside. "I told you—Rivermen *hate* conjurers. We would never help them." He grinned. "But don't tell the conjurers that. We smile and nod when they tell us to do something, and then we do our best to not help them. In fact, since Wailes specifically asked us to find you, Pax will *never* let him know you're here."

"You're sure?" Fae asked. "I don't want to put you and your people at risk, but I need to know if I'm safe here. I think Wailes will want me dead." Dead or in his power, which Fae thought would be even worse. Hewitt thought she'd make a good apprentice; Wailes would make her use magic that twisted her body so badly she'd wish she was dead.

"Rivermen hate conjurers," Aric repeated and stepped over to her. "With good reason." He leaned close to whisper directly into her ear. "If Wailes wants you, then keeping you from him will benefit Rivermen."

"Pax believes that?"

"We *all* believe that," Aric replied. He grabbed her hand and pulled her towards the cabin. "You'll be able to stay here, you'll see."

The inside of the cabin was dimly lit by a small brass lamp that hung from a chain. The deck of the boat swayed and Fae clutched the back of a wooden chair that sat in front of a desk. She sat down across from Pax, who was already seated, his hands flat on the scarred desk top.

"Why does Conjurer Wailes want you?" Pax asked abruptly.

Fae smoothed a hand over her damp and dirty skirt while she waited for Aric to pull up a chair and get settled.

"Because I know he has something he doesn't want the other conjurers to know about."

"And that is?"

"Spells," Fae said. "Hundreds, thousands of spells. Every single spell that a conjurer ever wrote down and had bound into a book." She met Pax's open-mouthed gaze and nodded. "He has them and he'll do *anything* to keep them for himself."

"Where did he find them?" Pax asked. He clenched his hands and Fae could see them shake a little.

"In my house," Fae said. "In a secret room that bookbinders have been filling with copied books for generations."

"You're sure they are spells?"

"Yes," Fae and Aric both answered at the same time, and Pax's gaze swivelled from Fae to Aric.

"You've seen them!" Pax said. "Why didn't you tell me?"

"Safely hidden they were no danger," Aric said. "Now, discovered by Wailes, they are a threat to everyone."

"No danger," Pax snorted. "A secret store of spells is nothing but danger."

"They'd been hidden for years," Aric said. He paused. "Since the last time whale skin was sent to a bookbinder on the bridge."

"Whale skin," Pax said. "We've never sent them a whale skin."

"Then explain this." Fae reached into her pocket and pulled out the journal. Despite the rough night, the binding was pristine. "This was among the oldest books. It's a journal, not a book of spells, but there were spell books bound in this same skin." She handed the book to Pax, who took and rubbed his hand across its smooth surface.

"I've never heard of books being bound in whale," Pax said. He flipped the book open. "Can you read this?"

"Yes," Fae replied. "But I haven't had time to read more than the first page. It mentions a Keetley. I'm hoping it explains why the spell books were all copied."

"Does it matter?" Pax asked. "Wailes has the spells. Who knows what he'll do with them." He spread his fingers out on the desk top. "Probably finish the job his ancestor started," he muttered.

"Finish what?" Fae asked. If the Rivermen knew what Wailes was planning, she wanted to know too. It might help save her life.

"Aric never told you?" Pax asked.

Aric shook his head. "My mother always said that it was not for outsiders," he said. "Not even for Fae."

"True," Pax agreed. "And perhaps even the conjurers have forgotten, but we haven't. And we do tell some trusted allies." He raised his spread hands to Fae, stretching the webbing between them taut. The light from the lamp glowed pink through the skin between his fingers.

"Conjurers did this to us," Pax said with a snarl. "Cursed us with webbed hands and feet and forced us to live on the water. Can't stay on shore more'n an hour or so." He looked at Aric. "It gets worse as you get older."

"That's why your village is floating?" Fae asked. Aric nodded and another thought struck her. That's why Aric wouldn't marry her—even when she was desperate—even if it meant Wailes would force her to marry someone else. Aric couldn't live on land. But the bridge wasn't land, exactly.

"Does the bridge affect you too?" she asked softly.

Aric nodded. "It's not as bad as land. I can stay longer on the bridge, but it's hours, not days."

"Aric, why didn't you tell me?" Fae asked. "We could have looked for that spell, or a spell to counter it." Fae closed her eyes. That spell—the one that cursed the Rivermen—it was there, she was sure of it. But it was too late. Wailes had the books and spells now. There was no chance to find it now.

"I looked," Aric said. "When we found the books."

"You can read?" Pax asked. "When did you learn to read?"

"Fae taught me," Aric replied. He sent a small smile her way. "The way her mother had taught her a few years earlier."

"It helped me remember how to read," Fae said. And repeating her mother's lessons for Aric had made her feel closer to her.

"Mmph," Pax mumbled. "Best not let the conjurers know either of you can read. They'd be mighty jealous of that."

"Too late," Fae said. "At least for me. Conjurer Hewitt knows." She bent her head and sighed. "He said it was one of the reasons he wanted me to become his apprentice." She lifted her head and met Pax's gaze. "I can't go back to the bridge, not with the conjurers looking for me. Can I stay here?"

Pax stared at her for a few moments before he nodded. "Aye. Can't ignore the sign. A ray marked you—a big one—and then you helped Rand bring it in. I read that as change heading our way and that we need you to help us weather it. You can stay. Aric, find her a place—but she can't be out on the river in the day."

Aric grinned and stood up. He grabbed Fae's hand and pulled her to her feet.

Fae closed her eyes in relief and resisted Aric's pull. She opened her eyes and turned to Pax. "Thank you," she said. "I'll stay hidden, I promise. I don't want to cause trouble."

Pax nodded and Fae let Aric pull her towards the door.

"Trouble is already here," Pax said softly.

THIS TIME WHEN Aric led her across boats and docks, Fae, feeling safer, could appreciate the way everything fit together like a puzzle. Boats tied together had steps that allowed people to easily climb over the gunwales and docks were fitted with ramps. They paused to let a woman carrying a baby step from a large boat onto a dock. The woman greeted Aric with a nod but the smile on her face faltered when she saw Fae.

"This way," Aric said.

As he tugged her forward Fae was aware of the woman's stare. She turned back and the woman quickly averted her gaze before hurrying away.

"We don't get many visitors," Aric said. He'd stopped and turned to face her. "And by now word of the ray will have spread."

"So everyone will blame me?" Fae asked.

"No," Aric assured her. "But many will be frightened."

"Of me."

"Of what's coming," Aric said. "But you heard Pax. He thinks we'll need you with us. People will respect his opinion on that."

"I hope so," Fae replied. Her optimism dimmed, she followed Aric across the boat and onto a dock.

This boat was at the very edge of the village and further downstream. The cabin that perched in the middle of the deck was painted dark blue, a sharp contrast to the reds and greens and whites of the other boats.

There were no stairs leading down from the gunwale to the deck. Fae had to hop down, using Aric's shoulder to steady herself.

"Is this yours?" she asked.

"My mother's," Aric replied. "Wait here." He opened the door to the small cabin and stepped inside, leaving Fae to worriedly stare at his retreating back.

Aric rarely talked about his mother to her, but she knew she didn't like Fae and her friendship with her son. The one time Fae had visited the village his mother had made it a point to *not* meet her. Aric had apologized and later he'd explained that his mother forbade her from visiting the village again. He was angry, but as shaman, her requests were respected.

Fae looked out across the bow of the boat towards the riverbank. It was only a few feet away and she could hear birds calling to each other from the trees. This boat was closer to shore than any of the other Rivermen boats. Was that because Aric's mother wanted to be close to land or just farther away from the rest of the Rivermen?

The door to the cabin opened and Aric stood in the doorway.

"Come in," he said. "And meet my mother."

Fae raised her brows as she walked towards him. Aric didn't meet her eyes as he stepped aside to give her room to enter the cabin.

Fae slipped past Aric and into a small room. A window looked out over the bow, a wooden wheel lashed to the wall below it. Narrow steps led down into a dim interior. Aric closed the door and the sunny morning was shut out. He averted his eyes as he edged around Fae and down the stairs.

Fae shook her head and followed Aric down a half dozen stairs until she stood behind him in a small, dark space.

Polished wood surfaces gleamed, and a small lamp, its wick turned low so that only a tiny flame burned, hung from the low ceiling.

"Mother, this is Faelin Keetley," Aric said. He stepped away from Fae and slid onto a bench behind a small table. "Fae, this is my mother, Sigrun Rawley."

"Bridger," said the woman who sat across from Aric. She was small, and her skin was a dark copper colour. She placed a hand flat on the table.

Surprised, Fae looked up into eyes so dark they were black. Sigrun Rawley's hands were so fully webbed that they resembled the feet of a duck.

"Not a Bridger," Fae corrected automatically. "I'm of the bridge."

Aric gestured to her and she slid in beside him on the bench. She couldn't help glancing at his hands—they were webbed, yes, but recognizable as hands.

"You live on the bridge," Sigrun said. "Makes you a Bridger all the same." She followed Fae's eyes to her son's hands. "Takes after his father," she said. "He was a lander—had hands like yours." She shook her head and frowned at Aric. "I was hoping a lander baby wouldn't have to live on the water. At least he wasn't born with these." She held up her hands and Fae stared at them, fascinated despite the woman's visible disdain for her own hands.

Sigrun tucked her hands under the table, out of sight. "My son tells me we have to give you a place to stay," she said. "That Pax said so."

"I'd be grateful," Fae replied.

"Not doing it for you," Sigrun replied.

The boat dipped and there was a sound from above.

"I'll see who that is," Sigrun said. She slipped out from behind the table and was out of the room before Fae understood that someone had stepped onto the boat.

"You never told me much about your mother," Fae whispered to Aric. She tried to catch his eye but he was staring at his hands where they rested on the table top.

"There's not much to tell," Aric said, and Fae was surprised by the bitterness in his voice. "She's the Riverman shaman—kind of an advisor—and we've never been close. She never really wanted a child. At least that's how I felt growing up."

"And your father?"

"I never knew him. She met him at a one of the town festivals." Aric turned his hands over before tucking them under his arms. "She won't even tell me which town he was from. My mother did not want a child who looked like her."

"All this time and you never said."

"Said what?" Aric turned to her. "That my mother hates herself so much that she can barely stand to look at the son who reminds her of what she is? That I practically had to raise myself? That even though my mother is a formidable fisher I had to find someone else to teach me how to fish?"

"But I . . ."

He reached for her hand. "I didn't want you to know. You were the only person who didn't look at me with pity, who didn't feel sorry for me because my mother so obviously didn't want me." He sighed. "And I loved hearing the stories of your mother and father—how much they cared for you—how they taught you what they knew even when they shouldn't have." He smiled. "And then you passed some of that knowledge on to me. I . . ." There were footsteps on the stairs, and Aric stopped talking and dropped her hand.

"Rand's come," Sigrun said as she entered the room. "He brought something from your catch."

Sigrun sat back down, and Fae twisted to see Rand, his hands wrapped around a rough, burlap sack, standing awkwardly in the doorway.

"I thought you should have this," Rand said. "Seeing that it was you who got stung."

He held the sack out and Fae took it. She undid the twine that held the sack closed, opened it, and looked in. It was the stinger—the long, thin tail of the ray—coiled up and tied with yet more twine.

"I'm not sure what to do with it," Fae said. Carefully she pulled the tail out. There was a nasty looking point on the end and she gingerly touched her finger to it. "But thank you."

Rand grinned. "Sure. Like I said, I never woulda landed that ray without your help."

"What ray?" Sigrun asked. Her eyes narrowed as she turned her gaze on her son. "You didn't say anything about a ray."

Aric shrugged. "That's why Pax said to help Fae. Change is coming and he thinks we're going to need her help."

Sigrun's gaze fixed on Fae until she had to fight to stop from squirming.

"You should have said," Sigrun said finally.

"I thought you knew," Rand said. "Or I woulda told you. I found Fae here when I was out fishing. She'd been hurt. Then we found what had hurt her. Biggest ray I ever heard of. It's hanging up over to the village square. You might wanta see it."

"I might," Sigrun agreed. "I'm sure it's a sight. Rand, you probably have things to do and I want to talk to my son, if you don't mind."

"Sure, I got the rest of my catch to sort out."

"Thank you again," Fae said. Rand rewarded her with another grin as he turned and left, and Fae smiled. Whatever might be coming, Rand had a story to tell.

"A ray," Sigrun said. "You helped bring in a ray."

Fae's smile dropped away and she turned to face Sigrun.

Whatever she expected, it wasn't the look of glee on Sigrun's face. "You're happy?"

"A ray means change," Sigrun said. "And the promise of *that* makes me happy. I would have rather caught it myself." She looked from Fae to Aric and back to Fae. "Even though being at the centre of change can be dangerous." She slid out from behind the table. "Let me get you some clean clothes to wear. And you can have my sleeping quarters."

"No, please," Fae said. "Don't put yourself out."

"I will sleep out here. Just let me grab a few things and then I'll show you my quarters." Sigrun hurried to the stern of the boat.

Fae met Aric's wide eyes. He shrugged.

"If I'd known she would act like this," he said. "I would have mentioned the ray sooner."

CLEAN AND WEARING a skirt and top borrowed from Sigrun, Fae sat on the edge of the small bed in her hostess' quarters, fingering the journal.

Aric had left to meet with some of the Rivermen leaders and Sigrun had gone to see the ray, so she'd told Fae. Even though she'd offered her a place to stay and the use of her own bedroom, Fae didn't completely trust Aric's mother—she wasn't sure he did! But she felt safer than she had since the day her father had died.

She smoothed a hand across the front cover of the journal. Even after everything she'd been through, it looked the same as it had when she'd found it. Not a scratch, not a watermark—nothing to indicate it had been dragged through the marsh. She'd think it some exceptional property of whale hide, except the pages were also pristine.

She flipped the book open to the page that mentioned Keetley Kellen. She started to read the faded script and her eyes drooped shut.

She snapped awake when her chin hit her chest. The journal would have to wait—she desperately needed sleep—but there was one more thing she wanted to do. Staring at the journal in her lap, Fae tried to remember her father's last words—the spell—he'd told her while dying.

Nervous, her hands trembling, she placed the book on the bed beside her.

"Geedcenne deanboc boc," she whispered while leaning over the book. The book lay where it was, motionless. Had she said it correctly? She reached a shaking hand towards the book. A spark arced from her fingers to the book, and startled, Fae snatched her hand back. It was warm where she cradled it against her chest.

And two books lay on the bed, side by side. Fae sucked in a breath and then exhaled, slowly. She held her hand out, staring at it. It didn't seem different—would she become misshapen? Or was this spell so small that it wouldn't change her? Her father hadn't shown any signs of disfigurement from using this spell, and based on all the books she'd seen, the ones she knew she or her father had bound, he'd been using it for years. She put her hands flat, side by side. If it had changed her she couldn't tell.

Fae focussed on the two journals. She couldn't tell them apart.

Gingerly she opened each one to the first page of writing. The same looping Ks, the same faint lettering, the exact same sentences and words. She flipped to a random page in the original journal and then found the same page in the copy.

There was no difference between the two books. Every sentence, every letter, every splotch of ink on the paper was exactly the same. She picked up the copy and turned it over. It too was in pristine condition. Should she make a third copy? No, Fae decided. She wasn't sure that reciting the spell hadn't affected her in some way: she didn't dare compound it. No, she had to hide this book, in case she lost the original. She glanced around the room for a moment before deciding that the simplest place to hide it was underneath the mattress. She lifted it up and positioned the book as far from the edge as she could before she let the mattress drop back into place.

After tucking the original journal under the pillow, she stretched out and lay down. Tired as she was, it took her a while to fall asleep. She'd done magic—real magic!

Chapter Nine

"FAE, WAKE UP."

Someone was pounding on the door. Groggily, Fae dragged a hand across her eyes.

Papa? No, not her father—he was dead. Fae sat up and shoved a rough blanket off and slipped her feet into her shoes.

"Fae!"

"Yes." She opened the door and Aric stepped in. "Is it dark already?"

"Yes," Aric said. "Almost dawn, actually. Tide's gone out."

Fae sat down on the bed and raked a hand through her hair, trying to smooth out some of the tangles. She looked up at Aric. "What's wrong?" she asked. He was pale, and he kept shuffling from side to side, clasping and unclasping his hands.

"Tide's out," he repeated.

"So you said," Fae replied.

"We found something," Aric said. "You need to see."

Aric wouldn't meet her eyes, and nervous, Fae grabbed a wrap that Sigrun had left on a hook and pulled it around her shoulders. Aric turned to leave and Fae, without thinking, grabbed the journal and tucked it into the pocket of her skirt. She'd be back, wouldn't she? Then why did she feel the need to take the journal?

In silence, Fae trailed Aric as he led the way across boats and docks—away from the bank towards the middle of the river. She tried to ask him where they were going but he shook his head. Thinking that he was worried about the sound of their voices carrying across the water, Fae remained silent as she followed him.

At last they reached a larger dock area. Rivermen were gathering; even as she and Aric reached the group, more had joined them, staring at something that lay on the dock. Fae glanced up and shivered. The carcass of the ray still hung there. The meat was gone but the hide was still stretched out, the wings spanning half the length of the dock.

"Make way," Aric said.

A few men looked up angrily but when they saw who it was, they stepped aside. Aric pulled Fae with him until they stood over the thing on the dock.

"What is . . . ?" Fae started to ask . . . then she stopped, her mouth open in horror. "By the Seven! It's Thorpe! What's happened to him?"

"Can't you guess?" Aric asked.

"Wailes," Fae said grimly. It had to be. Poor Thorpe. The last time Fae had seen him he'd climbed down the stairs to her father's secret room. He'd been twisted and maimed, but he'd still been able to walk—but now! His body looked like it had crumpled in on itself, and his back was so twisted that his head no longer faced forward. And his legs! They were curled up like the claws of a lobster. But it was the face that caused tears to form in her eyes. When he'd lived next door, Thorpe had been a happy lad who'd always had a bright smile for her and her father. Now in death his lips were stretched across his teeth in a horrible grimace. But it was Thorpe—the same blond thatch of hair, the same blue eyes that were now dull and lifeless.

"You recognize him?" It was Pax. He stood off to one side, looking down on Thorpe's body with fear and suspicion.

"Yes," Fae replied. "He was my neighbour until he became apprentice to Conjurer Wailes." She met Aric's gaze. "But he's used a *lot* of magic in the last few days."

Aric nodded. "That's what I said. He was found when the tide went out." He pulled Fae away from the body, towards Pax. "Could he have jumped?"

Fae closed her eyes, took a deep breath, and shook her head. "No, not with those legs. He's crippled worse than Wailes. He wouldn't have been able to move without help. No, he didn't get off the bridge by himself. He must have been thrown off."

"Wailes would do that?" Aric asked. "Order that done? What about the final ceremony? Thorpe was his apprentice, shouldn't that have been done?"

"Yes," Fae said. "It should have been. Wailes could be trying to keep the fact that he was misusing his apprentice a secret."

"Would he care?" Pax asked. "I thought he was the most powerful conjurer."

"He is," Fae replied. "But if the other conjurers saw how cruelly Thorpe had been used, they would have to confront him—especially those with their own apprentices. That could mean fighting amongst them." She grimaced. "I think Thorpe was so grotesque from using magic that Wailes didn't dare let the others see him. So he had him tossed off the bridge. Thorpe could even have been alive when they did it."

"Berhalla save him," Pax said. "Limbs like that, the lad would have sunk like a stone."

"Yes," Fae said. "But we can be pretty sure that Wailes is trying to figure out the spells in my father's house."

"Coward," Aric said. "Instead of risking himself he made Thorpe recite them."

"I'm afraid so," Fae said. Hesitant, she looked over at Pax. "What will be done? With Thorpe?"

Pax looked over to where Rivermen still crowded around Thorpe's body. "Usually we take bodies to the conjurers," he said. "If they're not one of theirs then they contact the towns." He shook his head. "I don't think it's safe to let Conjurer Wailes know we found him. We'll treat him like an unclaimed body. Aric, take him out to sea after dark. Weigh him down some so he don't drift back in with the tide."

Aric nodded and Fae felt her shoulders sag. She'd go with Aric and do what she could for Thorpe. He'd been—not a friend, not for a long time, but a boy she'd known growing up, and a young man who hadn't deserved this.

"Pax!" A man trotted up to the leader of the Rivermen. "We caught another one."

Curious, Fae followed Pax across the dock to a small fishing boat. Had they brought in another ray? Would it be as big as the one she and Rand had caught?

Pax sucked in a breath and stooped low, looking at what was in the boat, leaving Fae a clear view of the contents.

Not another ray; it was another misshapen body. A boy. Fae recognized him, and he was too young to be an apprentice, but here he was, afflicted by magic. Not the same twisted spine and crippled legs of Thorpe—no, this boy suffered from the raw, peeling skin of Conjurer Tadlow. The lesions were so numerous that there were only a few patches of intact skin.

"He was a Bridger," Fae said. "His name was Deven. He wasn't an apprentice, not to a conjurer." She paused. "I think he could read," she said, remembering something that the baker had said, that young Deven was being groomed to do accounts for the night watch. "At least a little." Worried, she looked at Aric. "Does anyone on the bridge know you can read?"

"No," Aric shook his head, and Fae relaxed a little. "No one knows, except for you, my mother, and now Pax. Why?"

"Because I think Wailes will be impatient, he'll be looking for anyone who can read, anyone who can recite those spells."

"We should be safe enough then," Aric said. "Wailes doesn't know you can read."

"No," Fae agreed. "But Conjurer Hewitt does. He might have told Wailes by now."

"Then it's a good thing you ran away."

"Yes," Fae agreed. And it was, for her. She just hoped that Aric, Pax, and the rest of the Rivermen didn't have reason to regret it.

NO MORE BODIES were found that morning. The next high tide was due in late afternoon and no one thought anyone would be dumped from the bridge in daytime.

"Tide's high again just before dawn tomorrow," Pax said. "That's probably the next time we'd find someone."

He was sitting in the cabin of Sigrun's boat, stuffed into the seat beside Fae. Aric leaned against the wall, and Sigrun sat on the other side of the small table.

"I'm not sure Wailes would even risk that time of day," Fae said. "The Bridgers of the night watch do his bidding, but too many people will have started their day by then. Pullen the baker is usually delivering bread before dawn. Wailes would definitely not want Pullen to see someone tossed off the bridge."

"Why would he be afraid of this baker?" Pax asked.

"He's Thorpe's father. What if he saw Bridgers throwing something off the bridge and connected it with the disappearance of his son? Wailes won't want anyone to know what happened to his apprentice, not until he has some spells he can use." Fae paused. "Or has figured out how to reverse the damage using magic has done to him."

"How many people on the bridge can read?" Aric asked.

"Other than the conjurers and their apprentices, there can't be more than half a dozen," Fae said. "And most of the rest are grown men—either key merchants or Bridgers. They would be more difficult for Wailes to use against their will."

"And the other apprentices?" Pax asked. "Will he be able to persuade them to help him?"

"He might," Fae said. "Although he'd have to convince the conjurers they're apprenticed to first."

"Conjurers!" Sigrun spat. "I hate them all." She raised her webbed hands. "I wish I could curse them!"

"Sigrun," Pax said. "Now is not the time."

"When will it be?" she asked. "We are Rivermen yet we don't control the river. We let the conjurers control it, and us! I'm tired of letting them tell us when we can visit upriver, of dividing our people. We need to stop them!"

"Enough!" Pax yelled.

Sigrun's face twisted in hatred. Fae looked from her to Aric, but he refused to meet her eyes.

"You will do nothing," Pax said and leaned over the table until his face was inches from Sigrun's. His voice lowered to a whisper. "They've used the river as a weapon against us before. Remember that. So do nothing or you might get us all killed."

Sigrun shook her head and leaned back, her arms crossed over her chest. "I won't do anything. Except hate them."

LATER, AFTER PAX had left, Sigrun grabbed her coat and stomped up the stairs and out of the cabin.

Fae sighed and ran her hands through her hair. "What did Pax mean, that she could kill us all?"

Aric slid into the seat across from her. He placed his hands flat on the table and spread them out so that the webbed skin between his fingers stretched taut.

"All my life my mother has threatened to kill the conjurers," he said softly. "She hates what she is and blames the conjurers."

"Well," Fae said. "They *are* responsible. At least one of them cursed your people a very long time ago."

"Yes," Aric agreed. "But Pax worries that if we kill the conjurers the spell will do worse than it already has. Kill us, or intensify our deformities." He looked up and met Fae's gaze. "We just don't know."

"And what about what Pax said; that the conjurers used the river as a weapon?" she asked.

"They can dam the river," Aric said. "They did it once, years ago. It flooded the river upstream and left the downstream village more susceptible to the tides. I've been told that fishing was ruined for weeks."

"But they released the river?"

"Eventually," Aric replied. "Once they got whatever it was they wanted."

"They could do that again," Fae said. She had no doubt that Wailes would use any means at hand to get what he wanted. "I'll try to find out more about the curse," she said. "My book—the journal I took from my father's secret room." She fumbled with the pocket in her skirt and pulled it out. "Maybe it says something about the curse."

"We can hope," Aric said, but Fae knew that he really didn't have any hope. "Tide should be in," he continued. "It's time to say goodbye to Thorpe."

Fae sighed and stood to follow Aric, tucking the journal back into her skirt pocket. "All right," she said. "I need some rocks. Something from the bridge would be best."

"I'll ask around to see if anyone has some from the piers," Aric said. He led the way out into a clear night. "We use them as weights for the nets sometimes."

FAE SETTLED THE pile of rocks in the middle of the piece of rough fabric and tied the edges together. The young Riverman who had given them to her swore that some of the smaller stones were from a bridge pier, but there was no way to know. And did it matter? Thorpe hadn't been given a proper ceremony and all she could do was her best. She spotted Aric coming towards her.

Thorpe, covered in a grey blanket, was draped over his shoulder. He stepped into the boat and it dipped and rolled from the weight. Carefully, Aric lay Thorpe down at Fae's feet and busied himself untying the boat and shifting the oars into place.

Fae reached out and lifted the blanket. Either Thorpe's face had relaxed in death or someone had tried to make him look more peaceful. In any case, the grimace was gone, replaced by, not a smile, but at least he no longer looked like he was in pain. Fae could only be grateful. As Aric rowed them out into the river, she tied the bundled rocks around Thorpe's neck.

She covered him up, trying not to stare at his twisted body. Beyond Aric, lights on the bridge glowed and she pretended that she could tell where the window to her old room was. But the room she'd grown up in would be dark: Wailes wouldn't allow anyone to live in her house, not with the treasure that sat a few floors below.

"Is someone else taking care of the Bridger?" Fae asked quietly. He hadn't been someone she'd known, not like Thorpe, but he deserved a proper send-off too.

"Rand offered," Aric replied. "He felt a little responsible since he was the one who brought in the ray."

"And me," Fae said, glad that someone was tending to the Bridger. It wasn't his fault he'd been born into that life, just as it wasn't his fault he'd been forced to do so much magic that it killed him.

They rounded a bend and Fae could no longer see the lights of the bridge. The wind picked up and waves swelled, causing the boat to dip and rock. Aric kept the boat close to shore for a few more strokes, then he steered towards the middle of the river.

Soon they reached the marsh. A deep pool was beneath them now, maybe even the same one where she'd been stung by the ray.

Another half hour of rowing and they were out past the riverbanks. A wave hit the boat and sprayed them. Fae tasted salt where the spray had hit her lips.

"We should be far enough out," Aric said. He pulled the oars in and laid them beside Thorpe in the bottom of the boat. "What should I do?"

"Just get him ready to go into the water," Fae said.

Aric tugged Thorpe's body to the side of the boat. Fae stood up, one hand on the pole that held the lamp, and leaned over Thorpe.

"Thorpe Wailes, born Thorpe Pullen, was of the bridge," she said. "And the bridge was of him. Thorpe Wailes has left the bridge for the final time." She nodded to Aric, who hoisted the body over the gunwale and let it slip into the sea.

The body bobbed on the waves for a few moments and Fae worried that there wasn't enough weight to make it sink, but then it slowly slipped under the water.

"That's it," she said to Aric. "If the conjurers do more, I don't know what it is."

"Better treatment than his master gave him," Aric said. He sat back down, slipped the oars into the locks, bent his head, and started rowing them back.

They were heading against the tide so it took them longer to return. Fae stared at the sea until it disappeared behind a bend in the river, wondering if she should try to find out when the next ship was due and whether she should try to get on it and leave Cleebrock. But she couldn't fathom the thought of leaving everyone and everything she knew. At least not so soon after her father's death.

HEWITT OPENED HIS front door and stuck his head out, looking each way before shuffling through it. No one was on the roadway, at least not that he'd seen, and hopefully no one was looking out their window at him.

He clutched his pack tight against his body as he hurried past Conjurers Hall. He knew Wailes wasn't there—he'd seen Tymm push the man to the bookbindery. Interestingly, a young Bridger had followed them inside.

Hewitt glanced over his shoulder, making sure that no one was watching, before he ducked into a doorway. Without knocking, he opened the door and slipped inside.

"Dabel," Hewitt called out. "Dabel!"

"My master is resting," Gerick Dabel said, peering at him from a doorway. "And you have not been invited in."

"I don't have time for this," Hewitt said. "Fetch Dabel at once."

"No. You are not expected and are not welcome." Gerick crossed his arms over his round belly, his hands resting on it. Middle-aged, Gerick was the oldest apprentice and from the lack of warts, Hewitt suspected he did very little magic.

"Thorpe Wailes is missing," Hewitt said.

"Missing, what do you mean missing?" Gerick asked. "He's probably just visiting his folks."

"The baker hasn't seen him in two days," Hewitt said. "He's been gone almost as long as the bookbinder's daughter."

Gerick's face paled, and he waved Hewitt through the door and into a large office. A fire burned in the grate and Hewitt stepped close, trying to warm his chilled hands.

"Both of them gone?" Gerick said. "But Conjurer Wailes said the bookbinder's daughter had gone to live with her mother's relatives."

"The relatives who had never once set foot on the bridge until Wailes spoke to them a few days ago?" Hewitt asked. He'd come to Dabel because he and Wailes were old adversaries—and Dabel had an apprentice. Without an apprentice of his own he wanted the security of another's. Gerick was the oldest apprentice, so Hewitt had known him the longest.

"I did think that strange," Gerick said. "But not really my concern. But Thorpe? Are you sure he's missing? Perhaps he's simply recovering from a spell."

"Perhaps," Hewitt agreed. "I hope that's the case but I can't inquire after him. Another conjurer's apprentice is, as you say, not my concern. And yet *I am* concerned." And he was, not just because the youth was missing. Hewitt had been making his own discreet enquiries, trying to find a suitable candidate to be his own apprentice, one who could read, at least a little, but all three people he'd spoken to had already been approached by Wailes.

The only reason the head conjurer would need more apprentices was if he was having them recite the spells in the books. And poor Thorpe Wailes looked like he couldn't recite too many more spells—especially powerful ones—and survive.

"I will go," Gerick said. "It is not unusual for me to talk to him."

"As long as Wailes does not suspect anything," Hewitt said. "If something unpleasant has happened to Thorpe, we do not want Wailes to be suspicious of us."

"He won't be," Gerick said. "At least not of me. Thorpe is my cousin. I need to find out if he's safe."

Chapter Ten

HEWITT PACED THE small room, waiting for Dabel to wake or Gerick to return. He paused and ran a hand along the spine of one of Dabel's spell books, rubbing the rough turtle skin binding.

The fact that Gerick had left him alone with his master's books spoke volumes about the young man's concern for his cousin. Or perhaps it said more about the power and usefulness of Dabel's spells. If the apprentice didn't think anything tucked away on the shelves was worth protecting, then perhaps *that* was the reason both Dabel and Gerick showed so few signs of disfigurement from using magic. Maybe all of the Dabel spells were trivial. Hewitt let his hand drop and continued pacing.

He wasn't sure if that would be good or bad. If none of the conjurer's spells were powerful, then Wailes was expending a lot of energy on nothing. But until he knew for sure, he had to assume that at least one of them had a powerful and dangerous spell. And that Wailes had it now.

There was a noise from the hallway and Hewitt turned to see Eilwen Dabel staring at him.

"Gerick let me in," Hewitt said.

"Where is he?" Dabel tottered into the room and sat heavily on the chair behind the desk.

111

"He's gone to see Thorpe," Hewitt said. "To check on his health."

"And what would be wrong with his health?"

"I'd rather not say anything until . . ." Hewitt began.

The outer door burst open and Gerick rushed into the room.

"They wouldn't let me see him," Gerick said. "My own cousin. They said he was resting after reciting a spell, but they wouldn't let me see him."

"Who?" Dabel asked. "By the Seven, who are you talking about?"

"Wailes," Gerick said. "Or at least the Bridger who was at his quarters. Said his name was Shiv—that he was a friend of Conjurer Wailes—but he didn't look friendly to me. He barred the door and wouldn't let me see Thorpe."

Gerick swept past Hewitt and stood by the book shelf, his face worried.

"I've always been allowed to see Thorpe, no matter how ill he was."

"Perhaps this Bridger Shiv simply doesn't understand Conjurer Wailes' instructions," Dabel said.

"No." Gerick shook his head. "He said he was told to keep everyone out—especially nosy conjurers and apprentices."

"I'm afraid we may be too late to save Thorpe," Hewitt said.

Dabel and Gerick both turned to stare at him. Hewitt walked to the door and closed it tight.

"I believe I know what has happened to Thorpe Wailes."

"If you know something, then tell me," Gerick said. "I need to know." He looked over at Dabel. "Master?"

Dabel nodded and Gerick relaxed. Hewitt sighed. He feared that the man's relief would be short lived.

"I believe Thorpe is dead," Hewitt said. "I have no proof, but he has already been pushed beyond acceptable physical limits by Wailes. And now Wailes has found a secret room that contains copies of all of our spell books. I believe he's trying to confirm what the spells do and how powerful they are. I think he made Thorpe recite some of them and that Thorpe's body failed him."

"It did not take Wailes long to turn the boy into a cripple," Dabel said, nodding his head thoughtfully. "I agree that he has already shown himself capable of causing damage, but the apprentice always has the right to refuse. Are you saying Wailes forced him?"

Hewitt looked at Gerick. "You met Shiv. Do you think he would allow Thorpe to refuse?"

"No," Gerick said. "He looked like he'd slit a man's throat for looking at him the wrong way."

"I think so too," Hewitt agreed. "I believe Thorpe would not have been allowed to refuse."

"What of this room full of books?" Dabel asked. "Are you sure they're all of ours? Where did they come from?"

Hewitt reached into his pack and pulled out the two identical spell books. He placed them on the desk.

"This was the last book Lachlan Keetley bound before he died," Hewitt said, not bothering to explain that Faelin had bound the book and Lachlan had only embossed it. "I was there with his daughter and she claimed that only one book was bound but two books were on the worktable inside the locked workroom. And Lachlan used his dying breath to tell his daughter a spell—a spell I think he used to make copies of every book he had ever worked on."

"A spell," Dabel said. "Impossible. The man had no symptoms, no deformities."

"And fathered a daughter," Hewitt added. "I do not know why he was not afflicted by the use of magic; I only know that these books are identical. And there are more." He paused and met Dabel's gaze. "I went to see Faelin. She had already fled, but Wailes was there with Tymm and Shiv. There were dozens of books laid out on the bookbinder's floor. Books bound in our signature hides—copies of books that contain our family spells. Wailes has them all."

"He would want to know what each spell did," Dabel said. "No matter the cost."

"But Thorpe was his apprentice," Gerick said. "He wouldn't use him so poorly."

"He would," Dabel replied. "He already *has*—Thorpe has been his apprentice for only a few years and already he can barely walk." He looked up at Hewitt. "The question is what—if anything—should we do about it?"

Hewitt shook his head. "I don't know," he said. "But I thought it better to share this." Better for him in any case. He wasn't as confident that knowing about Wailes and the spells would benefit

Dabel and his apprentice.

"Yes, of course," Dabel said. "But I still think we need proof that something has happened to Thorpe. They will let Gerick see him tomorrow."

"Let me know if that is the case," Hewitt said. He picked up the two books and shoved them back into his pack. He was sure Thorpe was dead, that Gerick would never see him again, but Dabel had to realize this himself, had to believe that Hewitt was telling him the truth.

Hewitt stepped out onto the street for the short walk home with his head high and back straight. If he was being watched, he wanted them to know he'd been to see Dabel. He hoped that Gerick asking about Thorpe coupled with him being seen leaving Dabel's home would make Wailes realize that killing a conjurer—killing *him*—would only raise more questions.

Still, by the time he reached his own home the hairs on the back of his neck were standing up and his heart was pounding. He closed his door and lit a lamp, quickly checking each room to see if anything was missing or out of place.

Only when he'd searched his whole house did he relax. But it was a long time before he was able to fall asleep.

By the angle of the sun that shone in through the tiny cabin window, Fae thought it must nearly be noon. She yawned and stretched, still tired from the long night just past. She sat up and swung her legs out from under the blanket. She'd done her best for Thorpe—his death wasn't her fault, although she did feel guilt that the discovery of the books had led to it. But she hadn't copied a book and placed it in that hidden library, and she hadn't instructed any offspring to continue the work started so long ago. And she certainly hadn't made Thorpe recite spells in order to see what they did.

No. Her family had to bear responsibility for the existence of the spell books, but Wailes had made his apprentice use magic until he was painfully crippled, just as Wailes must have given the order to throw Thorpe off the bridge.

She shook her head. She was almost afraid to go out, in case more bodies had been pulled from the river.

She quickly dressed, tucking the journal into her skirt pocket, and stepped from the small chamber to the main living area of the boat.

Warmth lingered from the fire and when she placed a hand on the tea pot, it felt warm. She poured herself a cup of tepid tea, grabbed a day old biscuit, and sat down at the table.

Chewing on the biscuit, she pulled the journal out, put it on the table in front of her, and opened it.

Her tea was cold and the light was dimming before she looked up a few hours later, blinking. She sat back and closed her eyes.

She was a conjurer.

At least her family had been. Kellen was the name of a conjurer family that had died out, in part, because her ancestor, Keetley Kellen, had decided not to become a conjurer. Instead, he'd found joy in binding books. Books of spells *created* by the conjurers of the day, not simply spells copied from one book to another.

According to what she'd read, all conjurers had created spells—that was what *made* them conjurers. And the strength and complexity of the spells they could create were how they were judged. Keetley Kellen—*a non-conjurer*—was the one who'd created the spell to copy books.

Fae blinked and rubbed her eyes. They were dry and tired from peering at the faded script. She was about half way through the journal. Keetley Kellen had just detailed the death of his older brother—the last Kellen conjurer. That was when he'd written his brother's name in the front of the journal. He'd also vowed to never bind a book in whale skin again.

Fae closed the journal and ran her hand across the binding. Whale skin. The binding for the Kellen conjurers—for *her* family. She would use it one day, she decided, and bind a book for herself and keep a family legacy alive. She could have reprised another legacy if she'd agreed to become Hewitt's apprentice. She laughed—and she, the only woman conjurer ever, would have been the only one who carried the blood of conjurers.

She stopped laughing and hurriedly flipped the book open to the last page she'd read. Yes, here it was.

"Sons have never been harmed by the spells created by their fathers, but for those without the blood, reciting their master's spells has terrible consequences. I only have daughters, so my brother has decided against an apprentice not of our blood. Others are not so ready to give up. Conjurer Hewitt apprenticed

a lad from the fishing village, but when he worked the spells, his feet and hands grew large. And when Hewitt forced his apprentice to create a spell, the lad died of his efforts."

Was that why the seven conjurers were afflicted when they used magic? Because they didn't carry the blood of those who had created the spells they recited? But she had Kellen blood. Did that mean she could recite Kellen spells—wield magic—safely? Without suffering any afflictions?

She wished she'd taken another whale skin bound book, one with spells. But she hadn't known that the conjurer who had written those spells down so many years ago was related to her. That she might be able to safely recite the spells the book contained.

The boat shifted and she heard footsteps on the deck above.

"Fae? Are you here?"

It was Aric. Fae put the book back down on the table as the Riverman entered the small space.

"There you are," Aric said as he slid into the seat across from her.

He smelled of fish and the sea and his hands were chapped. He tucked them into his armpits and shivered.

"The boats are back from dragging the marsh pools and the tide's coming in," Aric said. "No bodies were found. Pax was wondering if Wailes is done and I told him no, but he wanted me to ask you, since you know the conjurer best."

"He's not done," Fae said. "He won't stop until he's had someone cast every single spell in those books."

The boat rocked violently and there was a flurry of steps overhead. The door to the cabin was flung open and the wind gusted down the stairs.

"Get out!" It was Sigrun. She practically jumped down the stairs, her chest heaving as she stopped in the doorway. "They're coming, you have to get out."

"Who's coming?" Fae asked as she slid off the bench. She grabbed the journal and shoved it into her skirt pocket before crowding behind Aric, who was in the narrow aisle, staring at his mother.

"The conjurers," Sigrun said. "They're here and asking for Aric. You need to hide."

"Come on." Aric grabbed Fae's hand and they squeezed past

Sigrun and hurried up the stairs.

Once on deck, Fae pulled Aric down to a crouch. There was a cluster of lamps a few boats away, their light glowing in the early evening. With Aric following her, she crept to the far side of the cabin. The riverbank was only a few yards away. She gripped Aric's hand and gestured.

"I can't," he whispered, shaking his head. "You go."

"Not without you." Fae tugged him hard, her lips a thin line. She wasn't leaving him. Wailes might not know Aric could read but he knew that he was Fae's friend. He had to come with her.

"Fae." Aric faced her and met her gaze. "The curse—I don't know how long I can stay on land. If I go with you, I might end up doing something that gives away your hiding spot."

"But you were on the bridge for hours," Fae said.

"The bridge, yes." He looked away from her toward the knot of lanterns coming closer. "I can stay there longer."

"The water then," Fae said. "Both of us. We should stay together." She could see the hulking bulk of Wailes' assistant Tymm now, carrying a lump that must be the conjurer.

Aric nodded and grabbed both of Fae's arms as she stepped over the gunwale. Slowly he lowered her into the cold water. Her skirt was heavy and it became tangled in her legs until she drew the hem up and tucked it into the waistband.

Fae held her breath until Aric slipped over the side of the boat and into the river beside her. She hadn't been certain he would come. He reached an arm around her waist and pulled her tight against him as he steered them towards the bow of the boat. With his free hand he grabbed hold of a rope that was looped over the side.

Fae clamped her teeth together as a shiver wracked her body. In response, Aric pulled her more snugly against him and she tightened her grip on him, grateful for the warmth of his body.

The bow of the boat tilted up as people got on at the stern. Aric shook his head at her, but Fae didn't need him to remind her to be silent.

Wailes was here. The glow of lamps reflected off the water at the side of the boat and she saw a head peer out and look towards the riverbank. A voice chanted something and there was a flash of light in the trees and someone grunted in pain.

"No one's on shore," a man gasped.

"Are you sure?" That was Wailes.

"I recited the spell correctly," the first man replied, his voice low. "And have paid for it. No one is over there."

Fae heard clumping footsteps and then Wailes' voice came from close by. "And he's not on board this sad excuse for a boat, either. Bring me the mother."

"Conjurer Wailes," Pax said. "Sigrun has already told you that she does not know where her son is."

"Yes," Wailes replied. "But he's been here."

"Of course he has," Sigrun shouted from just above them. "He was born on this boat. But he hasn't been here in days."

"Why not?" Wailes asked. "Where could he be? I know he hasn't gone into one of the towns."

"He's gone upriver," Sigrun said.

"No," Wailes replied. "He hasn't. He'd have to get past the bridge to do that and I know he didn't go past on the river." He paused. "And I don't think he can stand to be on land long enough to reach the closest landing point upriver. You see, I know all about your curse." Wailes chuckled, and Fae heard someone, maybe Sigrun, spit.

"It's a Wailes curse, in case your people had forgotten. But what you might not know," Wailes chuckled again, "is that only the first half of the spell was recited. The second half—the part that will complete your transformation—has been carefully handed down from one Wailes conjurer to the next. Now, I want your son. And if you do not send him to me by tomorrow evening, I will recite the second part of the spell."

"He's not here," Pax said. "I haven't seen the boy in days. I'll need to send men out to look for him so I cannot have him to you by tomorrow."

"A week then," Wailes said. "And don't try to run. The spell will find you wherever you are, even across the sea."

"A week," Pax agreed, and Fae could hear the resignation in his voice. The boated dipped as Wailes and his group stepped off it.

"We also have stories that have been handed down," Sigrun called. "There is a way for us to reverse this curse forever and make it rebound back onto you and yours."

"A historian," Wailes said, his voice farther away and full of scorn. "Not that knowing will help. I don't believe a way to reverse the curse exists. If you had it, you would have used it already. See that the boy is sent to the bridge within the week."

Fae shivered and leaned into Aric's warmth. A few moments later, someone stomped on the boat three times.

"That's the signal," Aric said. "It should be safe enough."

He pulled her away from the bow to the side of the boat and soon they stood on the deck, staring out across the boats of the Rivermen village. River water dripped off them and puddled at their feet and a chill wind raised goose bumps on Fae's exposed skin.

"I have to give myself up," Aric said. "He'll finish the spell."

Fae ran a hand through her wet hair, trying to tame the worst of the tangles.

"He'll finish it anyway," Fae said. "He probably just wants to watch you while it happens."

He nodded. "But it might buy my people more time," Aric said and sighed.

"I'm afraid Fae is right," Pax said from the dock beside the boat. "Wailes will finish the spell anyway." The head of the Rivermen stepped heavily onto the boat and joined them at the bow. "You cannot buy time that Wailes won't let us have."

"But the week he gave us might be enough time for you to find the way to reverse the curse," Fae said.

"Wailes was right about that," Pax said. "The way to reverse it has been lost." He glanced upriver towards the bridge. "They did all of this on purpose, because they hate us." He sighed and looked back at Fae and Aric. "But the conjurers have suffered too."

"By their own hand!" Aric said. "And we did nothing to deserve this."

"Perhaps one of us did, at one time," Pax said sadly. "Although those alive today have never harmed a conjurer."

"Wailes can't finish the curse yet," Fae said. "We have more time. The second part of the spell must be powerful."

"I expect it is," Pax agreed. "But how does that give us time?"

"The more powerful the spell, the more damage is done to the one reciting it," Fae replied. "Reciting the rest of the curse could kill them even before they completed it. And we know Wailes won't risk himself doing that. And whoever he had recite the spell tonight might not do it either."

"It was a Bridger—full grown. I didn't know any of them could read but from the way he limped off I doubt he'll volunteer to finish the curse. No, Wailes will need to find someone to do it," Pax said. "But you said there are a few more people on the bridge who can read, so I suspect that won't be a problem."

"I think it might be," Fae replied. "Even Wailes won't be able to hide the disappearance of so many from the bridge. Especially if someone realizes that all those missing—including Thorpe— could read."

"He'll search off the bridge," Aric said. "To find more people who can read."

"Yes," Fae agreed. "He has no choice. Unless he wants to teach people from the bridge to read."

"Which will take too long," Aric continued. "As well as cause more suspicion to fall onto Wailes. It would be strange to suddenly encourage a skill that has been closely held by the conjurers." Aric looked towards the riverbank. "If we can warn people in the towns, take away Wailes' supply of people who can read and recite spells, we may be able to delay the completion of the curse."

"It's possible," Fae said.

"Can you do it?" Pax asked. "By yourself?" He looked from Fae to Aric. "I can't go. I can't spend more than a few minutes on land and that won't be enough time. Aric?"

"I can stay on the bridge for a day," Aric said. "On land? I'm not sure but I'm willing to try."

"We need to go now," Fae said. "Before Wailes has time to convince someone to help him." She eyed the night sky. "How far are we from Waglenn Landing?"

"It's just around the bend in the river," Aric said. "A few minutes away."

"I mean on foot," Fae said. "Oh, you wouldn't know. Aric, do you even have shoes?" He shook his head and she sighed. "All right. Just before dawn we'll get as close as we can to the town by boat without coming into view of the bridge. Then we'll need to go on foot to the town."

"Who should you talk to?" Pax asked.

"I'll start with the baker," Fae said. "He'll be awake and would know who we should see." She glanced at Aric, who stood staring at his feet. "We'll return to the boat as quick as we can."

"No," Aric said. "We should get back on the river upstream of the bridge. Wailes won't expect it. The Rivermen there will help us cross over to Durnham."

"All right," Fae said. "If you're sure you can make it."

"I'm not sure of anything," Aric replied quietly.

A FEW HOURS later, Fae and Aric stepped into Pax's small boat. It was almost dawn and the sky was starting to brighten.

"Should you tell Sigrun you're going?" Fae asked as she settled into the seat in the bow.

"The less she knows the better," Aric said. He sat down with his back to her and grabbed the oars. Pax crouched in the stern, his hand on the small tiller.

"Even if Wailes doesn't find someone to recite the spell, he could come back," Aric said "I can't trust my mother not to say something."

"She wouldn't, would she?" Fae asked. "Although . . ." she paused and looked past Aric's head towards the cluster of boats and docks that was the Rivermen's village. "He might have a small spell that uses very little energy." The spell Hewitt had used to unlock her father's workroom hadn't seemed to hurt him much. And the Bridger who had illuminated the trees had spoken right after reciting that spell. Wailes probably had more small spells, as well as a few people who could cast them.

"One that forces people to tell him things they didn't want to," Fae continued.

"If he gets her mad enough Wailes wouldn't even need to use a spell," Aric said. "My mother would tell him what we were doing just so he knew we were working against him."

"She wouldn't, not really." Fae refused to believe Aric's mother would put her own son in jeopardy.

"She wouldn't want to, but she might not be able to help it. She hates the conjurers."

"I noticed." Sigrun was so angry that Fae felt sorry for her, but she didn't think Aric would be willing to hear that. She'd lost her mother early and her father had been absentminded, but what must it have been like to grow up with a parent who hated so strongly?

"Shhh," Pax whispered from the stern, and Fae huddled into her seat, wrapping her arms around her.

It was a still morning and the current was slow this close to the river bank. Trees, their leaves trailing in the water, loomed over the small craft as they hugged the shore. A few birds flitted in the branches, their cries piercing the quiet predawn.

The boat edged in underneath the canopy of a willow tree and Fae had to push away the branches that threatened to tangle in her hair. There was a soft thud and the boat stopped, resting against the gnarled roots that arched from the tree and disappeared into the water.

"Town's just over that ridge," Pax said.

Aric wedged the blade of one oar underneath a loop of tree root and swivelled to face Fae. He stepped up and past her, straddling the water, one bare foot planted on the bottom of the boat and the other on the tree root. His toes flexed as he gripped the wet bark and Fae wished she had thought to carry her shoes.

She steadied herself against Aric and half crouched as she stepped out of the boat.

And almost slipped off the tree root and into the river. Aric steadied her with a hand on her shoulder and moved up beside her, keeping them both on their feet.

Fae gripped a branch and edged towards dry land. After a few shaky steps she was close enough to the bank to jump and she landed with a squelch on soft dirt. She turned back to see Aric use one foot to shove the boat away. Pax rowed the boat out from under the trees and away from the riverbank.

Aric jumped onto the bank beside Fae and grabbed her hand.

"Come on." Aric towed her towards firmer footing. "I'm not sure how much time I have."

Fae followed, slipping and sliding, as Aric led the way up the steep riverbank. She lost her footing on a wet fern and with a grunt, landed on her knees.

Aric tugged her upright and she shook her head. She'd thought he'd be at a disadvantage without shoes, and here she was the one having the most trouble staying on her feet.

Another few steps and she slipped again. Wet branches whipped around her face, drenching her hair. She paused to drag her hair out of her eyes and looked up at Aric. Finally! Aric was crouched low behind a pine tree, staring out above the lip of the slope.

Fae joined him, keeping low and out of sight.

A narrow road was cut into the side of the riverbank. To their right the road led down towards the marsh and the mouth of the river, to their left, the rutted and pitted road led up towards the town. Beyond the flat width of the road, evergreen trees marched up a steep hill.

"I don't see anyone," Fae whispered. "Or hear them either." She clambered up to the road and stood up straight, shaking her skirt to dislodge the mess of twigs and leaves and mud that clung to it. The journal in her skirt pocket banged against her knee and she sucked in a breath. When she lifted her skirt to look, the knee was red and swollen from falling too many times.

"Are you all right?" Aric asked. He bent over to look and she let her skirt drop.

She felt strange letting him look at her leg now that they were alone.

"I'm fine," she replied. "How about you?"

Aric rolled his shoulders. "I'm fine."

"No," Fae said. "I mean, how are you from being on land?"

"I said I'm fine," Aric snapped. "Let's go."

He headed left at a brisk pace and Fae had to run to keep up. He must have heard her panting, because he stopped and waited for her.

"Sorry," he said when she reached him. "It's just . . . my mother always asks me that, whenever I've been on land." He sighed. "I think she hopes that if I keep forcing myself, one day I'll be able to live somewhere other than on the river."

"Because your father was from one of the towns?"

"He wasn't my father," Aric said. "He was just the man who fathered me. There's a difference."

They trudged on in silence and soon the trees had thinned enough for Fae to see the top of the ridge. They would be coming to the town soon.

Aric sighed and Fae reached for his arm.

"What does it feel like?" she asked. "The curse."

"It depends," he replied. "On the bridge I slowly start to feel like I can't get a full breath." He glanced over at her. "That doesn't happen for hours. But on land." He looked up towards the dawn sky. "It usually comes on quicker. One minute I'm fine and a minute later I feel like I'm drowning." Aric stopped walking and turned to her. "I'm not though," he said, gripping her shoulders, meeting her eyes. "Drowning. If you can keep me calm and get me to the river, I'll be fine."

"All right." Fae nodded. "I'll get you to the river if it . . ."

"When!" Aric said. "Not if, when."

"All right, when it happens, I'll keep you calm and get you to the river."

"Thank you," Aric said. Then he started walking faster. "Let's go. We're wasting time."

ONCE AT THE top of the ridge, the road veered away from the river to the town. Aric craned his neck at the buildings that crowded the street. He'd never been as far as one of the towns—had only recently stepped on the roadway of the bridge. The structures here were not orderly, like on the bridge, where the fronts of buildings all lined up along the roadway—here everything was built haphazardly. On one side of the street the houses were built side by side and the doors opened right onto the road, while on the other side, houses were set back from the road with an expanse of grass or flower beds in front.

"We need to stay close to the river," Aric said. He sucked in a breath, feeling his chest tighten. It had started already.

"Yes," Fae replied. "But we'll also need to stay out of sight from the bridge: Bridgers man the gates."

The narrow street widened the closer they got to the bridge. The buildings here were better kept and grander as well, larger than anything Aric had ever seen before. The road jogged to the right a little and he glimpsed an open space ahead.

Fae grabbed his arm and pulled him into the shade of a shrub that grew at the corner of a house. He peered out at a large square. The pattern of the intricately laid cobbles led across the open space to two stone gateposts on the other side.

"The bridge gates," Fae said and pointed ahead. "For Waglenn Landing. I've never seen them from this side."

Aric inched further into the shrub. He dragged a hand across his forehead, wiping sweat away. He took a shallow breath, covering his mouth to muffle the wheezing cough.

Fae studied him for a moment. "Are you all right?" she asked.

Aric gulped and nodded, closing his eyes briefly. "So far."

"All right." Fae craned her neck to see out into the square. "I don't need to find the baker. There are some vendors opening up their stalls—I'll talk to one of them and find out who I should speak with. You stay here."

Aric nodded and slid down to sit with his head on his knees. He could hardly breathe now. He tried to gulp some air but although his mouth was open wide, his chest barely rose. He took another quick breath, feeling like a fish out of water, gasping futilely as it tried to survive.

I am breathing, he reminded himself. *I am breathing*. He stifled a cough. It didn't feel like any air was getting to his lungs but he knew it was. He sucked in another breath and closed his eyes, hoping Fae would return soon. He wasn't sure he could make it to the river without her help, no matter how many times he told himself he was fine.

Chapter Eleven

FAE FROWNED WHEN she glanced back at Aric. He was slumped over his knees and barely looked alert. Was he all right? He raised a hand to her and she squared her shoulders. There was no time to search out whoever was in charge. The best she could do was warn these vendors of the dangers from the conjurers and hope they spread the word. Wailes would search for readers closest to the gates anyway, wouldn't he?

She smoothed her hands down over her muddy skirt. She just hoped they believed her.

The nearest vendor, a small woman, was busy setting out knitted socks and scarves and gloves to help ward off the chill of the coming winter.

"Excuse me, mistress," Fae said softly.

The woman grunted but continued hanging her goods across the front of her small booth.

"Mistress? Can I have a word?"

"I got nothin' to give away," the woman said. She finally turned around, a pair of tall, thick socks clutched in her hands. Small eyes darted over Fae, taking in her muddy but finely made woollen skirt and blouse. "What can I do for ya?"

"I have a message," Fae said. "For whoever is in charge of Waglenn Landing."

"D'ya think I knows who that be?" the woman snorted. "I got no cause to deal with them."

"Please," Fae said. She glanced at the bridge. If she lingered too long, or the woman was too loud, would the Bridgers come to investigate or would they be forced to stay on the bridge—on their own territory? "The conjurers will be looking for those who can read—you must not let them take anyone."

"Read!" The woman's voice was shrill with laughter, and loud enough that one of the other vendors looked over at them. "Don't need to read to knit." She stared at Fae for a moment. "Buy somethin' or be off. Ye look like trouble, elsewise."

Fae ducked her head and pretended to study a scarf. This woman had no idea what she was trying to say—nor did Fae think she would care even if she did.

"Thank you for your time," Fae said and slowly turned to the next stall.

The next vendor straightened as she approached and placed himself between Fae and the vegetables he was stacking.

"What do ye want," he said.

"Just to warn you," Fae said. "To warn all of Waglenn Landing." She met his eyes. He didn't look friendly, for all he was smiling at her.

"'Bout what?"

"The conjurers," Fae said, dropping her voice to a whisper. "They will be looking for those who can read. You must not let anyone go to the bridge."

"Why?" The vendor looked nervously at the bridge. "What will happen to them?"

"They'll never be seen alive again," Fae said. She looked into the vendor's face, expecting derision and contempt. Instead she saw fear and worry.

"They already come askin'," he said to her. "Didn't think good would come of it, I told the council so just yesterday." He glanced at the bridge again. "Told my sister to keep her son away from them. He's trainin' to do accounts. It's numbers, but close enough to readin', is what I was thinkin'."

"Probably," Fae said. "And the council, did they believe you?"

"Council don't like the bridge, or the conjurers who control it.

They didn't need me tellin' 'em not to trust 'em."

"Good," Fae said, relieved. Waglenn Landing was already on the alert. She could go get Aric and head to the river.

"Well, Bleddyn, what ya got here?"

Startled, Fae turned to find a large man in a once-white apron hovering behind her.

"Nothin' that concerns you, Mallinder. Customer was just wondering when the berries will be back." He paused and shifted his body so that Fae was partially behind him. "Told her berries is done until spring."

"Berries," the other man, Mallinder, repeated. "She don't look familiar. Where you from?"

"How is that your business?" Bleddyn asked. "Just 'cause you want to know, don't mean people gotta tell you."

"I'm just makin' conversation," Mallinder replied. "If your customer got nothin' to hide, then why wouldn't she tell me?"

"I'm from across the river," Fae said. "Now if you'll excuse me." Fae turned and started to walk back across the square to where she'd left Aric.

"Hey, you didn't come across the bridge," Mallinder called out. "How'd you get over here?"

Fae shrugged and kept walking. A few steps later she heard Mallinder call out again, but not to her. She risked a glance over her shoulder. *By the Seven!* He'd called for the Bridgers. Two of them were running towards her, fast. Fae picked up her skirts and ran.

"Aric," she called out. "Aric, get ready to run!" She reached him just as he staggered to his feet, and Fae grabbed his arm to steady him. He choked and stumbled against her and she tightened her grip on him. He had to be able to run, he had to!

"This way!" she panted as she steered them away from the river. It was the wrong direction for Aric but she was hoping that the Bridgers wouldn't search too far inland.

Aric wheezed and stumbled, forcing Fae to slow down.

Aric bent over, gasping for breath. "Keep going," he managed to say.

Fae looked past him, towards the square. Two Bridgers stood at the end of the street with the vendor Mallinder hovering behind them. Even from here she could tell that the vendor was urging them on. One shook his head and relaxed, but the other glared at her. Fae sucked in a breath. It was Shiv, Wailes' favourite Bridger, the one with the son she was supposed to marry.

He said something to the other Bridger, who shook his head and crossed his arms. Shiv shrugged and started down the street towards her and Aric.

"Aric, come on," Fae said. She pulled him upright.

His eyes were wild and his face was pale. "Not drowning," he gasped. "Remember."

Fae nodded, not sure if he was reminding her or himself. They had to get to the river but evading Shiv meant they needed to move deeper into the town.

Fae pulled a staggering Aric down the first cross street she came to. For a few steps it led left, towards the river, the way they wanted to go. Then the street ended and the only way forward was toward the hillside. She hurried Aric as fast as she could, but he stumbled and gasped for breath as he ran.

The street spilled out into another, smaller square. Fae kept them to the edge of the open space, in the shadows of the buildings that lined the square, always heading upriver. More vendors had set out their wares here but there was only one stall—the rest had laid blankets out on the flagstones and goods were piled up on the blankets.

There was a shout from behind them—Shiv was calling for people to stop them. A few vendors looked her way, curious, but none did more than look.

Desperate, Fae dragged Aric behind her. She headed out across the square, sidestepping blankets piled with goods. There was a street across from them she thought would take them upriver. Aric stumbled and Fae dragged him across a blanket, scattering potatoes in their wake. The vendor shouted at them but didn't try to stop them.

"Get them," Shiv yelled, closer now. "There's a reward for the girl."

A man stepped in front of Fae, and before she had time to go around, she collided with him. He grabbed her arms and Aric dropped to the ground. Afraid, Fae looked up at him.

"Help us," she said in a small voice. "He's a Bridger—he works for the conjurers."

The man's face clouded with anger as he looked over Fae's

shoulder. "I have no quarrel with the river folk," he said with a nod to Aric. "They have always dealt fairly with me."

"Bridger!" the man called out as he stepped in front of Fae. "You have no reason to be in Waglenn Landing."

At the mention of the word Bridger, the people closest to Fae and Aric looked up. A few, most frowning, headed towards them. Fae pulled Aric into the gathering crowd, who formed a protective ring around them.

"Aric, you're not drowning," Fae said to him, willing it to be true. He lifted his face to her and nodded as he struggled to take a breath.

"Not drowning," he repeated.

"The girl is wanted by Conjurer Wailes," Shiv called out. "Let me pass."

"Conjurer Wailes," the man said, "may hold sway over the bridge, but he does not have any say over what goes on in this town."

"You dare obstruct Head Conjurer Wailes?" Shiv asked. "I want to speak to your head councilman."

"You're already talking to him," the man replied. "And I've heard enough of Conjurer Wailes' demands. He's getting no more of our young who can read and *invited* guests to Waglenn Landing can stay as long as they like. *You* are not invited."

"I will tell my master," Shiv replied. "He will not be pleased."

"No, I suppose he won't be," the councilman said. "But he does not rule this town."

"No he doesn't," Shiv agreed. "At least not yet."

"Is that a threat?" the councilman said.

"Consider it a promise," Shiv said. "Conjurer Wailes will not be kind to any who helped the girl escape."

"What'd she do?" someone from the crowd asked. "If Wailes' is so powerful, what could one young woman have done?"

"Conjurer Wailes has his reasons," Shiv said.

Fae peeked over a woman's shoulder in time to see Shiv's hard gaze sweep across the crowd. She shivered and ducked her head, not wanting to meet his eyes. Aric dropped to his knees, and she knelt down beside him.

"Aric, Aric." Fae shook him, but when he started to cough, she stopped. His breath was little more than a wheeze.

"Aric, you are not drowning!" she said firmly. "You are not

drowning!"

"Not drowning," Aric mumbled. He took a slightly deeper breath. "Not drowning."

He kept repeating the words to himself and his breathing seemed to steady.

A shadow loomed over them and Fae looked up. Had Shiv found them after all? But no, it was the Waglenn Landing councilman. He hovered over them with a worried look on his face.

"I suppose you can tell me what's going on with the conjurers," he said.

Fae nodded. "But I need to get my friend to the river," she said. "Upriver from the bridge."

"All right. And then you'll answer my questions."

It was a statement, and Fae simply nodded. She wanted them to know, but if they realized the true danger would they decide to hand her over to Wailes? She looked at Aric's pinched face. She had to trust they wouldn't, for his sake. He might not be physically drowning but if he couldn't take a breath he would die all the same.

The councilman led them across the square, a small knot of townspeople crowding around them. Fae could no longer see or hear Shiv, but she was certain he was watching the small group. Wailes would want to know where they went.

Aric stumbled against her, and Fae gripped his shoulders more tightly, taking some of his weight onto her. The councilman turned right, down a narrow street that led them away from the bridge.

"We'll get you back to the river," the councilman said. "I figure you didn't want the Bridger to know exactly where you're going."

"No, we don't," Fae said. The councilman took Aric's other arm, and Fae sighed in relief.

They walked a few blocks before making a sharp left. The roadway sloped downward past a few ramshackle huts before it faded to a rocky, well-worn path.

The councilman stopped and turned to the half a dozen people who were still following them. "All right, everyone," he said. "Thanks for your help. I'll just see these good folk safely away. I'm convening a meeting for tonight at sundown."

A couple of men in the crowd stepped up and, with their backs to Fae, Aric, and the councilman, blocked the way forward for the others. There were a few mutters about needing to know what was going on, but soon the small group headed back up into town.

"Can't be sure the conjurer's reach doesn't extend this far," the councilman said. "Now, let's get this young man back to the river." He pulled Aric upright and led them down the rocky path.

They followed a bend in the path and after stepping past a few pine trees, the councilman stopped.

They were on a cliff that overlooked the river. The Aberhayle glinted in the sunlight far below. Fae craned her neck—she could just make out the church steeple of Durnham, on the other side of the river, but the bridge itself was hidden behind a bend.

A small wooden platform was in front of them, and the councilman hunched over it.

"Do you think your friend can manage the ladder?" the councilman asked.

Fae helped Aric slide to the ground—his breathing seemed a little stronger—before she stepped over to the councilman. Thick ropes were secured to the platform and he was carefully feeding a rope ladder over the edge.

Fae looked past the councilman and over the edge. It was a sheer drop to the river—about half the height of the stairs from her workroom. A smaller, wooden platform perched below, built into the cliff face. The river was at low tide, she guessed, since the platform looked to be a foot or so above the water.

"Is there another way?" she asked. If Aric slipped he would fall onto rocks.

"Not one that will keep where you went a secret," the councilman said. "I'll go down with him." He let the last of the rope ladder slip off the platform and stood up, wiping his hands on his shirt. "I've done it before with my children."

"What about when we get down to the river?" Fae asked. "I don't see a boat."

"Not to worry. Rivermen keep a close watch on these platforms." He bent and pried a board off the floor of the platform and pulled out a length of rope. "In case I need to consult with them. Here, you go first, then I'll send the lad." He wrapped one end of the rope around his waist before reaching down to Aric with the other. Once the rope was securely tied, the councilman tugged. "Go on," he urged her. "I won't let him fall."

Fae tucked her skirts into her waistband, thinking that it would be so much easier if she wore trousers, like the men did. The councilman steadied her as she sat down and swung her legs out over space. Carefully, she set her feet onto a rope rung and firmly gripped the lip of the platform.

She took one foot off the rung, reaching down with it until she found the next step. She ducked below the platform and grabbed hold of the sides of the ladder.

Forty three steps, that's how many she counted before her shoe finally hit the wood of the platform. She stepped down with her other leg and her knees gave out and she sank to the wood. She took a deep breath and looked up. The councilman gave a jaunty wave and then she saw Aric's bare foot slip over the edge of the upper platform.

Fae stared as Aric inched slowly down the ladder. He was four rungs down when he paused. The councilman quickly swung over the edge and stepped onto the ladder. It swung wildly for a moment, and Fae grabbed it, trying to keep it steady.

Another glance showed her that Aric had moved down another rung. The rope that tethered him to the councilman hung slack beside the ladder.

The ladder bounced and twisted beneath her hands as the two men steadily climbed down. Halfway down, Aric placed a foot on a rung and then suddenly the ladder bucked and his foot slipped off. With a yelp he twisted his leg around as he tried to find a place to put his foot. The motion caused the ladder to buck again, and this time it twisted from Fae's hands. Aric's other foot slipped off the ladder and he hung by his arms. He coughed and gasped, wriggling his body, trying to get his feet back on the ladder.

"Careful now," the councilman called from above. "Try not to swing so much."

Fae grabbed at the ropes and hung on despite the pain of them sliding across her palms. She leaned back, letting the weight of her body stabilize the ladder. She heard Aric gasp once more, then he let out a strangled cry. She looked up in time to see his hands slip off the ladder.

The rope that tethered Aric to the councilman snapped taut and both men grunted in pain. The ropes jumped in her hands but she held on, practically sitting as she put all of her weight into keeping the ladder taut.

Chapter Twelve

"LAD, ARE YOU all right?" the councilman called from above him. "Grab onto the ladder."

Aric breathed out once, the pain from where the rope dug into him making him wince. He clutched at the rope, shifting it until it rested more on his ribs instead of the soft flesh of his belly. He spun slowly on the rope, the ladder just out of reach of his outstretched hand.

He looked down at Fae, her face pale, and nodded. He would not fall on her, he wouldn't.

Ignoring the pain, Aric swung back to the ladder. He reached out and his fingertips brushed a rung, and then momentum brought him close enough to grasp the rope. He grabbed it and pulled himself onto the ladder, twisting his legs as he searched for footholds. Once he had his feet back on the ladder rungs, he let out a big breath. The ladder jumped and he looked up to see the councilman take two steps down towards him. The tether line was slack again and Aric loosened the rope from around his chest and stomach. He would have bruises, but at least he was alive.

"Thank you," he said to the councilman. "I hope I have the worst of it."

The man grinned. "It's a good system," he said. "It's worked before."

More slowly now, Aric made his way down the ladder. Finally he was close enough for Fae to grab him. She steadied him, her hands on his waist, as he stepped onto the platform. Exhausted, he slumped to the ground as the councilman climbed the rest of the way down.

Gingerly, Aric untied the rope from around his waist. His hand touched a rib and he sucked in a breath. He looked up at Fae, who hovered over him, a worried look on her face.

"I can breathe now," he said. "I didn't notice while I was on the ladder."

"Thank the Seven," she said. "I was worried the effect wouldn't reverse so quickly."

The councilman stepped off the ladder. "That could have gone better," he said as he untied the rope from around his waist and let it drop to the floor of the platform. "Don't think there's any permanent damage, but it's a sight more painful than the time my son slipped." He stretched his arms over his head. "But he was just a lad of eight, not a full grown Riverman." He turned to Aric. "Are you all right?"

"Just bruised I think," Aric replied. He stood up, wincing.

"Me too, a rib or two," the man said. "At least we're at the river."

"Yes," Aric agreed. "And I can breathe." He took another deep breath, trying not to wince from the pain in his side. Even if he'd cracked a rib, he couldn't let it slow him down.

"Good," the councilman said. "We can talk now. It might be an hour before someone comes." He sat at the edge of the platform and dangled his feet out over the edge. "I'm Larwood, by the by. As I told the Bridger, I'm the head councilman for Waglenn Landing."

"I want to thank you, Councilman Larwood," Fae said. "I'm Faelin Keetley."

"The bookbinder's daughter?" Larwood asked, his eyebrows raised.

Fae nodded.

"I heard about your father," Larwood continued. "I am sorry."

"Thank you," Fae replied. "Did you know him?"

"No. But much of our livelihood depends on the bridge so we on the council keep abreast of their news." Larwood fixed his gaze on Aric. "Much like Rivermen."

"Yes," Aric agreed. "We also are at the mercy of the conjurers."

"How?" Fae asked. "I thought . . . I assumed that the towns were independent."

"The bridge controls trade," Larwood said. "Goods traded between Waglenn Landing and Durnham must all cross the bridge. And since there are no suitable places to dock downriver of the bridge, goods travelling to and from the Dark Sea need to pass under it."

"Can't the Rivermen take goods across the river?" Fae asked.

"No." Aric shook his head. "The conjurers forbid it. I told you that they can dam the river."

"Yes," Fae said. "And flood upriver and disrupt the fishing."

"And worse," Aric said. "If they flood upriver they can release all the water at once. That surge of water could smash the upriver village into the bridge and sweep the downriver village out to sea. We cannot risk angering them." Especially not Wailes, he thought. Wailes had threatened to finish the curse—Aric didn't think flooding the Rivermen out of their homes would concern Wailes.

"It harms the towns as well," Larwood said. "Last time the river was dammed trade was disrupted for weeks and there was very little fish. People starved—*children* starved."

"I didn't know," Fae whispered. "Why didn't I know?"

"Your father would have been a boy," Aric said. "Perhaps he was never told? Or people on the bridge didn't notice?" Or it just hadn't concerned them. Aric was the very first Riverman to befriend someone from the bridge, so his mother had told him. They sold them their fish, but never before had one of them set foot on the bridge.

"Ah, here come friends," Larwood said.

Aric peered upriver. Yes, there was a boat. Not a dory, like they used near the mouth of the river, this was a canoe, a long narrow boat that sliced through the water. Some of them had sails, but if this one did, he didn't see a mast.

As it got closer he recognized one of the two people paddling it. It was the head of the Rivermen upriver. He'd met him a few times with his mother.

Aric stood up and waved to the paddlers. "Chart Upton, well met," he said.

Chart paused and rested his paddle on the gunwales, shaded his eyes, and stared up at him. "Aric," he said. "I should have known."

A chill ran down Aric's spine at Chart's words and he shivered. The only reason Chart would know that he would be here was if he'd been told to watch for him. And the only one who would tell him to was Wailes.

"Chart," Larwood called. "Happy we are to see you. Toss me the line."

Larwood grabbed the rope that was thrown and quickly pulled the boat into the small dock.

Only Chart jumped out, leaving the other paddler in the boat, one hand on the dock, steadying it against the pull of the current.

"I cannot claim the same happiness," Chart said. "Although I am relieved to find the shaman's son safe and whole."

"Shaman's son . . ." Larwood's voice trailed away as he looked from Chart's sombre face to Aric's. Then his eyes darted to Fae. "And the bookbinder's daughter," he said. "This does not bode well."

"No," Chart agreed. "Let's sit and discuss." He sat down cross-legged.

Larwood sat and dangled his feet over the edge of the platform again, and Fae looked at Aric.

He took her hand and gingerly settled down onto the platform with her at his side.

"I take it Conjurer Wailes has asked you to watch for us," Aric said.

"Ask isn't the word I'd use," Chart replied. "He sent some of his Bridgers through Durnham to find me." The older Riverman looked away. "One didn't think I came quick enough. He broke the arm of the lad sent to fetch me." Chart looked down at the river, shaking his head. "A grown man hurting a ten-year-old boy."

"We expect they're doing worse," Aric said. He met Fae's eyes and nodded, silently urging her to take up the tale.

"After my father's death, I found a secret room," Fae said. "It looks like it holds a copy of every single spell book ever bound by a Keetley." She sighed and raised her eyes. "Wailes has them now and we think he's been looking for people to read the spells."

"Are they dangerous?" Larwood asked. "These spells?"

"Yes," Fae replied. "There are so many that we have to assume that some will be very dangerous. And they certainly are to those reciting them. We found two bodies already, downriver. One was Wailes' own apprentice."

"Could they have jumped?" Chart asked. "Every year people jump from the bridge."

"Do they?" Fae asked. "That's what you're told, but do they jump or are they tossed? Because it looked like Thorpe Wailes couldn't even walk by himself, let alone climb out of a window to jump and end up downriver."

"I knew two men who were found downriver from the bridge," Larwood said. "I never believed that they jumped, but I couldn't say anything, not against the conjurers." He sighed and shook his head. "I have no reason to trust them. It didn't feel right, the conjurers looking for folk who can read, so I told them no."

"Did anyone go?" Aric asked. If Wailes had more people who could read he could possibly complete the curse. His hand rested on the dock beside Fae's, and he stared down at the webbing he had that she didn't. What would he turn into if the curse was completed? Would he even look like a person? He feared that his mother wouldn't—she already looked inhuman—but his father was from one of the towns. That part of him would be unaffected, wouldn't it?

"I think a lad went, before we knew to warn people," Larwood said. "There's not so many folk with that skill—I spoke to every one left. I'll talk to them again now that I know why Wailes wanted people who can read." He spat into the river. "He'll not get any more from my town."

"Good, that just leaves Durnham," Fae said. "We need to warn them."

"Chart, you'll need to lend me a boat so Fae and I can cross the river," Aric said. "We'll go when it's dark, so no one on the bridge can see us."

"Aric," Chart said. "I don't see this as Riverman trouble. Does your mother know you're doing this? Going against the conjurers?"

"Yes," Aric replied. "And this *is* Riverman trouble. Fae was stung by a ray—a big one—and my mother says changes are coming. And now Wailes has threatened to complete the curse."

"Complete the . . ." Chart started to speak but then he stopped, his mouth open. The colour had drained from his face and his eyes were wild. "Sweet Berhalla, is that even possible?"

"Yes," Aric replied. "I heard him say he has the second part of the spell. We have to assume he'll use it."

"But it must be a powerful spell," Fae said. "Powerful enough that it could kill whoever recites it. Wailes won't recite it himself. He needs someone else, but he's already used up two people from the bridge—he can't afford to lose many more before people get angry. He still needs the merchants."

"So he's looking for someone from off the bridge to recite the curse," Larwood said. "If they die in the process, he doesn't need to explain their absence."

"We'll get you a boat," Chart said. He glanced over at the Riverman who still sat in the canoe. "But we need to keep this quiet. I do not want to panic my people."

"Agreed," Aric said.

"Councilman Larwood," Fae said and turned to face him. "Do you have a contact in Durnham that can be approached?"

"Yes," Larwood replied. "They don't have a council as we have, but I have dealt with the head of their church, Cleric Kenway. He's a fair man, and smart too. I can send a runner with a message today and let him know you're coming."

"Over the bridge?" Fae asked. "You can't. You've said no to Wailes—anyone you send across the bridge might be found downriver tomorrow. I'll have to convince Cleric Kenway myself."

"Oh," Larwood said. "Yes, I suppose you're right."

He patted his jacket pockets before reaching his left hand in and pulling out a pipe. He knocked it against the dock, but instead of finding leaf to fill the pipe, he handed it to Fae.

"Here, give him this," Larwood said. "We've met a few times and he has admired this old pipe of mine. Perhaps he'll recognize it."

"Thank you," Fae replied and tucked the pipe into her skirt pocket.

Aric shaded his eyes and looked at the sky. Just after midday, he thought.

"Councilman Larwood," Aric said. "I think it's time for us to part. Thank you for your help." Aric stood up, trying not to wince at the pain in his side. Carefully, he held out a hand to Fae and she scrambled to her feet.

Larwood stood as well and placed a hand on the rope ladder.

"I did it more to keep the Bridgers from getting what they wanted than to help you," Larwood said. "But I'm glad I did. Chart, thanks for turning up. I'll see you in better times, I hope."

Larwood stepped onto the ladder and started climbing up it faster than Aric expected. He was halfway to the top before the other Riverman had pulled the boat in closer.

Chart helped Fae step into the boat and waited while Aric followed her. He crouched in the middle of the canoe while Chart and the other Riverman paddled them upriver. At the bend in the river, Aric looked back in time to see the rope ladder being hauled up. At least they knew one town wouldn't give Wailes anyone else who could read. Hopefully Durnham would do the same. Then his people would have a little more time—and he and Fae could figure out how to break the curse.

Hewitt exited his house and glanced across to Conjurers Hall. He didn't see anyone and the windows were curtained on the inside, but his skin prickled as though he was being watched.

Gerick Dabel answered his door, and Hewitt knew by the look on his face that his fears were confirmed.

"He's dead," Gerick said as soon as the door was closed. "Wailes said there was no body, that the spell burned him to ash."

"Do you believe that?" Hewitt asked as he followed the apprentice to Dabel's office.

"No," Gerick replied. "I don't believe any conjurer has a spell that will do that. I know we don't."

Hewitt had to agree. None of his spells were so destructive.

"Could it be because it wasn't a Wailes spell?" Hewitt asked. "Could it have interfered with his existing condition?"

"I don't think so," Dabel said from where he sat behind his desk. "At least I've never heard of anything like that." He paused, a worried look on his face. "I approached Tadlow."

"What?" Hewitt hadn't expected Dabel to involve the others. "We don't know if Wailes has talked to anyone, promised them new spells."

"A dead apprentice concerns us all," Dabel said.

"I suppose," Hewitt replied. "What did Tadlow say?"

"He doesn't believe a spell could destroy a man so completely either," Dabel said. "But since Wailes says that Thorpe is dead, he insists we force him to pay the family, just as he had to."

Tadlow's first apprentice had died while gathering ingredients for a complex spell. He'd been angry when the rest of the conjurers forced him to compensate the man's family.

"Yes," Hewitt said and sighed. "I suppose that's all we can do for poor Thorpe." He glanced at Gerick. "I wouldn't visit Wailes alone again."

"He would never act against my apprentice," Dabel said.

"I'm not so sure," Hewitt replied. "I believe he has all of our spells. Once he's gone through them he will know our strengths." He glanced at the books that lined the shelves. "And our weaknesses. I do not have any particularly useful or powerful spells."

"Nor I," Dabel said. He spread his hands on the desk top and stared down at them.

"Maybe none of us do," Gerick said. "Maybe Wailes will find nothing useful in all those books."

"What about Sherston?" Hewitt asked. "He claims his master saved a life all those years ago." Hewitt didn't believe it, but he didn't know for certain.

"It was a small spell that stopped the bleeding," Dabel said. "That Sherston was already practically blind. He just made it seem so much more impressive than it was."

"We have to assume that Wailes knows that we are defenceless," Hewitt said. "And that his Bridgers can do whatever they want to us."

"He will have total control of the bridge," Dabel said. "And us."

"He already does," Hewitt replied. He sighed. He'd felt a fraud for as long as he'd been a conjurer—maybe it was time they died out. If none of them could do more than concoct a love potion or make a flower bloom in winter, maybe they didn't deserve the power and prestige their position afforded them.

FAE TOOK A deep breath. The air smelled of fish, of course, but on this side of the bridge, so far from the marshes and open sea, there was no tang of salt. The wooden cabin bobbed as the river surged below the flat planks of the raft it sat on.

"I am going alone," she said, interrupting the conversation that had become a heated debate over who would accompany her to Durnham. Three sets of eyes turned to look at her but only Aric blinked and looked away, his eyes downcast. The other two—Chart and his second in command, Safi—glared at her.

"We're wasting time," Fae said. "It's not as though any of you can stay on land for very long."

"We could get one of the younger ones to go," Safi said. "They are able to stay longer."

Fae squinted in the lamplight, trying to decipher the look that passed between the older woman and Chart.

At first Fae had been surprised that a woman was second in command of this Riverman village, but Safi was intelligent and had a good grasp of the politics of the bridge. And Aric's mother, as shaman, was the most revered Riverman on either side of the bridge. It was just that a woman with power—and the respect of men—was so different from life on the bridge that she'd never thought about Sigrun Rawley's authority.

"No," Fae said. "One of your youngsters was already hurt by a Bridger; they'll do worse if they know they're helping me."

"Fae."

Aric's voice was soft, and when she met his eyes she saw pain and worry. For her. She grabbed one of his hands in her own.

"They don't want me dead," Fae assured him. "They want my talent as a bookbinder."

"They won't care about bookbinding, not now that they have all those old spell books. Hewitt knows you can read," Aric said. "Which means Wailes does too. You can't go."

"I'm the only one who *can*," Fae replied. "Durnham has to be warned."

"She's right," Chart said. "Durnham won't listen to us." He frowned. "Think we're river flotsam, though they eat the fish we sell them."

The fight went out of Aric's eyes and Fae knew she'd won, although it wasn't much of a victory. She had Councilman Larwood's pipe, but that didn't mean Cleric Kenway would believe her even if she was able to find and speak to him.

"I'll take you as close as I can by boat," Aric said. "But not so close that you can be seen from the dock."

She eased open the shutter of the small window and peered out into the night.

"I need to be at the church at dawn," Fae said. "Someone will be there to ring the bell. If it's not the cleric, they'll know where to find him."

"I'll get you a canoe," Safi replied. "And a map of the currents and landings." She and Chart both left.

"You should get some rest," Aric said. "Who knows when you'll have another chance?"

Fae sighed and headed for the small cot that sat in the corner of the room and stretched out. She didn't think she would sleep but after what seemed a moment, she felt herself being shaken awake.

"Fae."

She looked up into Aric's eyes.

"Time to go."

Fae nodded and sat up. Aric settled beside her.

"You don't need to do this," he said. "You can leave—the bridge, the Rivermen, both towns—and go somewhere and keep yourself safe."

"And Wailes will finish the curse," Fae said. "I can't let that happen."

"None of that will be your fault," Aric said.

"No," she replied. "But it will be my family's fault. My ancestors have been keeping copies of books—*of spells*—for generations. With those, Wailes has the power to do whatever he likes, including finding someone who can complete the curse."

FAE PULLED HER shawl tighter around her shoulders, trying to ward off the chill. The moon was still up, a silver crescent that highlighted the ripples the canoe made as it silently glided through the water. The boat rocked as Aric switched the paddle to the other side and she heard him suck in a breath.

Frowning, she turned to face him. "You're hurt," she whispered.

Aric shrugged. "My ribs. When I lost my grip on the rope ladder."

"You should have let Safi bring me."

Aric shook his head and looked up at her, his eyes shadowed in the moonlight. "This is my fight."

"You don't trust her," Fae said. "Or Chart either."

"Not with you," Aric replied. "To them you're an outsider. Worse, a Bridger."

"I'm not . . ." Fae stopped and sighed. Anyone not from the

bridge would think they were all the same, would think that she was a Bridger. Just as those not of the river assumed that all Rivermen were the same. "But you'll be safe?"

"Yes," Aric said. "I'm the shaman's son."

"They won't want to anger your mother." Fae could understand that. Sigrun Rawley, small as she was, was intimidating.

"Or me," Aric said. "Chart wouldn't keep his position long if the upriver village found out he'd harmed the father of the next shaman."

"The father of the next . . ." Shocked, Fae stared at him. How had she not known that Aric's child would inherit his mother's position? Because she hadn't asked him. Now Aric was staring at her, his eyes no longer in shadow.

"But the next shaman won't be my child," he said in a strained voice. "It will be me."

"You'll be the shaman?" she asked. "How do you know?"

Aric looked away. "I don't, for sure. It's not something I ever expected. My mother believes that the next shaman will be my daughter. But now I'm *sure* that it will be me; that I will become shaman."

"Shamans are only women?" Fae asked.

"According to our history, according to my mother." Aric shook his head. "But I *will* be shaman."

"Will it hurt? When you become shaman?"

"I don't know," Aric replied. He winced as he shifted the paddle to the other side of the canoe, his eyes focussed on it. "But it will change me."

"How?"

"I don't know." Aric raised his anguished gaze to her.

Fae let out the breath she'd been holding in. "You'll still be you," she said with certainty and was rewarded when relief replaced anguish in Aric's eyes.

She turned to face forward again. "I'm pretty sure your mother wasn't all smiles and laughs before she became shaman." She heard a chuckle from behind her and the canoe surged forward.

A few moments later, Aric steered them under the overhanging branches of a willow tree. He nudged the canoe up to a thin branch and Fae grabbed onto some trailing fronds.

"This is as close as I can get," Aric said. "Durnham's dock is just beyond those trees."

"All right." Fae peered out towards the river. She guessed that it was about an hour before dawn. Time to go. "Hold steady while I climb out." Taking care, she half stood and grasped a thick branch. With her skirt tucked up out of the way, she swung one leg over the branch. The canoe bounced as she pushed off and hopped onto the tree.

"I'll wait here," Aric said.

"All right," Fae replied. She inched along the branch until solid ground was below her. She dropped onto the riverbank and looked back. She knew Aric was there but she couldn't see him through the tangle of willow fronds. She turned back to the steep bank, leaned forward to grab a clump of grass, and started to climb.

Fae stepped out onto a narrow path. Just wide enough for a wagon and lined with trees and bushes, the path curved around a large oak and headed towards the town. The journal knocked against her knee when she pulled her skirt from her waistband and smoothed it out. Worried, she patted the pocket. The pipe was still there and she closed her eyes in relief. She'd forgotten about it. If the pipe had fallen into the river she would have had an even worse chance of convincing the cleric that she had spoken to Councilman Larwood.

She ran a hand through her hair, dislodging a few twigs, before starting towards the town.

ARIC SQUINTED OUT at the river. It was dawn and a few boats were already out. How long would it take Fae to speak to the cleric, convince him of the danger, and make her way back to him? The lighter the day got, the more danger she would be in. Bridgers had gone through the town when they'd been looking for Chart; they might be there even now.

He sighed. He'd told Fae that he was going to be shaman based on a feeling. It wasn't something his mother thought possible, but he *knew*. And despite what Fae had said, he wasn't certain if he would still be himself once the change happened.

His mother had told him very little about her own transition but once, long ago, she'd said it had been gradual. Her powers had emerged while her mother's had faded, just as it had happened for generations. Did that mean his mother's abilities were waning?

Aric sighed and looked back out at the boats. His mother thought her inability to bear a daughter a dark omen for the Rivermen. What would she think about him being the first male shaman ever? Was that part of the change the ray signified?

He shivered. Fae had been caught with the ray—stung by it—marked. And he knew that was an omen. He shivered again and his vision blurred. He gripped the sides of the canoe as his body shook. Then the chill passed and he found himself staring at the tree branch Fae had used to get to shore. Mist swirled along it and then dissipated.

Something was wrong. Fae was in trouble. As soon as he thought it, he *knew* it to be true. Was this a premonition? Was this the beginning of his transition into a shaman?

It didn't matter. All he knew was that he had to find Fae, had to get her as much help as he could. He tugged on the line that tethered him to the tree, pulling the canoe closer. He stepped onto the branch and quickly ran along it to the riverbank.

The moment his feet hit the ground a wave of dizziness washed over him. He dropped to the ground and his chest heaved as he tried to suck in a breath.

Forcing himself to stay calm, Aric swung back up onto the branch and made his way back out over water.

He gulped in a deep breath, wincing at the pain in his ribs. The sense of drowning had been immediate—and strong. Was this tied to his shaman powers? Was that why he hadn't even been able to take a step on land? Or had his struggles yesterday used up any reserves he may have built up? He'd been able to stay on the bridge for hours, and travelling through Waglenn Landing with Fae had been difficult, but possible. But he couldn't do it today. He looked back up at the bank of the river.

Fae was in trouble and he could do nothing to help her. He stared out towards the fishing boats. He couldn't leave: he'd promised Fae he'd be here and now it was even more important that he keep his word, but maybe he could flag down one of the boats and have them bring Chart. Would he be willing to send children to Durnham now? He had to find out what had happened to Fae.

Chapter Thirteen

THE CHURCH HAD been easy to find. Taller than any other building in Durnham, she'd seen the steeple even before she'd stepped into the town proper. For the past few minutes Fae had been peering around the corner of a squat house at the front doors to the church. A bird sang nearby and she eyed the sky.

It was getting light. The cleric would have to arrive soon if he was to ring in the dawn. Unless he was already there? Hesitating, she shifted from foot to foot. She had to get into the church now, before it got too light, before the townsfolk started their days.

She closed her eyes briefly and stepped out into the lane that ran beside the house to the church.

"An early riser, I see," a man said from behind her.

Fae paused and clenched her hands. "Yes, I thought I'd say a quick prayer before I started my day." She tucked her chin to her chest and took a step, forcing herself to walk slowly. One step, two steps.

"Not from Durnham, are you?"

The voice was closer now, he was following her. "How did you know?"

"Church doors aren't unlocked until the bells are rung."

He was almost beside her now. Fae continued to walk toward

the church, her head down. A booted foot entered her line of sight as he stepped up beside her. With the doors shut, the church was no longer the haven she thought it would be. She stopped and turned to her companion.

"You!" the man said.

He grabbed her arm and Fae tried to wrench free, desperate to get away from him—from Graylon Burrage.

"Let go!" Fae said. She twisted, trying to get loose, but her cousin's stepson held on.

"Ah, you recognize me," Graylon said. He tightened his grip and twisted her arm behind her back.

Fae sucked in a breath and stopped struggling. He was bigger and stronger than she was. She'd have to talk her way out of this.

"Cousin," Fae said. "I was hoping to find you and your mother. I have a proposition to discuss."

Graylon laughed. "I hear that you are in no position to bargain. But Mother will be delighted to see you. Come on." He yanked her to his side, and with one arm around her shoulder and the other twisting her arm behind her back, he steered her through the early morning streets.

He hauled her up two steps of a small house. Dirty white paint peeled from the siding, and a light glowed in one window. Fae had a glimpse of Oleda Burrage before she was pushed through the door.

"Mother," Graylon said as he slammed the door shut. "We have a visitor. Our dear cousin from the bridge."

Fae was shoved so hard that she stumbled and fell to her knees. When she looked up, she saw surprise flit across Oleda Burrage's face. Then the woman smiled and Fae shuddered.

"Our dear, dear cousin," Oleda said and rose to pace in front of Fae. "Who just a few days ago welcomed us so . . ." she paused. "Disrespectfully. I believe we shall treat you the same."

"Let me go," Fae said.

"No," Graylon said. "You owe us."

"For what?" Fae replied. "Because you lived with my mother's cousin? Made him part of your family?"

"I put up with that disgusting oaf," Oleda said. "Because he promised that we would inherit the bookbindery. You owe me that!"

"You're the one who believed him," Fae said. She stood up and faced Oleda. "You trusted your life, your future, to a drunkard, not me. Besides, I don't have anything anymore. The conjurers have everything."

"You will marry my son," Oleda said. "Then the conjurers will give us the bookbindery."

Fae shook her head. "If I marry your son, Wailes will kill him too."

"He needs you," Graylon said. "You told us that yourself."

"Not anymore," Fae said. "He has all the books he could ever want. Now all he needs are people to read them." Fae saw the startled look that passed between mother and son and laughed. "He's been asking for readers, hasn't he? Same as at Waglenn Landing."

"Waglenn Landing?" Oleda repeated. "He asked there as well? We were told that Graylon had impressed Conjurer Wailes . . ."

"Don't go," Fae said. She didn't like these Burrages, but she didn't want Wailes to have even one more person to read the spells.

"Don't tell me what to do," Graylon snapped. "It's my chance to become a conjurer."

"No," Fae replied. "It's a chance at a painful death. You've seen what conjuring has done to Wailes but you haven't seen the rest of them."

"What do you mean?" Oleda asked. "Conjurer Wailes has an unfortunate affliction but that didn't stop him from becoming the most powerful man on the bridge."

"Then go," Fae said. "You'll find out soon enough. But remember that I warned you. Now, let me go."

"You're not going anywhere," Oleda said. "Put her in the cold room."

"Come on." Graylon grabbed Fae's arm and spun her towards a doorway. He pushed her through a rundown kitchen to a small door. He pressed her against the rough wall and leaned into her.

"Can't let you in there with a weapon," he said, his breath hot on her neck.

Fae cringed as his hands patted her skirt.

"What have we here?"

He stepped back from her and she spun around to face him. He held the journal in one hand and the pipe in another.

"What are you doing with a book?" Graylon flipped it open.

"Whose is this?"

Fae looked at her feet and Graylon shook her until she looked at him.

"Whose is this? Why do you have it?" He shook her again, this time hard enough that she lost her balance. She would have fallen except he forced her up against the wall.

"I won't ask again," he said, leaning close to her.

"It's a book Wailes wants," Fae said.

"Then perhaps I should give it to him," Graylon replied. He opened the small door and pushed Fae through it. She heard what sounded like a bar being slid across the door then footsteps receded.

She pushed and pulled at the door for a few fruitless moments before giving up. Fae clenched her fists and waited for her eyes to adjust to the dim lighting.

She heard the faint rumble of voices from beyond the door. No doubt Oleda and Graylon were plotting how to use the journal to their advantage. She hoped Graylon *did* give Wailes the book, because Wailes might very well kill him just for knowing about it.

There was enough light for her to see that shelves lined two walls of the small room. Three large wooden bins were set against the wall opposite the door. The wooden slats of the ceiling were a few inches above her head and a dirt floor muffled her footsteps.

Partly by sight, partly by touch, she started to investigate the contents of the room. A few crocks of what looked like preserves, a mound of turnips in one of the bins and two empty burlap sacks. If this was all the Burrages had to their name then they were desperate. And more dangerous than she'd realized.

They would probably trade anything—including her—for money and position.

Her search complete, Fae piled the sacks on the dank earth and sat down, trying to figure out what to do. She had to escape if she didn't want to be handed over to Wailes.

There would be no rescue by Aric and the Rivermen. Even if they could stay on land long enough to get to Durnham they would have no idea where to look for her.

She squinted at the back wall. Light seeped in from outside. Could she get out that way?

She knelt down beside the bins. A faint breeze blew in through a gap between two boards, and when she placed her hand flat on the wood, it felt damp. Was it rotten? She dragged the bin away from the wall. When she scraped a finger across the wall, wood flaked away.

The door rattled. Fae shoved the bin back in place and hurried to sit on the sacks. Light spilled in when the door opened.

"What is this?" Oleda held out the journal, her son hovering behind her. "Graylon says it's a journal of some kind. That it belonged to a mage."

"Then you don't need me to tell you what it is," Fae said. "I can't read it anyway."

"Then why do you have it?" Graylon asked.

"Because it's a book," Fae said. "Wailes wants them all, so I figured it must be worth something."

"Why does he want all the books?" Oleda asked.

"You don't want to know," Fae said. She shook her head. It would be funny if it wasn't so dangerous.

"Tell me!" Oleda shouted.

"Why should I? You don't plan on letting me go, so why would I tell you anything?"

Fae didn't get out of the way fast enough and the journal hit her cheek with a loud smack.

"I will hurt you if you don't," Oleda said. She pulled her hand back, readying the book for another strike.

"I still won't tell you anything," Fae replied. If they took the journal to Wailes, Fae might have enough time to escape. It meant Wailes would have the information in the journal, but so would she. She had the other copy.

"What is the pipe for?" Graylon asked. He gave his mother a stern look and edged past her, holding up the pipe. "You only had two items with you so both of them must be important."

"Ask the cleric," Fae said.

"She was trying to get into the church," Graylon said to his mother. "That's where I found her." He turned back to Fae. "Why would the cleric be interested in an old pipe?"

"Ask him." Fae shrugged. She wasn't sure the cleric *would* be interested in the pipe—that he would recognize it without her explanation that it came from Waglenn Landing's councilman. But it might take them out of the house long enough for her to get away.

"I'll go," Oleda said. "You stay and read the journal." She

looked over her son's shoulder and fixed her gaze on Fae. "And make sure she stays locked up."

Graylon nodded and left the room, shutting the door. Fae heard the bar being slid back into place and she jumped to her feet.

She dragged the turnip bin away from the wall and sat down with her shoulder against the wood. But as hard as she pushed, the wood wasn't weak enough to split. She tried kicking it, wrapping her shoe in a burlap sack to muffle the sound, but still the wood held. She'd have to make some noise then, which meant Graylon would come to investigate.

She piled all the turnips into one sack and swung it around, testing the weight. She thought it would be heavy enough to smash through the rotten wood, if she had enough time. The other sack she filled with the crocks of preserves. The shelves were fixed to the walls, but she pushed the empty wooden bins in front of the door, hoping that in the low light, Graylon wouldn't see them. He'd be a much easier target if he was on the ground.

With the sack full of preserves at her side, Fae hefted the turnips and with a grunt, swung it in a wide arc.

It hit the back wall with a thud and damp wood cracked and splintered. Another swing, and another. The small crack was bigger now, almost large enough for her to put her fist through. Encouraged, she kept swinging the turnips at the wall.

She heard a shout from outside the door and dropped the turnips to pick up the other sack. The door opened and Fae stood up and faced it: Graylon was silhouetted in the doorway.

"Hey!" he yelled and took a step into the room. He stumbled over a wooden bin and went flying, landing in a heap.

More furious than frightened, Fae swung the sack of crocks over her head and sent them smashing down onto Graylon. He grunted in pain as the bundle hit his shoulder. Fae dragged the load up and drove it down again. Less forceful, this time a jar glanced off his temple. His body went limp and Fae dropped the sack in relief.

Without bothering to check to see if Graylon was dead, Fae picked her way past him. She closed and barred the door and hurried to the front window. A few people were on the roadway. And Oleda was coming towards her.

Fae paused at the front door. The journal! Should she look for it? She peered outside. Oleda was close now. Banging on the cold room door told her that Graylon had recovered. She couldn't get out that way. She would have to leave the journal behind, which meant it would be in Wailes' hand soon. She ducked out of the house and slipped around the back and into the woods, Oleda's shouts following her. The town would be on alert and no doubt Bridgers on their way soon. She'd find a place to hide until it was safe. Then she'd make her way back to Aric.

HEWITT STROLLED INTO Conjurers Hall, trying to mask his fear as he passed the two Bridgers who flanked the door to Wailes' office. Were the guards there to keep others out or to keep those invited to this meeting in?

It had only been a few days since Wailes had taken control of the bookbinder's hidden books and the Head Conjurer was no longer bothering to hide what he was doing. Bridgers stood guard in front of the bookbindery and Wailes was often heard shouting orders from within. Hewitt had to assume that he'd looked at enough of the books and had determined that the rest of the conjurers were no threat.

Was that why he'd convened every conjurer and apprentice in his office today? To tell them that they had no power?

Hewitt looked over at the door. The Bridgers stood, arms crossed, in front of the now closed door. It definitely looked like they were there to keep them all in.

Tymm pushed Wailes' wheeled chair into the centre of the room then backed away to stand in the nearest corner. Shiv stood along the rear wall, beside two men, one of them a Bridger Hewitt recognized. He was showing obvious signs of spell casting—the raw skin of a Tadlow and the oversized hands of a Hewitt. He assumed the other man was a new Wailes apprentice from one of the towns.

His fellow conjurers stood in a half circle in front of Wailes. Some looked bored but Dabel looked afraid. And was he sporting a few more warts on his face? Had he been casting spells himself?

Hewitt's gaze rested on Wailes and his blood chilled when he met the other man's fevered eyes. The huge smile told him that Wailes didn't care who knew what he was doing or who was being hurt by it.

"I see you've replaced your missing apprentice," Hewitt said.

"I trust you compensated your previous apprentice's family?" He would stick to something he knew the rest of the conjurers would support him on.

Wailes' eyes narrowed and Hewitt knew he'd taken the man by surprise.

"You did say he'd died while reciting a spell," Hewitt said. "I believe the term was *reduced to ash*?" He glanced past Wailes to the two new apprentices and stifled a smile when they paled. Shiv frowned and shifted his weight from foot to foot. So, even Wailes' collaborators were uncomfortable with what he was doing. Could he use that to his advantage?

"I had to compensate when my apprentice fell into the river while collecting ingredients," Tadlow said. "I expect you to do more, since your apprentice died while actually conjuring."

Wailes looked from Tadlow back to Hewitt. He gave him a slight nod, but Hewitt knew it wasn't an agreement about his request to compensate Thorpe's family.

No. Quillan Wailes had just declared war on him. Hewitt let out a breath and his shoulders relaxed for the first time in days. They knew where they stood, he and Wailes. Now it was just a matter of time before one of them was dead.

"You are right, Tadlow," Wailes said. "I will compensate the baker for the loss of my apprentice. Now, to the reason why you were all invited." Wailes waved a hand and the Bridgers all stood straighter. "I have found a spell book, a very old spell book. One that does not seem to belong to any of us seven." He looked at Tadlow. "Poor Thorpe couldn't contain his excitement and I'm afraid he took it upon himself to try to work with the spells. The result was disastrous, as you've heard."

"Can we see the spell that killed him?" Hewitt asked. What did Wailes mean, the spell book wasn't for one of the seven? No other conjurers existed. Or had they? And why was Wailes telling them he'd only found one? He'd seen dozens of books on the floor of the book bindery—was this the only one with old spells? "We don't want that happening again."

"Unfortunately Thorpe was working in secret," Wailes replied. "I don't know which specific spell he recited. Shiv."

The Bridger stepped forward and handed a leather bag to Wailes. The conjurer slipped a book out of the bag and held it up.

"This book," Wailes said. He held the book up in one gnarled and twisted hand. "The language is archaic and I do not recognize the binding as one of ours. I was hoping one of you knew more."

"Can I see?" Hewitt asked. Wailes nodded, and Hewitt stepped forward to take the book from his outstretched hand. Dabel shuffled over and peered at the book.

Hewitt ran a hand across the leather. Wailes was telling the truth. The binding did not match anything used for conjurers today. How could that be? Who had this book belonged to? Would Faelin have been able to tell them what skin this was? Excited now, Hewitt opened the book.

"And it contains spells," Dabel said. "You're sure?"

"Of course I'm sure," Wailes replied. "But the language is archaic enough that I cannot be sure what the spells are for."

"Or *who* they are for," Hewitt said, fascinated despite himself. Another family of conjurers! He had to know more. But now he knew why Wailes was showing them this book. He didn't have the knowledge to read the old language. Hewitt leaned down to peer at the script on a page.

Archaic, yes, but he could decipher the text easily enough. He looked up and met Wailes' eyes. Wailes knew he could do it as well.

"Dabel," Wailes said, and his smile chilled Hewitt. "You are a bit of an expert on old languages. Care to try it?"

"Don't," Hewitt whispered.

"I would love to," Dabel said. He took the book from Hewitt's hand and flipped through a few pages. "Ah, this spell seems clear enough." Dabel looked up. "And benign. A simple spell to light a candle."

Hewitt stepped away from Dabel. He didn't trust that anything was simple. Wailes would have had more than one spell from this book read aloud before bringing it to the rest of them. He was desperate, which meant that what Dabel was about to do was dangerous.

"Let me see," Dabel said. "It would help if I could sit at a table."

"Shiv," Wailes said, and the Bridger pulled a table away from the wall and set a chair down in front of it. He grabbed a candle, blew out the flame, and placed it on the table. Dabel sat down without taking his eyes off the page in front of him.

At a signal from the head conjurer, Tymm pulled Wailes' chair away from Dabel. Shiv and the two apprentices shuffled back a few steps. Hewitt crept back as well, trying to motion to the other conjurers that they were in danger. But just as for Dabel, the old book of spells was proving to be too enticing. Except for Gerick. With wide eyes, he looked from his master to Hewitt and then to Wailes and his allies before edging towards the door.

"Let me see . . . this word is . . ." Dabel muttered under his breath. "Ah, yes." A few more mumbles and he seemed to relax. "Of course."

"Can you read it?" Wailes asked.

"Yes," Dabel replied, nodding.

"Then do it," Wailes commanded.

"But I . . ."

Hewitt followed Dabel's gaze as he looked around the room. Shiv stood with his back to the wall, a knife in his hand. Dabel glanced at Hewitt and Hewitt shook his head, hoping that the other conjurer would stop. It was one thing for Wailes to ask a fellow conjurer to recite an archaic spell but it was quite a different matter to knife him if he refused. At least for now, Wailes needed at least some of them to cooperate.

Dabel took a deep breath and Hewitt's heart sank. The old man was going to recite the spell.

"*Byrnewielm dieaplieg*," Dabel said. "*Byrne* . . ."

A gout of flame engulfed the conjurer. Hewitt shielded his eyes but he felt the searing heat on the back of his hand. The flame extinguished as quickly as it had flared. Someone whimpered. Could Dabel have survived that? With spots still starring his vision, Hewitt lowered his hand.

Dabel was gone. The book lay on the table, in front of the unlit candle, seemingly unscathed, and there were singe marks on the chair, but the only thing left of the conjurer was a small pile of ash.

Reduced to ash, Hewitt thought in amazement. He hadn't believed Wailes but it was true. Oh, maybe Thorpe hadn't died this way, but someone had. And it had happened before they'd discovered that Thorpe was gone.

The whimpering continued, and he looked over to see Sherston lying in a heap, his hands covering his eyes.

Hewitt looked back at the book. Who had the conjurer been who had written down these spells? He must have been powerful! He met Wailes' gaze and nodded. War or no war, he needed to know more.

FAE STIFLED A scream as a surge of pain erupted in her head. It faded quickly and she sat up, gingerly rubbing her temples. A wave of dizziness almost caused her to topple over and she gulped in a breath and squeezed her eyes shut. After a few moments, the dizziness abated and she opened her eyes.

The sun that filtered through the trees was weak, and from the position and length of the shadows, she thought it was late afternoon. Had they stopped looking for her? She held her breath and listened intently, but all she heard were birds singing and the wind rustling through the trees. No sounds of anyone tramping through the thick trees, no carts rattling by on the road.

She took a deep breath and tried to relax. It was time to find Aric. Holding onto a sapling, she struggled to her feet as another, less severe bout of dizziness gripped her. What was wrong with her? She'd never felt pain like that before. Finally feeling steady, she crept down towards the river, keeping well away from the dock.

Navigating through the trees that lined the river would be more difficult than taking the road back to where she'd left Aric, but she couldn't risk being seen.

Had the Burrages raised an alarm in Durham? They were the ones who had imprisoned her—they were the ones who had stolen from her. Would the townspeople side with them? Maybe not, but they would have gone to Wailes with the journal. Bridgers could be looking for her by now.

She climbed over the root of an oak, her hand on the trunk of the massive tree. She could see the river now. All she had to do was follow it to Aric.

ARIC SWATTED AT a fly and looked up at the sky for the thousandth time that hour. The sun would be setting soon and still there was no sign of Fae.

He'd only left this spot once, right after the feeling that Fae was in immediate danger had given way to a general uneasiness. He'd paddled out to the nearest fishing boat. He hadn't recognized the Riverman, but Kester had recognized the son of the shaman.

Chart had sent word that they didn't want to risk sending any youths into town until dark. Until then, the whole river was being watched by Rivermen pretending to fish. At least if Fae made it to the bank of the Aberhayle, someone would see her.

Kester, in his sail-equipped canoe, was going from boat to boat, gathering and giving news. On his last visit to Aric he'd reported that Bridgers were searching the roads and the Durnham dock. They were looking for Fae, they had to be, which Aric took as a good sign. If they were looking, it meant they didn't have her.

So where was she? He hated feeling so helpless. He was worse than useless on land; he was a burden.

"Shaman's son."

Aric peered through the trees. Kester was back.

"I have what you are seeking."

"Aric?"

Fae's voice. Aric blew out a breath. She was safe.

"Fae," he called out softly. "Thank Berhalla." Aric quickly untied his canoe and pushed off from the tree. Once out from under the willows, he saw the square sail of Kester's canoe. And Fae, sitting in the bow on a pile of nets.

"Kester, my thanks," Aric said. He grabbed the side of the other Riverman's canoe and lashed his to it before crawling across.

He settled beside Fae and hugged her. She hugged him back.

"I was worried," he said. "I had a feeling that something had gone wrong. Right around dawn."

"It did," Fae agreed. "I never made it to the church. My mother's cousin's son—the one who would have married me? He caught me."

"What do you mean, he caught you," Aric said. "He held you prisoner?"

"Yes. He and his mother." She looked away. "They took the pipe." She met his eyes. "And the journal," she whispered.

"All right," Aric said. He wasn't letting her go back to Durnham, so losing the pipe meant nothing. He knew she would regret losing the journal though. It was a tie to her family. But now the most important thing was getting somewhere safe. He turned to Kester. "Can you take us back to the village? We need to see Chart."

"Yes, shaman's son," Kester said. He paddled them out from

under the trees and soon wind filled the square sail, taking them upriver, Aric's canoe trailing them.

"Did they hurt you?" Aric asked Fae.

She shook her head—then grinned. "I knocked Graylon out cold." Her smile faltered. "He and his mother will give the journal to Wailes."

"I think they already have," Aric said. "Bridgers are looking for you. In Durnham."

"Oh Aric, I'm so sorry." Fae hung her head but he forced her to look at him.

"It's not your fault," he said.

"It is. I'm the one who insisted on going to Durnham. Now I've put your people on both sides of the bridge in danger. I'll leave."

"Yes," Aric said. He smiled at the worried look on her face. "We'll both leave. Just for a while. Sooner or later Wailes will stop looking for you." He sighed. "And Rivermen were already in danger: Wailes threatened to finish the curse. Maybe," he said and shrugged, "the journal will even distract him from that."

"Maybe," Fae said.

Aric didn't think she sounded very hopeful. An intense feeling of certainty flashed through him and he relaxed. Leaving was the right thing to do, he felt it. He frowned. This was the second time today he'd had such an intense feeling. Were they premonitions? Shaman abilities? He'd ask his mother the next time he saw her. Would she be happy he was to be a shaman? He hoped so. But it would be a surprise, which meant she'd never had a premonition about him.

HEWITT STARED AT the book on the table, his tea cooling beside it, forgotten.

The rest of the conjurers had left, taking what was left of Dabel with them. Gerick—the new Dabel—was going to arrange the final ceremony. The rest of them had been horrified, but Hewitt was fascinated. A spell that was so powerful that the backlash reduced a man to a pile of ash in moments. It was incredible!

He ran a hand across the pebbled hide that covered the book. The skin was silvered with age and a few cracks marked it, but he knew it was not any hide he was familiar with. What treasures were written inside?

"There are more books bound in that hide," Wailes said. He

sat in his chair across the table from Hewitt, his body twisted so that his head faced forward. "But I think you already knew that."

"Guessed," Hewitt said absently. "I knew there were more books, but I thought they were simply copies of all our existing spell books. I never dreamt that there was so much lost knowledge."

"Yes," Wailes agreed. "Conjurers were powerful once. With your help we can be again."

"Why do you need me?" Hewitt asked, looking up from the book.

"You were always better at the old language," Wailes said. "And my eyesight is failing."

"You think misreading and mispronouncing words might cause the severity of the backlash," Hewitt said. He relaxed a little. Wailes needed him—he would be able to strike a bargain. "What about your Bridgers?"

"Most of them can't read," Wailes replied. "And the ones who can, Shiv says he can't spare. They have other uses."

"I'm sure they do." For now, Hewitt thought, but Wailes would force them if he had no one else who could read. He ran his hand across the book again. What was this made of? "The bookbinder's daughter might have known what this was bound in."

"Interesting that you mention her," Wailes said. "Tymm."

Tymm shuffled forward from the corner he'd been standing in. He reached into his jacket and pulled out another, smaller book and set it down on the table.

"I was given this earlier," Wailes said.

Hewitt picked up the smaller book. It was bound in the exact same hide as the larger one. "Who gave it to you?"

"People hoping for my favour," Wailes said. "They got it from the bookbinder's daughter."

"Faelin? Where is she?" Even now, Hewitt would offer her his protection if she agreed to be his apprentice.

"Where she is now, I do not know," Wailes said. "But this morning she was in Durnham. I have men looking for her. But I am more interested in what this book says. It's a journal. My eyesight is too poor and I do not have anyone I trust who is able to read the more archaic wording."

"Ah, so you do miss Thorpe," Hewitt said. He'd thought the new apprentices looked more afraid than capable.

"I have someone to replace Thorpe," Wailes replied. "But I need to be sure of him before I make him privy to such secrets."

"How am I a better choice?" Hewitt asked. "You don't trust me." He was longing to open the journal, could barely stop his fingers from flipping it open. He needed to know the secrets it held.

"No," Wailes agreed. "But I know you. You *need* conjurers to be more than we are. That would justify spending your life and your health copying and reciting and selling weak spells for weak people. These books," Wailes gestured at the table with one crooked arm, "could give you that. I think they hold the key to powerful spells that could be used to do great things."

Hewitt nodded. Wailes did know him. But he also knew Wailes. "As long as you controlled the knowledge, as long as you wielded the real power."

"You would have real power," Wailes replied. "But I would be the final authority."

"Yes," Hewitt said. "I'll do it." He was never going to say anything else, even if Wailes' terms were more restrictive. He still didn't trust the man, just as he was sure Wailes wasn't going to trust him completely.

"Excellent," Wailes said. "You will live under this roof, of course. And no books are allowed out of this building."

"That's acceptable," Hewitt said. He flipped open the journal. "You will understand if I don't simply start reading this out loud, considering what happened last time words from a book bound like this were recited."

Wailes chuckled. "Of course, but I expect an account of what it says."

"I can do that," Hewitt replied. He paused, his finger on a word he didn't recognize. "I will need a few things from my house."

"I'll send Shiv," Wailes said.

Chapter Fourteen

"I WILL GET word to your mother, shaman's son," Kester said and backed out of the cabin.

Fae and Aric were in the same cabin as before, waiting for Chart. Fae sat down on the bed while Aric spoke to Kester. She'd been able to borrow a pair of trousers from Safi and she wasn't quite used to having fabric encase her legs. They were a little more restrictive than her skirt, but not as heavy and cumbersome.

Kester left and Aric sat down beside her.

"Since my mother doesn't know I'm becoming a shaman," Aric said. "I'm not sure she'll care where I am."

"Maybe not," Fae said. "But she has to be better than the people who call me family." Oleda and Graylon Burrage were probably in Wailes' hands by now, but it was hard to have sympathy for them after what they'd done to her.

"Neglect is better than imprisonment," Aric agreed, and Fae laughed. "At least you had a father who loved you."

"He also kept secrets from me." But her father *had* loved her, which was more than what Aric had grown up with.

"To keep you safe," Aric replied.

"I'd be safer if he'd told me," Fae said. "As it is I have no idea what those secrets are or what kind of danger we're in now that Wailes has the books and the journal."

"I'm sorry about the journal," Aric said. "I know it was a connection to your family."

"I think it's the key to everything," Fae said. Aric tensed beside her and she looked at him in alarm.

"You're right," he said, his voice tight. He turned to her and his eyes were wide. "Without it we are lost."

"What do you mean?" Fae asked. Aric simply stared past her, not replying. She shook his shoulders. "Aric? Are you all right? Aric?"

Suddenly he let out a breath and hunched over.

"Aric?" Fae gripped his hands. They felt cold in hers. "What is it?"

He straightened. "My abilities," he said. "They are manifesting."

"Abilities?" Fae repeated. "Shaman abilities?"

"Yes." He shook his head. "Earlier I had a feeling—a premonition—that you were in danger. I had another one when we decided to leave together. And now the journal. We have to get it back."

"No, we don't," Fae said.

"It's the key," Aric replied. "I know it is."

"Then it's a good thing I made a copy of it. I hid it on your mother's boat."

"I can ask Kester to get it," Aric said.

"No," Fae replied. "It's safe for now. I mean . . . would you be able to tell if it's all right if we wait to get it?"

Aric closed his eyes for a moment. He nodded and opened them. "I think we can wait for the journal. And we should still leave for a few days. At least, that's what I *feel* we should do."

"Then that's what we'll do."

ARIC SMILED AS Fae dipped her paddle into the river. She wasn't skilled but she was trying. A bundle of supplies wrapped in otter skin lay in the middle of the canoe—blankets, cooking utensils, and fishing gear. Chart had told him where to find a raft upstream. He couldn't guarantee what condition it was in, but if it couldn't float it might at least supply some timber to use in a new raft.

Aric swept his paddle through the water and the boat surged forward. Ahead, the river glinted in the moonlight. They'd reached the second bend Chart had described. Aric submerged the blade of his paddle, steering the canoe towards the bank. The river had cut into the earth here and trees leaned out over the water.

"Watch your head," he called softly to Fae.

She ducked as the branches of the willow trailed across her and the canoe. Aric leaned out and grabbed a handful of trailing fronds, hanging on to slow them down. It was dark under the trees and they had to be careful. They couldn't afford to hit a submerged trunk or large rock and damage the canoe.

"Fae, here, hang on," Aric said.

She grabbed the fronds from him and he swung his paddle out towards the shore. It should be here, under the first big willow tree—there. His paddle struck something solid and he reached out. The wood was wet under his hand, but it was flat—they'd found the raft and it was still floating.

"I've got it," Aric said. He pulled the canoe up beside the raft, dragging them along it until he found the rope that tethered the raft to the tree. The knot was wet and too tight to untie, so he cut it with the small knife tied to his belt. He quickly looped the rope around the stern-most thwart in the canoe and tied it off.

"All right, Fae, you can let go."

"Done," came the reply.

Aric set his paddle against the willow and pushed, and the canoe started to edge out from under the trees. He flipped the paddle to the other side of the canoe, reached out, set the blade into the water and pulled straight towards him. Slowly the canoe moved out from under the trees and further out into the river, towing the raft behind. Suddenly the raft caught the current and started dragging them downstream.

"Paddle, Fae," Aric called. He pulled with all his strength and the canoe started to inch upstream. A few tiring minutes later and they were past the bend in the river. According to Chart a beach was just ahead. They should be safe enough there.

EVEN THE FEW minutes it took to set up the shelter left him gasping for breath.

"Is this because you're becoming a shaman?" Fae asked. She

stood with her hands on her hips, staring at him. The moonlight cast a shadow on her face so he couldn't see her expression.

"I'm not sure," Aric said. He hunched over, gasping. "My mother didn't tell me much about what happened when she became shaman." He grabbed the canoe's painter line and secured it to the nearest tree. "But I'm pretty sure it didn't involve spending time on land."

"You would never be able to climb the stairs to the bookbindery now," Fae said. She wrapped her arms around herself.

"I would if I had to," Aric replied. There, the canoe was secure. He hung onto the rope as he made his way back to the beach. Fae stepped over to help but he waved her off. He was supposed to save her, not the other way around.

When both his feet were in the river, he took a deep breath.

"Your mother should have told you what to expect," Fae said.

"My mother should have done a lot of things," Aric said. "Including bearing a girl. Remember, there is no history of a male shaman. She'll be as surprised as I am.

"I'll be just a few feet away," Aric continued, ignoring Fae's snort of derision. He waded out to the canoe and climbed in. His weight caused it to sink into the sand but he was surrounded by enough water that his breathing wasn't affected. "Get some sleep, Fae," he called. He saw her nod and step back towards the shelter. He slid lower, keeping his head above the gunwales and stared out at the beach.

He'd meant what he'd said to Fae—he would *want* to make it up to the bridge—or this beach—if Fae was in danger. But he hadn't been able to help her when she'd been caught in Durnham. The flap on the shelter closed and still he continued to stare at it.

Fae tied the flap closed and crawled over to the blanket. She was worried about Aric. Two days ago he'd been able to stay on land, well away from the river, for more than an hour. It hadn't been easy, but he'd been able to do it. And the day of her father's ceremony he'd been with her on the bridge almost all day. Now both of those would be impossible.

What else were his shaman powers going to take away?

He'd told her that becoming shaman would change him. She lay down and closed her eyes. And she'd assured him that he would still be him. And he would be, but would he be like his mother too? Would his skin darken and his hands become more webbed?

It didn't matter, not to her. She trusted Aric. Since her father's death he was the *only* person she trusted. She'd asked him to marry her as a way to stay on the bridge, but now she just wanted to be with him, wherever they could live together. If that meant she lived in a Riverman's floating village, then she better get used to it.

SOMETHING LARGE WAS being dragged past her head. Fae rolled over and lifted the edge of the canvas. A log slid along the beach a few feet from where she lay, sand piling around it as it scraped a path.

"Aric?" Fae called. It wasn't quite dawn and her voice carried in the still air.

"I'm here," Aric replied, sounding out of breath.

She pulled her shoes on and after fumbling the tent flaps open, she crawled out.

Aric stood with his feet in water, pulling on a rope that was tied to the log. The raft was pulled up on the beach and the canoe drifted in the river behind it.

"Where did you find the log?"

"Just past the beach," Aric replied. "I had to run, but I was able to tie the rope."

"You should have woken me." Fae looked along the trail the log made towards the edge of the woods. She could see a few more fallen trees.

"Just because I couldn't sleep didn't mean you shouldn't."

"I'll tie the next one," Fae said. She wandered towards him. "How many trees do we need?"

"Three more should do it," Aric said. "The raft is in pretty good shape but it's a little unstable. I think adding one log to each side will steady it." He nodded towards the forest. "Can you find some kindling and make a fire? I caught some fish earlier."

"Sure." Fae headed along the beach to gather wood. She was careful to collect the wood furthest from the beach. Aric had made tying the log sound easy, but she was pretty sure it hadn't been.

FAE PUT THE flint back into the pack and fed a few more sticks into the fire. The wet stones she'd placed in the middle sizzled as the flames heated them. She'd set the fire as close to the river as she could, but even so, Aric's breathing was laboured as he knelt down across from her.

"Here." He held up two cleaned fish. "We'll need to watch them." He skewered one fish on a stick and set it down on one of the stones before repeating his actions with the second fish.

"Chart packed plates," Fae said. She pulled two battered tin plates from the pack and set them down in the sand. "And knives and forks."

"Good," Aric said. Grabbing one end of the sticks, he flipped the fish over.

After a few moments, he poked one of the filets. "Fish is ready," he said

Fae held the plates up while Aric deposited the fish. She handed him a plate and a fork before picking up her own breakfast.

The skin of the fish was crisp and the white flesh flaked off it easily. The first bite burned her mouth a little, but it was delicious even without any seasoning.

"Was that trout?" Fae asked when she'd finished eating.

"Yes. Those two were." Aric rose and went to the canoe, returning with another two cleaned fish. "These are perch." He set about putting them on the rock to cook.

"Perch is good too," Fae said as she spooned the last morsel into her mouth.

Aric laughed. "You've eaten both types before, I'm sure."

"Probably," Fae agreed. Fish was a staple for everyone who lived along the river. "But not this fresh."

Aric nodded. "They always taste better outdoors." He set his plate and fork down and sighed. "I need to finish with the raft."

"Not yet," Fae said. She reached out and grabbed his hand. When she entwined her fingers with his, the web between his fingers felt warm. "I want to know what abilities your mother has." She met his eyes. "What abilities you're going to have."

"Do we need to talk about this now?" Aric sounded angry, and he tried to pull his hand from hers but she held it tight.

"Yes." She looked down at their hands before looking back up at him. "You can barely stay on land anymore and I've seen you go into a trance. What if something else happens? I won't know what to do."

Aric sighed and closed his eyes for a moment. When he opened them, he stared out at the river. "My mother didn't tell me much, but I asked others, like Pax. Here's what I have been told. The shamans in my family have all had the same abilities, although the strength and accuracy are different for each one." He looked at her and raised one finger. "One, they have premonitions, feelings about how current events will affect future ones. My mother's have always been related to the Rivermen. So far mine seem to be related to you." He held her gaze and Fae sucked in a breath at the intensity in his eyes. Aric held up a second finger. "Two, there is knowledge that has been passed down through the generations. This usually starts early but my mother never bothered with me."

"Because you weren't a girl," Fae said.

"Three, up until me, shamans were always women, and four, shamans always only gave birth to women."

"So what does it mean?" Fae asked. "That you weren't a girl?"

"I don't know," Aric replied. "She never expected me to be shaman after her. Not only am I not female but I'm not . . ." He paused and pulled his hand from hers, holding it up between them, spreading his fingers and stretching the webbing between them. "Shamans in my family have always been like my mother. More . . . changed than other Rivermen. My grandmother told me that it was to remind us of the Wailes curse—to ensure that we never stopped looking for a way to break it. But I'm less like my mother than most Rivermen. Yet another reason why she never thought I would become shaman."

"But you are."

"I am," he agreed. "I've had premonitions." He paused. "I am the first male shaman ever, and I have no idea what *that* means."

"All right. You might have abilities never seen before," Fae said. She grabbed his hand and squeezed. "Thank you. I just wanted to know if I should expect you to, I don't know, faint or walk when you're in a trance." She dropped his hand and stood. "I'll clean up and you get back to the raft. I'm sure you don't want to sleep in the canoe again tonight."

HEWITT PUT THE journal down, careful to leave it open to a page much earlier than the one he'd been reading. Tymm was a simpleton, had been since birth, but he'd been employed by Wailes long enough for the conjurer to have trained him to spy. And he didn't want Wailes to figure out just how fast he was reading the journal.

"I'll be right there," Hewitt said, rising to his feet. The only reason Tymm ever came to this room was to summon him to see Wailes.

Not that Tymm ever actually set foot in the small room Wailes had assigned to him for reading the journal—he hovered in the doorway until Hewitt noticed. Shiv, on the other hand, simply walked in, whether the door was open or closed. Hewitt *was* certain that the Bridger was sent to spy on him.

The journal had not left this room since Wailes had put it on the small table yesterday. And every hour when he left to report to Wailes, and for the few hours he'd taken to eat and sleep last night, Shiv had been here, guarding it. The rest of the time Hewitt had spent poring over it.

And what secrets! It was a bookbinder's journal, but interspersed among the minutiae of a mundane life were astonishing revelations. The bookbinder had been born into a conjurer family. That in itself was amazing—that conjurers' had families—but this was a family not heard of since that time.

Only one member in each generation of a family was allowed to become a conjurer, so Keetley Kellen had become a bookbinder. But when neither Kellen brother had fathered a boy, Vandon had become the last Kellen conjurer. Faelin Keetley was a direct descendant of this forgotten line of conjurers.

Hewitt had kept this last bit of information from Wailes. The man was already searching for Faelin; if he knew about her bloodline he would double or triple his efforts.

Because only those who carried the blood of conjurers could perform spells unscathed—and then only the spells created by their kin. Yet another revelation! Every conjurer had created their own spells! Unthinkable today, when all they did was copy spells handed down for generations.

Both the journal and the book that Dabel had read from were bound in the same hide. Since she had the blood, Faelin Keetley should be able to recite those spells without being harmed. *That* he was keeping from Wailes as well.

Hewitt had to be the one to find Faelin. And he needed her alive. *She* was the salvation of conjurers. She could wield powerful spells; she could marry and produce children. Faelin Keetley could be the matriarch of a whole new cohort of conjurers. Ones with real power, real magic.

If Wailes knew the truth about Faelin, unless she submitted to him, he would want her dead. Even if she never knew about her potential, even if she wasn't aiding Hewitt, he would see her as a threat. And kill her.

Hewitt followed Tymm into Wailes' office. The head conjurer sat facing the door. He waved at him over the heads of two people sitting across the desk from him. One head craned around to look at him and Hewitt had a glimpse of a woman's face, pinched into a frown.

He'd seen her before, in Wailes' office. Ah yes, it was the woman who'd thought to have the book bindery because she'd married a relative of Faelin's. The one whose hopes he'd dashed when he'd informed Wailes that Shiv had an unmarried son.

"Conjurer Hewitt, these are Faelin Keetley's closest relatives," Wailes said. He motioned to a third chair in front of the desk, and uneasy, Hewitt sat down.

Wailes' smile might fool these two, but he knew it meant danger. He relaxed. But not for him.

"There was a cousin in Durnham at one time," Hewitt said. "Of the mother's." Lachlan had talked about the man a few times. His wife had hated him. And not a drop of Kellen blood in him. Hewitt's attention waned; these people did not matter to him.

"My poor Thaddeus," the woman said. "He so wanted my son Graylon to succeed."

"Graylon reads," Wailes said.

Hewitt looked at the young man, hoping his pity didn't show in his eyes. He looked proud to be sitting here with the head conjurer; his mother looked as though all her prayers were coming true. Hewitt didn't believe in the lander's gods, but he hoped they could comfort these two during what was in store for them.

"Congratulations," Hewitt said. He tried to ignore Wailes' widening grin. "It's such a rare skill."

"Yes," Wailes said. "Oleda and Graylon brought me the journal. They got it from Faelin." Wailes leaned crookedly over the desk. "Graylon said he read some of it—out of curiosity—before handing it over."

Hewitt nodded, trying to keep his fear from his eyes. Had he made the connection between Faelin and Keetley Kellen? Had he told Wailes? No, if he'd caught Hewitt in a lie, Wailes would either be furious or gloating.

"And did you have difficulty with the archaic text?" Hewitt asked, grateful that his voice was calm.

"I read very little," Graylon said. "I thought it more important to hand it over to Conjurer Wailes as soon as I could."

"And critical for you," Wailes said to Hewitt. "He confirmed that there was a conjurer family by the name of Kellen—which is the name you told." Hewitt nodded once, to hide his relief. Graylon Burrage must have read the name Vandon Kellen and not the note from his brother Keetley.

Wailes turned to Graylon. "Thank you, Graylon. You and your mother are my guests for the foreseeable future. Tymm, fetch Shiv."

Tymm lumbered out and Hewitt caught the pleased look on Oleda's face.

"I'm sure Graylon will be very useful to you," Oleda said to Wailes. "He's bright and ambitious."

Hewitt glanced from Oleda's smiling face to Wailes' contemplative one. She had no idea that she'd just guaranteed her son's death.

"I'm sure I will find a use for him." Wailes said. "Shiv—take them somewhere secure."

Oleda's smile vanished when Shiv approached, but she and her son stood and politely followed him out of the room.

Wailes turned to Hewitt. "Tell me something fascinating."

"Well," Hewitt said. "Conjurers created their own spells."

Wailes sat back in his chair. "All of them?" Hewitt nodded. "Was it dangerous?"

"Sometimes," Hewitt said, leaving out the fact that it was only dangerous for those without conjurer blood. "From what I can tell. This was the bookbinder's life, after all."

"Yes, one of the other books must describe how to create spells." Wailes chuckled. "Perhaps I'll give young Graylon Burrage a chance to prove how useful he can be."

ARIC PULLED THE rope tight. He'd had to trim a few branches off it, but finally the last log was in place. He jumped, and the raft shuddered when he landed, but it stayed high and buoyant. He did the same at each corner, testing to see how deeply the raft dipped.

He wouldn't trust it to hold a wooden hut, and he didn't plan on building a fire on it, but it should keep him, Fae, and their small pile of belongings afloat.

"Ready for the shelter," he called to Fae.

Fae waded into the water and handed the rolled up canvas to him. "Can I help?" she asked.

"Sure." Aric grabbed her hand and helped her scramble onto the raft. He smiled. She'd finally shed her boots and her bare feet flexed as she found her footing. "Tie the corner to that loop of rope over there." He watched as she followed his instructions before quickly tying his own corner down. He'd already moved to the second corner by the time she looked up from her task.

"How did you do that so fast?" Fae asked.

Aric grinned and tied the last corner off and edged over to stand beside her. "Fishing requires a lot of knots. I'm pretty fast at it."

"I've been fishing with you, and I haven't seen you tie that many knots."

"Before and after," Aric said. "Repairing nets, rigging the sale, securing my boat at the village." He bent over and picked up the centre post for the shelter. "Hold this." He handed the post to Fae. He found the top edge of the door to the shelter, lifted it, and crawled in.

"All right," he said.

Fae handed him the centre post, and he pushed it up, stretching the shelter above his head. He secured the post to the raft and turned to exit, only to find Fae standing beside him.

"It feels different on the raft." She reached out and trailed a hand along the canvas. "The light is different, and it feels more temporary." She laughed. "That sounded silly even to me. This shelter is always temporary."

"The light is different," Aric said. "Depending on where you are on the water. There are fights in the village over who gets to dock where."

"Really?" Fae asked. "It makes that much of a difference?"

"Yes. And the time of year changes the light as well. So good light in the spring may mean a dull, dark winter."

"Is being close to land good?" Fae asked. "I wouldn't think so, but your mother is shaman."

"Yet she ties up closer to the riverbank than anyone else," Aric said. "I'm not sure why. I asked her once but she said she had a feeling that it was the right spot." At the time he'd assumed she was shutting him out, as always, but now, after having had a few feelings himself, maybe she *had* told him the truth.

"I'm not sure I'd want to be in the middle of the river," Fae said. "Even with all the other boats and docks tied together, I'd feel better closer to shore."

"You would be comfortable on my mother's boat?" Aric asked. She'd always wanted the bridge—always. That's part of what they were fighting for, wasn't it? But if Fae was willing to live on the water . . .

"I think so," Fae replied. She stepped away and headed to the shelter opening. "I'll get the rest of the gear from the beach. You need to find us something for supper."

FAE DROPPED MORE wood onto the pile. It was mostly driftwood, silvered and weathered from the elements. It was easy to gather and it was dry, but it burned quickly. She'd foraged in the wooded areas that surrounded the beach looking for greener wood and had come across a few berries. But since she didn't recognize them she'd left them on the bushes.

All her life she'd had food delivered to her on the bridge: she'd never had to pick anything herself. She'd never seen where food grew, whether in a garden or in the wild. Aric wasn't much help when it came to anything other than seafood and seaweed. Any foraging he'd done had been years ago and on the other side of the bridge.

Fae added some wood. When the flames died down, she dropped the two flat rocks into the middle of the coals.

"Trout again," Aric said. He tied the canoe to the raft, stepped out of it and into knee deep water. "I didn't want to go too far upriver looking for something else." He held up three cleaned fish as he waded towards her.

Fae grabbed one and placed it on one of the rocks. It sizzled for a moment. Aric sat beside her and put a fish on the second rock.

It didn't take long for the fish to cook and they ate in silence. But by the time the last fish was cooked, Aric was wheezing.

"You get on the raft," Fae said. "I'll make sure the fire is out."

"Thanks."

Aric waded towards the raft without an argument. Which worried her. Was he getting worse? Or was he just more comfortable with her knowing how much he was struggling?

She rubbed sand on the plates and rinsed them in the river before using them to drench the fire. It sizzled and sparked when the water hit it, sending smoke and steam into the air. Once it stopped sputtering, she kicked sand onto it, careful to keep her bare foot away from the still hot rocks.

The campsite tidy, she turned towards the raft.

Aric sat cross legged at the edge of the raft, watching her. When she headed towards him, he grabbed the rope and tugged the raft closer to the beach.

After one step into the river, the raft was close enough for Fae to sit beside him. Aric let the rope out and the beach receded. A cool breeze blew and she shivered.

"Sorry there's no fire on board," Aric said.

Fae leaned into him and he wrapped his arm around her shoulder. She sighed. "Is it getting worse?" she asked. "Being on land?"

"Yes," was the reply. "But is it because I'm older or because I'm becoming a shaman?"

"A few days ago you could stay on land for an hour," Fae said. "Less than a week ago you were on the bridge almost a whole day."

"All right," he agreed. "It's because I'm a shaman. Almost."

"You don't want it."

"No. I feel like it's the only thing my mother ever gave me." He laughed, but there was no sound of joy in it. "Although it's an unwilling gift."

"It's a family legacy," Fae said. "You can't always hide from them." She stared out at the river until Aric finally turned her face to his.

"This isn't about me anymore," he said. "Tell me."

Fae nodded. Aric was the only person in the world she trusted. Even her father had kept secrets from her.

"You're not the only one with hereditary abilities. The journal talks about ten conjurer families."

"Ten," Aric repeated. "What happened to the three that are gone?"

"I know what happened to one of them," Fae said. "The conjurer side died out." She reached for his hand and gripped it. "But the bookbinder side survived. My ancestors were conjurers. And like shaman abilities, conjuring is in the blood."

"You can do magic?"

"I already have," Fae said. "I copied the journal using the magic spell my father told me."

"But I thought that . . ." Aric paused then nodded. "Of course, it's magic, it has to be. So all this time your father has been doing magic and none of the conjurers knew."

"Yes," Fae replied. "Which makes me think they can't really do magic. Not real magic. They certainly can't create new spells."

"Your father was just as much of a conjurer as any of them."

"More. He had the blood. I have the blood."

"They'd welcome you back," Aric said. He dropped her hand and looked out at the river. "You could live on the bridge. That's what you've always wanted."

Fae's hand felt cool after being held in Aric's. "No," she said. "I mean, yes, that's what I've always said I wanted—to live on the bridge, run the book bindery. But what I really meant was that I want to be able to choose where and how I live and not be restricted because I'm a girl."

Aric laughed. "We're a pair. If you were born a boy and I was born a girl none of this," he waved a hand downriver towards the bridge, "none of this would have happened."

"We wouldn't be friends," Fae said softly. "I would have been too busy being an actual apprentice to my father to watch my neighbour buy fish from the Rivermen. Even if you had been the girl selling."

"It's all worth it then," Aric said. "To have you as my friend."

"I think so too," Fae said. "But we're more than friends. At least I'd like to be." She ducked her head, not daring to look at Aric. He'd already turned her down once, but that had been because he couldn't live on the bridge, wasn't it?

"Fae." Aric tilted her head up until she had no choice but to meet his gaze. "I can never live on land."

"I know," she replied, her heart in her throat. "But you can live near it, like your mother."

"Yes." He paused. "I will be shaman, and even I don't know what that means."

"And I am a conjurer, whatever that means." Fae lifted her face and Aric kissed her. She could feel his smile on his lips and for a moment she wore a matching one. Then passion and need and desire surged through her and she melted into him.

She broke away, gasping, and held his head in her hands, staring into his eyes.

"Sweet Berhalla," Aric said. Then his mouth met hers again and he pulled her over onto him.

The moonlight lit his face when she rose up enough to straddle him. She felt him fumble with the rope belt on his trousers and laughed when he swore again. She stopped laughing when she felt her own trousers being pushed down and a hand reached between her legs.

Aric rolled her onto her back, dragging her trousers off her completely. He paused and she met his heated gaze. She ran a hand across the planes of his face before trailing it down to his chest. Then he pushed and he was in her, and she wrapped her legs around him as he sank into her. She pulled him into her, with her legs, her body, her eyes, as they rocked together. She felt a burst of intense pleasure, and then she collapsed, Aric on top of her.

It took her longer to recover her breath. By that time Aric was planting soft kisses over her face, along her jaw line, down her neck. He opened her blouse and took one nipple into his mouth and Fae arched her back, again.

"You like this?" he whispered onto her chilled nipple, and all she could do was nod and pull his head closer.

"And this?"

He thrust into her again and she whimpered and arched into him.

"Yes," she said. "That." She kissed the top of his head as he continued to nuzzle her nipples, keeping a slow tempo as he plunged into her. He froze and tensed and Fae strained against him. Aric's lips met hers just as she felt the release. Her body relaxed, then his did, but still they kissed.

Aric rolled to his side, his head touching hers and his arm

across her chest. His fingers fumbled to close her shirt against the chill night air. He grabbed a blanket from somewhere and pulled it over them.

Fae sighed and rolled over to stare into his eyes. She was aware of the sound of the river lapping against the raft, aware of the gentle rocking of the raft, but mostly she was aware of Aric. Of the way his skin smelled, of the way his hair curled around his ear, of the way his eyes burned into hers until there was nothing outside of the two of them.

Chapter Fifteen

HEWITT DROPPED THE book onto the table and rubbed his eyes. Even with three lamps he could barely read the faint script.

This was the third spell book he'd found that started the same. With a name and then a declaration that this was the first spell created by the conjurer; or more accurately, by the apprentice.

It seemed they didn't start writing a book until they'd actually created a spell. The apprentices were quite proud of themselves for accomplishing that—Hewitt would have been too. But the steps that led up to being able create the first spell were not included.

There *must* be other books hidden among the spell books; books with instructions that helped apprentices create their first spells. Had finding these instructions been assigned to Graylon Burrage? Wailes had implied that, but had he done it?

Wailes must be getting impatient with the lack of progress. Should he ask again to look through all of the books? Or would it be better to have Graylon fail and have Wailes ask *him* to look again?

He picked up the journal again. He was almost finished reading it. Unfortunately, after the death of the bookbinder's conjurer brother, the entries had become even more mundane.

But the man had fathered two daughters. One had married and stayed with the bookbindery. That line seemed unbroken— why else would bookbinders be named Keetley?

Hewitt needed to find out what happened to the other girl so he could trace her descendants. It was possible that Faelin Keetley wasn't the only Kellen conjurer alive today. If he found one he could train them, teach them to read, give them a chance at real power. He expected they would be very grateful to him. Grateful enough to help him defeat Quillan Wailes and his Bridgers.

He flipped a page and ran his finger down it, looking for names in the faded script. He had to find another Kellen.

Wailes knew that Faelin could read and that if he found her, he'd make her read from one of the spell books. Hewitt could try to make sure she read from a Kellen book—he was certain she would survive that—but Wailes, even more eager, would have her read from other books. Which would kill her, just as it was killing the others.

Hewitt could save Faelin. He could tell her to read only Kellen spells, but what if she still ended up under Wailes' control? He would have the greatest weapon in existence—a powerful conjurer with powerful spells.

Hewitt leaned back in his chair. Would he sacrifice his own ambitions, his own life, to restore conjurers to their glory? He'd thought his answer was yes, but *he* wanted to be the one in power, the one to bring conjurers back to greatness. And he did not want Wailes to have that glory.

To keep Wailes from having both the power and the credit, Hewitt might have to kill Faelin himself. If it did come to that, he wanted to have another Kellen conjurer working with him. He just needed to find one. Leaving the conjurers in their current, pathetic circumstances wasn't what he wanted either, but he would rather that than have Wailes hold all the power.

ARIC COULDN'T STOP smiling. The past day and a half had been the happiest of his life. He and Fae had spent the time talking, laughing, and making love with only a few breaks for fishing and eating. Right now he was supposed to be teaching her to float, but he was distracted by the way her wet shirt clung to her.

"Focus, Aric," Fae called. She splashed water at him.

"I am focussed," he replied. She was standing in water up to her waist, the beach behind her, while he floated in front of her. "Just lay back and wave your arms in the water."

She lay back and immediately her face sank below the water. She stood up, spluttering.

"You didn't wave your arms."

"I did," Fae complained. "It didn't work." She held up her hands, her fingers spread wide. "Maybe I don't have the right physical attributes."

Aric launched himself at her, lifting her off her feet and into his arms. "I think you have exactly the right physical attributes," he said. He rolled onto his back, dragging her on top of him. She hugged him and he let go of her, sweeping his hands from side to side to keep them both afloat.

"See," he said. "It's easy."

"So you say."

Fae's breath was warm on his neck. She kissed him and he forgot to move his arms and they both started to sink.

Fae laughed and jumped up, leaving him to sputter and flail until he got his feet under him.

"I thought it was easy," Fae said.

"You did that on purpose."

"Yes," Fae admitted. "I kissed you on purpose."

"To distract me." He reached for her but she moved away, a slow motion escape as the water dragged at her legs.

"You're blaming me? I fail to see how it's my fault. You're the one who can't concentrate."

She was in shallower water now. If she made it to the beach he wouldn't be able to catch her. He dove towards her, skimming just under the water. When he surfaced the remark he was about to make died on his lips.

"Fae?" Where was she? He spun around. She wasn't on the beach and she couldn't have gone very far, not in this waist deep water. "Fae!" A hand floated to the surface a few feet from him. Frantic, he dove towards it and grabbed her, pulling her limp body up.

"No, no, no, no, no," he chanted as he turned her face up. Her eyes were open and her mouth moved but she didn't draw a breath. Aric hauled her back against his chest, wrapped his arms around her and pulled up hard. Fae spit out a mouthful of water and then drew in a deep, wheezing breath.

"Thank Berhalla," Aric said. He held her as she continued to suck in air, her body shaking against his. Her breathing steadied into a ragged gasp and her body started shaking more violently. "Can you move?" She nodded and he steered them over to the rope. With one hand he pulled on it, bringing the raft towards them. When it was close enough he lifted her up and climbed onto the raft beside her.

Once inside the shelter he stripped off her wet clothes and covered her with blankets. Her teeth chattered and he ran a hand through his wet hair. He didn't want to leave her, not even to make a fire and heat some water. Assuming he could gather enough wood to do that.

It was Fae. He'd do whatever he had to. Right now she needed to be warm.

He pulled his own wet clothes off and tossed them aside, rubbing his arms and legs, trying to dry off and warm up his limbs. When he felt he was warm and dry enough he slipped under the blankets and pulled her against him. After a few minutes, her shivering stopped and she settled her head on his shoulder.

With another prayer to Berhalla, Aric wrapped his arm around her, pulling her closer.

HEWITT LOOKED AWAY. That made five deaths that he knew of. The book the apprentice had read from was bound with the same hide as the journal. And just as when Dabel had read from a book bound the same, this apprentice had been incinerated in a flash of flames. It was the only *complete* destruction caused by any of the books.

The spells bound in hides of the current seven conjurers seemed to cause the current afflictions only amplified many times. The apprentice who had read from the ancient Hewitt spell book died after his hands and feet had ballooned so much that they'd burst. He could only assume it was because the spells were so much more powerful than the pitiful ones they currently owned.

Wailes was watching him during that, so he'd tried to keep the horror off his face, but he knew the Hewitt spell had been recited as a warning to him. None of them would be able to recite any of the spells, not even those they felt belonged to them.

What Wailes didn't know was that Hewitt had no intentions of reciting any of the spells, ever. Not when he couldn't be sure he carried true conjurer blood in him.

He sighed and looked around the room. So many new faces. He wasn't sure where Wailes was getting his new apprentices, but it wasn't from the ranks of the Bridgers.

And there was the Burrage lad. Idly he wondered what had become of the mother. Perhaps she was being taught to read? The son didn't look frightened enough, given that he'd just witnessed the death of one of his fellow apprentices. Had he made some sort of bargain with Wailes?

Hewitt forced himself to look away from Burrage and scan the faces of the other two apprentices. They were afraid—terrified, even. Burrage and Wailes must have an agreement. Did the man know where to find Faelin? Or was it because he was looking through the books for instructions on how to create spells?

"The next apprentice, step forward," Wailes called.

None of the apprentices moved, but one of them looked faint. So Wailes was going to kill two of them today. Hewitt glanced down at his hand, feigning boredom. He didn't expect this lad to have any more success than the last one.

"Apprentice!" Wailes yelled. "Step forward!"

"I won't," the youth said. "You can't make me read."

Wailes frowned. "Shiv." The name was said quietly, but Hewitt heard the menace.

The Bridger, a sickening smile on his face, took a step and in one smooth motion pierced the apprentice's chest with his knife. The youth's face went slack and he sagged against the Bridger. Shiv jerked the knife out and the body dropped to the ground. He leaned over and wiped his blade on the dead man's shirt before calmly re-sheathing it and stepping back to his place by the door.

"Next apprentice, step forward," Wailes said.

An older man stepped forward, making a motion with his hands and muttering under his breath. From Durnham then, Hewitt thought. Their church held a lot of power and the people could be quite devout. Too bad this man's God couldn't save him from Wailes.

Burrage looked nervous now, though. As he should. It seemed Wailes wanted at least two spells tried today. If Burrage was assuming that any agreement he had with the Head Conjurer would save him, Hewitt thought he was mistaken.

But Burrage was spared; rather than face Shiv's knife, the other apprentice recited a spell. At least he started to recite it. He was part way through when his head swelled and he fell to the floor. There was a sickening crunch when his head hit the ground and the body twitched once, then stilled. Lambskin binding, then. That was a Maykin symptom.

Wailes waved everyone away and Hewitt rose to leave. He had a dozen pages left to read in the journal and was still no closer to finding out what had happened to the second daughter. He had to discover that, and soon. Wailes was going through apprentices so fast that he would very soon run out of people who could read. Then he would turn to conjurers. Die by spell or die by Bridger. It was a terrible choice.

Fae tried to burrow further into the warmth. Her head throbbed and her throat ached.

"Are you awake?"

She sighed and ran a hand across the warm skin her cheek rested against. Aric.

"Barely," she replied. She sighed again. Why was she so tired? "What happened?" She raised her head and met Aric's worried gaze.

"You scared me to death," he replied. "What do you remember?"

"We were swimming." She'd been laughing. Aric was teaching her how to float in the river and then . . . "I had a splitting headache and I couldn't move." She felt the panic again. She hadn't been able to breathe or stop herself from sinking below the surface.

"You're safe," Aric said. He stroked a hand down her damp hair and held her tighter.

"You saved me."

"You were only under for a moment," Aric said. "And you're safe."

"Thanks to you," Fae said. Suddenly her headache disappeared. She frowned. "I had a headache like this once before. After I ran away from the Burrages."

"And before that?"

"No." She shook her head. "Even as a child I was rarely ill. Unless . . ." She had a horrible thought. "What if it's because I did magic? Because I used my father's copying spell?"

"It is," Aric said. He smiled sheepishly. "Sorry, I *feel* that's the truth. Your headache is related to magic." He frowned. "But I don't think it's bad. At least not for you."

"So I'm not going to suddenly grow another eye?" She'd meant it as a joke but once the words were out she found that she couldn't laugh. Some of the conjurer's deformities were too horrible to make fun of.

"Your father didn't have anything like that happen to him," Aric said.

"No, he didn't." Fae closed her eyes in relief. Her father had been using that spell for decades with no physical symptoms. "I don't remember him complaining about headaches either. It's just a coincidence."

"No."

Aric's voice sounded tight, and when Fae looked up, his eyes weren't focussed.

"The headaches are connected to the magic, but not necessarily to you reciting the spell." Aric shook his head and met her gaze. "My shaman abilities seem to come when they want."

"What did that mean?" Fae asked. "I didn't have a headache until after I recited the spell."

"Sorry," Aric said. He sighed and pulled her closer. "I have a very strong feeling that what I said is true, but I have no idea how or why."

"I need the journal," Fae said.

"Yes," Aric agreed. "We should leave tomorrow."

"Will it be safe? We told Chart we'd be gone four or five days. Maybe we could have the journal brought here?"

"No," Aric said. "We'd need to tell Chart about it."

"You don't trust him," Fae said.

"I don't think we can trust *anyone*," Aric replied. "Not with that."

"More shaman feelings?" Fae asked.

"Yes." He paused and took a deep breath. "There's more. I think my mother is in danger. I think that's why my abilities are manifesting."

"Do you think it's an immediate threat?" Fae asked. If Aric

couldn't trust Rivermen, they would truly be on their own. It meant that getting the journal—understanding what was in it, what it meant for her—was even more urgent.

"No. Maybe." He sighed. "I don't know. But my mother will never bargain with Wailes."

"But someone else might." Fae nodded. "If Wailes promised not to complete the curse. We don't even know if he *can* complete it."

"It doesn't matter," Aric said. He lifted his hand and spread his fingers. "The threat is enough."

"All right. We need to figure out how to slip past both the Rivermen and the bridge," Fae said.

IT HAD TAKEN Hewitt some careful questions, but he finally knew that the Burrage woman was being held one floor down in Conjurers Hall.

He'd known about the rooms, of course. They were small, secure rooms with no windows and iron hinged doors. When he was younger he'd often wondered what the rooms had been used for. His favourite guess was that they were storage for the gold and jewels conjurers were paid for performing great works of magic.

But there were no riches, no great works of magic. Now the dark corridors leading to the rooms made him think they had always been used for their current purpose: to hold people captive.

He'd finished reading the bookbinder's journal and finally had a name. The second daughter had married a man named Gallacher.

"Conjurer." A Bridger nodded and stepped aside to let Hewitt pass. Wailes had obviously warned them he was coming. Hewitt hated having to advise Wailes of his every move but the man controlled the Bridgers completely. He'd love to know why— whether he'd done them a favour or had issued a threat. If he knew he might be able to counter with his own offer.

Wailes may have all the spells, but no one had completed one before dying. Until he had someone who could do that, every single spell he had was useless. Hewitt was certain that the rest of his fellow conjurers would be willing to follow *him* instead of Wailes. They may not have powerful spells but they did have deep connections to, and the respect of, the residents of the bridge.

Would Wailes be willing to set his Bridgers against the baker and the fishmonger—against the very people who made life on the bridge possible? It would be interesting to learn the answer to that.

"Ah, you are one of Shiv's sons," Hewitt said to the Bridger who was guarding the door. "Are you the married one?" The Bridger's only response was a grunt, but he did turn to unlock the door.

Hewitt wondered if the man would do anything if he knew that Wailes had been willing to have Shiv's son's wife killed in order to free him to marry Faelin.

"Knock when you want out," the Bridger said. He opened the door wide enough for Hewitt to slip through it. The door was pulled shut and he heard it being relocked.

"Hello," Hewitt said. The Burrage woman looked up at him briefly before dropping her defeated gaze to the floor in front of her.

It was a small cell, with little room for more than the narrow cot the woman sat on. At least the cot was raised off the floor; she wasn't completely exposed to the cold and damp he could already feel, but it was not comfortable.

Hewitt leaned against the wall and waited until he could no longer hear the guard out in the hallway. He'd told Wailes he would ask the Burrage woman about Faelin, and he would, but mostly he wanted to know if any Gallachers lived in Durnham.

"Oleda Burrage," he said. "You were married to the cousin of the bookbinder's wife."

The woman sighed and looked up at him with dull eyes. "I never met the bookbinder," she said. "Or his wife. And I only met that girl when we came here to see about the inheritance."

"My understanding is that you imprisoned her in your home," Hewitt said. If she hadn't done that he might have more sympathy for her now. "And then she escaped. How?"

"She attacked my son," Oleda Burrage said, angry now. "Then she ran out the front door."

"I see." It seemed Faelin was more resourceful than expected. "And you took this book from her." He showed the journal. "Did she say anything to you about it?"

"Just that she had it because Conjurer Wailes wanted all the books. She thought it was valuable."

"So you took this book from her in order to strike a bargain with Head Conjurer Wailes," Hewitt said. "And regrettably for you, Faelin escaped. Do you know where she went?"

"No, but she'd already been to Waglenn Landing."

"She had?" Hewitt hadn't heard this piece of news. Was Wailes testing him, making sure he really was questioning her about Faelin? He couldn't imagine Oleda Burrage keeping any secrets from the Bridgers. "Do you know why?"

"She talked about people who could read," Oleda said bitterly. "She even warned us not to come here. We should have listened to her." She met his eyes. "Is my son alive? No one will tell me anything about him. Is he still alive?"

Hewitt leaned closer. "I will tell you if you answer one last question. But you can't tell anyone I asked this."

She nodded her head. "I need to know about my son."

"Have you heard of a family with the name of Gallacher? Or maybe Kellen? A woman's maiden name perhaps."

"No, I'm sorry." Oleda's face crumpled. "I don't know anyone with that name."

"That's unfortunate," Hewitt said. "I can tell you that your son is alive, but he's an apprentice to Conjurer Wailes. They have exceedingly short lifespans these days. I am sorry." And he was. He was sorry for all of them, himself included.

He straightened up and banged on the door. Shiv's son came and let him out and he trudged back through the corridors towards the stairs.

Now to find a way to talk to someone from Waglenn Landing. He must find another Kellen conjurer.

Chapter Sixteen

ARIC LOOKED AROUND and sighed. He and Fae were unsure of who they could trust or where to stay, but the past few days spent near this little beach had been the happiest in his life. And that was despite Fae's near drowning and his own inability to stay on land.

He didn't need shaman abilities to tell him that there were dangers ahead for Fae and him, but he would always be grateful for the time they'd had here.

Fae stacked wood on the fire up to the height of the ring of stones he'd dragged from the bottom of the river.

They wanted the fire to keep burning for a while but they didn't want it to jump to the forest. He didn't think anyone was keeping track of them—he didn't sense it—but that didn't mean Chart wouldn't send someone soon. He didn't want them to know exactly when he and Fae had left. Which was one reason why they were travelling at night.

Fae waded through the water to the front of the canoe and hopped in. She'd rolled the trousers up and her calves were bare, as were her feet. Her shoes were tied to a thwart, within easy reach if she needed them.

"Ready," Fae called back to him. Using his paddle, he pushed off against the sand. The raft drifted beside them, the canvas tent flapping in the evening breeze. With a few strong strokes they left it and the beach behind. Fae hunched down, a dark shadow in front of him as he steered the canoe.

He let the current take them downriver. The only sounds were the soft rush of the water and the splash of the occasional fish.

It had taken most of a day to paddle upstream; Aric guessed it would take half that to return to the Riverman village. He wanted to time it so that they went past it after the night fishing had ended but before the boats went out in the morning.

Which should put them at the bridge an hour before dawn. Getting past the bridge was the most dangerous part of the journey. He and Fae had counted the days, trying to determine if they would see a low tide or a high one—they needed a high tide.

The tides had been part of his subconscious for so long that he couldn't believe a few days upriver made him doubt the timing—but there it was. He couldn't be sure—he was close to sure—but not positive.

They planned on letting the debris that went out with the tide camouflage them as they slipped under the grate of one of the arches. It would be dangerous among the fallen trees and other flotsam that flowed out with the tide.

They'd be swimming at that point, and Aric pushed down the panic he felt at the thought of Fae getting another headache and drowning. She'd told him not to worry, that it was unlikely to happen at that exact moment, but he'd almost lost her once.

FAE SLIPPED INTO the water, stretching out her legs until she touched the bottom. She shuddered when her feet sank into the cool mud and weeds brushed against her legs.

She reminded herself that Aric said there was nothing dangerous on this side of the bridge—no sharks, no rays—only harmless plants and the odd curious fish. But she felt vulnerable without her shoes.

On the bridge, only small children went barefoot. But besides a few loose stones, there was nothing on the bridge roadway that could really harm a person. Did they wear shoes and boots in order to keep the cobbler busy—just as the conjurers ordered meaningless books and kept the bookbinder employed?

She'd never really questioned the way people lived: in part because she'd never had much to compare it with. Now that she'd seen both Riverman villages and the poverty of her mother's cousin, she wondered about her safe, comfortable life in the bindery.

Binding books may have been a worthwhile skill at one time, an act of creation that helped preserve knowledge—the old books of spells were a testament to that—but for generations nothing new had been created. What was the value of her father's life work when all he did was create new books that contained existing knowledge?

"I sunk the canoe," Aric said from beside her. "Filled it with river rocks."

"And it will float if we need it?" Fae asked. Aric hadn't admitted it but she knew he was worried they wouldn't be able to go under the bridge tonight. If they couldn't—if Bridgers were patrolling the stairs or they'd miscalculated the tide, he'd need a place to hide so they could try again another night. And it couldn't be on land.

Right now they were between Waglenn Landing's main dock and the small cliff-side platform where they'd first met Chart. Even getting back here at dawn would be risky; they wouldn't be able to go further upriver if they wanted to avoid the Rivermen.

"Yes, as long as it's not underwater for too long."

"We'll know in a few hours," Fae replied. She could barely distinguish Aric from the shadows. She caressed his face and he leaned over and kissed her.

When he moved away from her, he gripped her hand. They hadn't discussed the danger. They both knew the risks: from the river and the Bridgers. If one or both of them didn't survive this, at least they'd had a few days of joy together.

"Tide's in," she said. "There's salt in the air."

"Yes," Aric replied. "It should be going out soon. Time to go."

Aric towed her through the shallow water past a dozen willow trees, the trailing fronds scraping across her head and shoulders. At the end of the trees, Aric stopped.

"The river runs faster on this side," he said. "Time to tie us together." He pulled out a rope and looped it around her waist before securing the other end around his. He loosened her hands from the branch she gripped and Fae drifted past him, stopping when the rope grew taut. She grabbed the rope and pulled herself back to him.

"Good." Aric expelled a breath and hugged her, and she knew he'd been reliving her near drowning.

"I think I saw a downed tree," she said. "Just before the bend."

Aric towed her toward the bend in the river. She could see the bridge now. Lights dotted the length of the square and a few windows facing them gleamed. Right in front of them, the dock at Waglenn Landing was dark and there was only a small dory tied up to it. The pale moon was visible until a cloud scudded across it.

Aric pulled a partially submerged tree out from under the overhanging willows, the soft rustling merging with the sounds of the river.

"Exactly what I was hoping for," he said as he tugged it towards her.

Aric maneuvered the tree so that the branches with the most fronds and leaves were on their left. She draped her left arm over the thickest part of the trunk and hung on tight.

It wasn't a whole tree—there were no roots—and it was jagged and pale where it had split from the rest of the tree. Willow fronds waved around her, partially obscuring Aric. He started to swim, one hand on a branch, dragging both the tree and Fae after him. She fanned her right hand in the water to keep herself steady. Once in the middle of the river, the current started spinning them towards the bridge and the tree tried to roll.

Fae clung to the tree as Aric, working to keep them straight, slowly steered them towards the bridge arch closest to Waglenn Landing. There was a grate on it, to stop boats from passing below the bridge without paying the toll, but when the tide went out, it was raised to prevent debris from collecting at the grates and damaging the bridge.

Fae's father had told her that when the Bridgers first installed the grates, felled trees and logs had piled up at them, eventually knocking stones from the arches. The conjurers had forced the Bridgers to pay for the repairs, wiping out any profit they'd made from tolls. Bridgers had been raising and lowering the grates with the tide ever since.

Aric claimed the grates weren't raised very high even at high tide, unless a paying customer was going through. Young Rivermen challenged each other to go through the arches, slipping under and back with the tide. They didn't expect anyone to do that tonight, though, not with Wailes' threat hanging over them.

Despite their efforts, the tree started to spin. Fae caught a glimpse of Aric's worried face before something bumped her hip. She stifled a cry of pain; a half-submerged log nudged her and she shoved it away.

They were close, nearly in the shadow of the bridge. Another cloud covered the moon, taking away what little light they had.

The tree rolled and Aric pulled her against him, his left arm circling the tree. The tree spun and Fae saw the arch directly ahead.

Branches and debris crunched and bumped against the grate until they were dragged under, leaves and twigs tearing off. The tree they held onto tried to spin again.

"Now," Aric said. "Swim!"

Fae kicked with her legs, trying to move with Aric, trying to keep the tree heading straight. Aric's legs tangled in hers for a second, then she kicked again. She gasped as she struggled to point the stump end of the tree directly at the arch.

Willow fronds cushioned her as smaller trees and branches bumped into her. Something soft touched her arm and she shoved it away, trying not to dwell on the feel of cold skin and trailing hair.

The tree shuddered as it hit the grate. Aric turned her to face him and she clung to him as he pushed up on the branch he held, trying to force the far end lower, under the grate. They moved forward slowly as the tree edged under the grate. Branches whipped around her face and she buried it against Aric's shoulder.

"Hold your breath," he said, and she took a deep gulp and closed her eyes. The tree pushed her down into the water but she could feel Aric moving them forward. She felt him kicking and tried to help, one arm still clutching him.

A few seconds later they were through and he dragged her up to the surface. The willow fronds, sparser than before, calmly waved around her as she tried to quietly suck in air. Aric pulled her tighter against him and she felt him tense up.

She turned to look. In the moonlight, something white bobbed in the water a few feet from them. It was a woman, her dark hair streaming out from her head, her blank eyes staring up. She rolled over and disappeared under the water.

"FAE." SHE FELT herself being shaken. No, she was shivering.

"Fae, wake up."

Aric's voice. Fae opened her eyes. The sky was starting to lighten. Had she fallen asleep? They were still in the river, still clinging to the tree.

"There's a boat," Aric said. "I need to swim to reach it and you need to stay here. I'm going to tie you to the tree."

Fae nodded and thought she'd replied but he leaned closer.

"Fae."

Aric swore and then there was a tug on the rope around her waist when Aric looped the other end around the trunk of the tree. She tried to grip the tree but her hand slipped and she felt rough bark against her cheek. She lifted a hand but it looked like the hand of the dead woman and she pushed it away.

Aric was back. She told him how happy she was to see him and then she was pulled out of the water. Nets covered her and then Aric was there, holding her tight. She could feel his warmth where their bodies met and she closed her eyes.

HEWITT SIPPED HIS tea. He was in Wailes' study, and Shiv paced back and forth in front of the desk. The head conjurer had yet to arrive, and although Hewitt thought his own business more important, Shiv looked almost excited.

The door opened and Tymm lumbered in carrying Wailes. He gently put him in the chair and pulled a harness over Wailes' shoulders, tightening the straps that were tied to the back of the chair.

Hewitt took another sip of tea. Wailes' health was deteriorating. He could no longer keep himself upright even in his modified chair. Perhaps all Hewitt needed to do was outlive the man. He glanced at Shiv, who cleared his throat. He'd need the Bridgers on his side first though.

"What is it, Shiv?" Wailes asked in a tone of voice that made Hewitt grateful he hadn't spoken first.

"A body was spotted, conjurer," Shiv said. "A woman's body."

"Where?" Wailes asked.

"By the eastern arch," Shiv said. "We think it went through overnight."

"Is it her?"

"We've contacted a Riverman to fetch it," Shiv said. "We hope to have it soon."

"Hope!" Wailes said. "We need to know. I need to know! Tell the Rivermen that I will reward the one who brings me this body." Shiv hesitated. "Go!" Wailes said. "And don't come back until you have news."

"You think this is the bookbinder's daughter," Hewitt said.

"It must be," Wailes replied. "She has not been seen in days. She has no friends, no one to help her."

"I spoke to her mother's cousin." Hewitt knew Wailes was aware of that, but he thought he had an opportunity. "Did you know the girl told her she'd been to Waglenn Landing?"

"Yes," Wailes said. "Shiv gave me that information."

"Did Shiv tell you why the girl was in Waglenn Landing? Did he mention that she warned the Burrages about coming here? Warned that you were looking for readers?"

"No," Wailes sat up as straight as his twisted body would allow. "He said nothing about that. Why does it matter?"

"The girl must have had help from someone in Waglenn Landing in order to get to Durnham. Even if," he paused, "the body in the river is her, wouldn't you like to know who helped her? Who is acting against you?" If Faelin was dead it was even more important for him to find another Kellen conjurer. Wailes had to let him go to the town.

"The Bridgers have already been to Waglenn Landing," Wailes said. "They had only two people who could read, and I've apprenticed them already."

"Only two," Hewitt said. "The Bridgers confirmed this?" Wailes nodded. "Since they were less than thorough when they questioned Oleda Burrage, might I suggest that they may have missed something in the town?"

Wailes pinned him with a glare. "To what point? The body must be hers."

"If it is, then she likely came from Waglenn Landing," Hewitt said. "That arch is closest to that town. Someone there would know something."

"I don't care," Wailes replied. "As long as she's dead."

"If you change your mind," Hewitt rose, "I'd be happy to interrogate the townspeople for you. Perhaps gain some insight, just as I did with Oleda Burrage." He nodded. "Thank you for the tea." He let himself out the door and headed back to his small workroom.

He couldn't push Wailes—it would only make the man even more distrustful.

FAE SUCKED IN a breath. She was cold and wet. She'd never convince Aric she would be happy living on the river if she kept almost drowning. Although she hadn't drowned. Not this time. It had been the cold. It had seeped into her bones and made her sluggish and confused.

"Are you all right?" Aric asked. He wrapped something warm and dry around her and helped her sit up.

They were in a boat. She could tell by the rocking motion and the strong smell of fish. She sat in a small—it wasn't a cabin, not exactly, but she was out of the wind and covered. Her buttocks ached and she squirmed, trying to get comfortable on the pile of nets.

"Where are we?" she asked.

The worried look on Aric's face was replaced by a grin. "We're in the hold of Pax Oldham's fishing boat. He usually has fish in here." He looked up and her eyes followed his. There was a hatch. She could see the dawn sky above.

"We're lucky he was close." Aric's expression turned serious again. "I waved down a boat and they got Pax."

"We made it," she said. "We're past the bridge."

"Yes." Aric paused. "A body came through with us. We're lucky Bridgers didn't see us, but they spotted it."

"I remember," Fae said. "Poor thing. Did they get her?"

"Bridgers?" Aric snorted. "They don't go near the water. They asked the Rivermen to send them the body." He grinned again. "It will take us a few hours to find it." He leaned close. "Pax thinks they believe it's you."

Fae nodded, not wanting to admit that it could have been her.

"Thank you," she said. "For saving me. Again."

"My fault you were in danger," Aric said. A muffled voice came from above, along with three sharp stomps on the deck above. "We're almost home. Pax is going to bypass his usual dock and go as close to my mother's boats as he can. We'll find you something dry to wear then."

"And the journal," Fae said.

"And the journal," he agreed.

SIGRUN RAWLEY'S BOAT seemed smaller and more ramshackle than it had when Fae had stayed there before.

Aric's mother greeted her coolly, which made Fae wonder if Aric had told her anything, but she ushered her into the small bedroom with a clean pair of trousers and a warm shirt. Fae dumped them on the bed and lifted the bedding.

There. The copy she'd made of the journal. Or was it the original? She tossed it onto the bed and quickly changed into the dry clothes. Her wet clothing in one hand and the journal in the other, she exited the room.

"Where should I put these?" She held up her damp bundle.

Sigrun stared at her from where she sat at the small table. Aric stepped out from his small berth under the stairs, a similar wet clump of clothes in his hands. He grabbed her bundle and stuffed everything into a cubby by the door.

"We'll get them washed and dried next sunny day," he said. "Right, Mother?"

Sigrun crossed her arms over her chest and was about to lean back when suddenly she paled. Her gaze became unfocussed and her hands dropped to the table. She smiled an eerie smile—and then she blinked.

"Mother?" Aric went to her side. "What is it? Did you have a premonition?"

"I was wrong about you, bookbinder's daughter," Sigrun said. "You are needed if we Rivermen are to survive." She looked at Aric. "But we will be changed by this. All of us."

"Is it the curse?" Fae asked. "Does Wailes complete it?"

"I do not think so," Sigrun replied.

"I'm not sure," Aric said. "But it doesn't feel bad. At least not for Fae and me."

"You have had premonitions?" Sigrun asked.

"Yes," Aric stated. "It seems I am to be a shaman after all."

Sigrun stared at him, her mouth gaping. "It should be impossible! When did they start? And what were they about?"

"A few days ago," Aric said. "And they've been about Fae. She's important—the key to everything. Her and the journal."

"Yes," Sigrun said. "The ray marked her. But you! Men do not become shamans." She looked worried, frightened even.

Fae sat down across from Sigrun and Aric squeezed in beside her. She was aware of contact between them when he wedged up against her.

"Are you sure there has never been a male shaman?" Fae asked.

"There has been no mention of one in all of the memories that have been passed down," Sigrun said.

"Sometimes things, even very important things, are forgotten," Fae said. She ran a hand across the cover of the journal. "This journal was written by the first Keetley bookbinder. I've only read the first few pages but he was born Keetley Kellen, and Kellens were a conjurer family."

"You're a conjurer?" Sigrun asked.

"So it seems," Fae agreed. "As was my father. The ones who call themselves conjurers do not carry the blood."

Sigrun's eyes widened. "That is why Wailes has not completed the curse."

"It will kill him," Aric said. "And anyone else who tries to complete it."

"Not necessarily," Fae said.

"What do you mean?" Aric asked. "He isn't truly a Wailes."

"He's not," Fae said. "But there is a chance he'll find someone with conjurer blood."

"Ah," Sigrun said. "Like your first bookbinder, others with the blood of conjurers may have chosen different paths." She laughed. "We could even have conjurer blood among Rivermen." She slid out from the table. "Get up. Both of you, get up."

"Mother," Aric said.

Fae nudged him. "Do as she says, Aric." Sigrun had a wild look in her eyes, one that made Fae think this was another premonition. Aric looked at her, and then eased out from the bench. Fae slid along it and stood beside him.

Sigrun squeezed past them and shooed them out of the way, before grabbing the table and lifting the end up towards the wall. It inched up and then stuck.

"Aric." Fae gestured towards his mother.

Aric stepped up beside Sigrun and Fae was struck by just how unlike her he was. Where she was copper, he was golden. Aric put his hands on the table. The webbing between his fingers was almost invisible—his mother's hands were almost unrecognizable as such.

The table went higher until it rested against the wall.

"What is this?" Aric asked. "I've never seen this before."

"Shaman business," Sigrun said.

Fae craned her neck. A small compartment was set into the floor. Sigrun leaned over and pulled a wrapped package from it. She stepped back and Aric let the table drop back into place. Sigrun reverently placed the package on the table and pulled at the covering.

"Sealskin," Fae said. "And it's old." She peered at the hide. It had been expertly tanned—a level of skill that Rivermen didn't have today. Was it another talent lost through the years?

"Books!" Aric said. He reached past the sealskin and picked up a small book. It was bound in a different hide.

"Shaman legacy," Sigrun said. She flattened the sealskin wrapping, allowing Fae to see three books, each one bound in a different hide.

"But you don't read," Aric said. "Shamans never read."

"I tried," Sigrun replied. "As did my mother, and my mother's mother. In secret, we have approached people from the towns and traded with them for the chance to read, so we can finally know our legacy. But it has always failed."

"But Aric can read," Fae said.

"Yes." Sigrun smiled. "When you told me you could read I assumed it was more proof that you would not be shaman. But now." She gestured to the books. "There may be answers here."

Thoughtful, Aric looked from the book he held to his mother. "You said you traded with the townspeople. What did you trade?"

"I traded what a woman has," Sigrun said. "To a man who wanted it."

"My father?" Aric asked. "He was a man who traded with you?"

"My mother did the same with my father," Sigrun said. "He too was from the land."

Fae laid a hand on Aric's arm. He was tense and angry. "You should give us a moment," she said to Sigrun. Aric's mother looked from Fae to her son then she nodded. A minute later Fae and Aric were alone.

"She did what she was taught to do," Fae said. "By her own

mother." She leaned into him and he wrapped an arm around her. She felt the tension leave his body.

"You're right," he said.

"Of course I am."

Aric smiled, just as she knew he would.

"And we have more important things to worry about." Fae picked up the second book. "Between my journal and these books we have a lot of reading to do." She looked at him. "I think your mother is warming up to me."

"What makes you say that?"

"She didn't make me leave when she showed you the books. Even though she said they are shaman business."

"Because she knows that we need you if we're to survive."

Chapter Seventeen

THERE WAS A loud rap on the door and Hewitt smiled briefly before schooling his face into concern. He couldn't let even Shiv know that he'd expected this summons. And it *was* Shiv, knocking for once.

"Conjurer Wailes has asked to see you," the Bridger said when Hewitt opened the door.

"Of course," Hewitt said. "I'll come right away."

Shiv led the way through the hallways to Wailes' study. The single window they passed showed a sunny day and Rivermen fishing out towards the mouth of the river, but inside Conjurers Hall it was mostly dark. As usual, candles and lamps lit the way.

Shiv stopped at the door to Wailes' study and tentatively tapped it. The door opened and another Bridger—Hewitt thought it might have been another of Shiv's sons—exchanged a look with Shiv before motioning them in.

Hewitt suppressed a shake of his head. He wished the Bridgers had more sense than to be afraid of Wailes. The man was never going to risk what little health he had on a spell to harm them. The only leverage Wailes had over anyone on the bridge was Shiv and his men. He took a deep breath as he surveyed the room.

Wailes, his body twisted in his chair, glared at a third Bridger.

An angry Tymm stood behind his master, his hands fisted at his side.

Hewitt risked a glance at Shiv and his son. Perhaps he could reason with them. He would prefer to have some leverage, though. It would be easy if he had something they already feared—like an active conjurer. A Kellen conjurer.

"Get out!" Wailes shouted. "And don't come back until you have that body. I don't care if you have to kill a dozen Rivermen. Get me that body!"

The Bridger turned and made a hasty retreat, forcing Hewitt to step aside. Once the man was out the door, Shiv and his son flanked the exit.

"Trouble, Conjurer Wailes?" Hewitt asked calmly. "I do hope it's something I can help with. Although killing Rivermen is probably beyond me."

"Hewitt." Wailes settled back in his chair, pulling his tunic back into place. "I need you to go to Waglenn Landing. Find out everything you can about what the bookbinder's daughter did while in town. Who she spoke to, where she hid. And if she's missing. I need to know if the body that went under the bridge was her."

"Of course, Conjurer Wailes," Hewitt said. "Shall one of your Bridgers accompany me?" He'd given Wailes no reason to distrust him, but that didn't mean he *would* trust him. He desperately wanted to go alone.

"Yes," Wailes said sharply. He paused and stared at Hewitt. "On second thought, no. But do not try to plot against me, Hewitt. Shiv, take him to the gate. Now."

Hewitt bowed and turned to follow Shiv, hiding his relief. He'd spent hours thinking about what he'd do if given the chance to visit Waglenn Landing. He would take full advantage of this opportunity.

"Hewitt," Wailes called, and he turned to face him. "You have until the gates close. If you miss that I will assume you are working against me and I will send Shiv after you."

"Understood, Conjurer Wailes." Hewitt bowed his head and turned to follow the Bridger. Shiv smiled at him and Hewitt forced himself to stay calm. This man liked to kill. Hewitt might not be able to work with him even after he found a Kellen conjurer.

ARIC PICKED UP one of the books and opened it. The writing was faint and it flowed across the page in cramped loops. He leaned closer. "I can hardly make anything out," he said to Fae. They were seated across from each other, the three shaman books and Keetley Kellen's journal on the table between them.

"Let me see?"

Aric pushed the book towards her and Fae peered down at the script.

"It's very faint," she said. She pulled the lamp closer. "It's a name. Zevach, I think. Yes, that's it. Zevach." She looked up. "It says he is the last male shaman."

Startled, Aric pulled the book back to him. Fae was right. "*I am Zevach, of the shaman line Simen,*" he read aloud. For some reason the words were clearer to him. "*And today, with the death of my brother upriver, I am the last male in my line and the last male shaman on either side of the bridge. The Wailes curse has given us only daughters. They have the sight, as they are true daughters, but the shaman powers that are tied to men will die with me.*"

He looked at Fae and shivered. "Men *were* shamans." He flipped forward a few pages. "I can read it. As soon as I read his name I could read the rest of it." *Men were shamans.* He could hardly believe it, but here was the proof. "What do you think it means?" he asked. "I am the first male shaman since the Wailes curse and you are the first Kellen conjurer in generations. What do you think that means?"

"Though I have the blood," Fae said. "I may not be a conjurer."

"You are." As he said the words, Aric felt as though he was outside of his body, looking at the two of them huddled over the books. "You will be. You *must* be or all is lost. Powers on the bridge are building. You must oppose them."

"Aric."

He shook his head to clear it. Fae was staring at him, worry on her face.

"Was that a premonition?" she asked. "You said I must oppose the powers on the bridge."

"I did?" He knew he'd said something, but exactly what, he couldn't recall. "I don't know what I said. My mother only ever has feelings, like what I've experienced up until now. I've never heard of her making statements—forewarnings—like this."

"Maybe it's a shaman ability tied to being male?"

"We need to know," Aric said. "Fae, I'll keep reading this book, and can you take a look at one of the others? I know you want to read your journal, but I have a feeling that this is just as important."

Fae nodded and dragged another of the shaman books over to her, setting her small journal to one side. "We need to go through them all anyway," she said. "Can you make us some tea?"

"Yes," Aric said. "And I need to tell my mother what we've found so far." He slid out from behind the table and put the water on the stove before heading for the stairs. They'd arranged a set of signals so he and Fae didn't have to wander around the village. Wailes could have spies anywhere, including here.

At the top of the stairs, Aric took a small white cloth from a hook and tied it around the blade of an oar. Without going on deck, he propped the oar against the outside of the cabin, right beside the door. It might be a while before his mother arrived— only a few people in the village knew that he and Fae were here and only Sigrun and Pax knew to look for this signal.

HE AND FAE were on their second cups of tea when the boat dipped to one side.

"Someone's here," he said. They packed up the books and took them with them to the bedroom at the back. Aric peered out into the main room. His mother came down the steps and he relaxed.

"You wanted me?" his mother said.

Aric opened the door wider. "I have news." He moved back to the table and sat down, sliding along the bench to make room for Fae. She dropped the books onto the tabletop and sat down beside him.

His mother sat across from them. "It's dangerous for me to come and go too often."

"You don't trust everyone," Fae said.

His mother shrugged but didn't reply.

"The Wailes curse did more than make us amphibious," Aric said. "It was also the end of male shamans." His mother stared at him, startled. "This book," he picked it up, "was written by the last one. Zevach Simen was his name."

"Zevach Simen," his mother repeated. "I have heard the name

Simen. One of the greatest shamans was named Simen. But she was a woman. You're sure this Simen was a man?"

"So he writes," Aric said. "And speaks of talents specific to male shamans, although we haven't found what those talents are."

"But Aric had a foretelling," Fae said. "He said that powers on the bridge were building and I must oppose them."

"You spoke those words?" His mother looked frightened now.

"That's what Fae says," Aric replied. "I know I spoke but I don't know what I said."

"I have never heard of a shaman speaking like that," his mother said. "Not in all of the histories that have been handed down."

"Because those histories have all been passed down by women," Fae said.

"I found another reference," Aric said. He flipped open one of the books. "*None of the daughters can read, though I have tried to teach them,*" he read aloud. "This seems to be an account of his life. I think this Zevach was a very old man when he wrote it."

"The other books seem to be earlier," Fae added. "They mention men and women shamans."

"There used to be a lot more of us," Aric said. "Up and down river."

His mother nodded. "There were more families. That is why I had given up hope when I had a son and no daughters."

"Yes," Aric replied. "I know." He'd been the one to pay the price for his mother's lack of hope.

"Aric." Fae laid a hand on his. "Zevach is sad that he is the last of his kind. No doubt your mother has been as well."

He glanced at his mother. She didn't seem sad but maybe that was because she'd had years for her disappointment to set in. He'd only read half of Zevach's book and the musings were increasingly despondent. It made him think that his mother's hopelessness hadn't been about him, not personally. It had been about being the last shaman.

"Did you worry about the Rivermen?" he asked. "What they would do without a shaman?"

His mother stared at him for a moment before replying. "Yes. Pax and I often talked about this." She looked away. "He thought I should train someone else—that I *could* train someone else."

She met his gaze. "I told him it was in the blood—that my only hope was that you would have a daughter. Then you talked of marrying a Bridger."

Aric would have said something angry, but Fae squeezed his hand. He kept his mouth closed, his lips tight, as he stared at his mother.

"Then I was stung by the ray," Fae said.

"Yes," his mother replied. "A good omen. I had a feeling—a very strong feeling—that everything was as it should be."

"I've felt that too," Aric said.

"Good." His mother rose. "The current flows downstream, but you must navigate your own course."

His mother left, and he and Fae sat side by side in silence for a few moments.

"It must be hard to watch your world change and not be able to do anything about it," Fae said. "Keetley Kellen watched the conjurer side of his family die out, Zevach's people were altered because of a curse, and your mother expected to be the last shaman ever."

Aric leaned over and kissed her. "With luck we'll reverse all of those things."

"With luck." He would have kissed her again but Fae slid out from beside him. She laughed and sat down on the other side of the table. "And hard work. You need to finish Zevach's tale and I have to read the Keetley journal."

Aric sighed and pulled the open book closer. He stretched his legs out until they tangled with hers, and when he looked up she was smiling down at the page she was reading.

HEWITT STARED AT the gates that led to Waglenn Landing. He'd last been off the bridge two years ago and even then he'd only gone as far as the market in the square directly in front of the gates. He'd been searching for new quills, if he remembered correctly.

He stepped through the gates, nodding to the Bridger who stood guard. Shiv had already spoken to the man before leaving Hewitt at the gates. They wouldn't have let him leave without Wailes' approval.

In another three steps he'd crossed onto land. Market stalls dotted the cobblestones in front of him and tidy stone houses ringed the square. He studied the stalls before selecting one.

"Master Conjurer," the man in the booth said. "It is a privilege. What can I help you with?"

"I'd like a dozen of your best beeswax candles," Hewitt said. He didn't need the candles—he could buy those on the bridge—but he wanted this man friendly and relaxed.

"Excellent," the vendor said. "Let me just wrap them up."

By the time the man had the candles tied and packaged, Hewitt had three coins sitting on his palm. The vendor's eyes went wide and then he coughed.

"That's far too much, Master," the vendor said.

"They're yours if you tell me if you saw a girl a few days ago. Long dark hair—she's from the bridge."

"Is she? I wondered what the fuss was about. Bridgers was after her. Her and the Riverman. They got away, though."

"Did anyone help them?"

"Councilman Larwood did," the vendor said. "Kept them from a Bridger. Saw it myself."

"Did you?" It would have been nice if Wailes had shared this information with him. Or was this another test? "Do you know where I can find this councilman?"

"House with the green door, facing the square," the vendor said. "Is that the reward?" He gestured to the coins. "Bridger said there was a reward for the girl."

"This is separate from the reward," Hewitt said. He handed the coins over and the vendor nodded. He turned away, before casually turning back to him. "Do you happen to know anyone by the name of Kellen? Or maybe Gallacher? It could be a middle name or a grandmother's maiden name?" He reached into his pocket and pulled out another coin.

"Kellen or Gallacher, ye said." The vendor eyed the coin. "Don't know anyone goes by those names but Mistress Bleddyn is the one to ask."

Hewitt held out the coin and the man snatched it from him.

"Nosiest person on either side of the river," the man muttered. "I'll put out the word that a conjurer wants to talk to her. She'll find you whether you want her to or not."

"Excellent," Hewitt replied. A busybody was exactly who he needed to talk to.

THE GREEN DOOR opened and Hewitt smiled at the look on the woman's face. He had to admit, it was very unusual for a conjurer to simply arrive unannounced at anyone's door, even that of the head of Waglenn Landing's council.

"Councilman Larwood, please," Hewitt said. "Tell him Conjurer Hewitt is here to see him."

"Of course, Master Conjurer," the woman said. "Please, come in."

The room she led him to was large, by bridge standards—almost twice the size of his own quarters—but of course they had plenty of land to build on here.

"I'll fetch my husband," Mistress Larwood said and hurried out.

He stood by the window, watching the bustling market, wondering if Mistress Bleddyn was out there amongst all those people. He'd spent all of his life on the bridge and was familiar with every single person who dwelt there. It was odd to see a whole town of strangers.

"Conjurer Hewitt."

Hewitt turned as a man strode into the room. Middle-aged with grey hair, he frowned but extended his hand in greeting.

"Councilman Larwood," Hewitt said. He gripped the man's hand briefly. "You do not seem happy to see me."

"Conjurer's business is never a good thing for those of us not of the bridge," Larwood said. "Did Head Conjurer Wailes send you?"

"In a way," Hewitt replied. "We all must work within constraints." He moved away from the window and sat down on an overstuffed chair. Very good quality, he thought absently. He might want one like it for himself.

After a moment, Councilman Larwood sat down opposite him. "Can I get you tea?"

Hewitt smiled. "No, thank you." He'd wondered how hospitable the councilman would be. "I believe you know why I am here."

"The girl," Larwood replied.

"And the Riverman," Hewitt added. "She was here with a Riverman. Where did they go?"

"Him I took upriver," Larwood said. He glared at him. "It's a terrible thing, to see a man drowning on dry land. And it's your fault."

"Well, it's not my fault," Hewitt said. "Although a conjurer was to blame a long time ago. Not my family."

"No. I know it was the Wailes curse," Larwood said. "Heard it from a Riverman years ago. Unspeakably cruel."

"Yes," Hewitt said. "But I did not come here to talk about ancient wrongs that cannot be righted. I want to know where the girl went." He was fairly certain Faelin would have gone with her friend Aric but it would be nice to know for certain.

Larwood rose. "I'm sorry, I've said all I'm going to on the matter."

"I don't want to see her hurt," Hewitt said. "I considered her father a friend." He paused. "And I asked her to be my apprentice."

"A female conjurer?" Larwood was genuinely surprised. "Why would you do that?"

"Because I trusted her," Hewitt said. He sighed. He didn't trust her any longer. "Something in short supply on the bridge."

"On land as well," Larwood agreed. "So you'll understand why I will not say anything more."

Hewitt rose. "A pity. I will have to tell Wailes that you were not completely co-operative." He paused at the door to the hallway. "I know the girl went with the Riverman. They've been friends since they were children." Larwood stared and Hewitt nodded. He wasn't going to get the confirmation he wanted, but neither did Larwood deny it. "I'll let myself out."

Hewitt glanced at the sky. He had another hour before he had to be at the gate. He picked up an apple and studied it before putting it back down.

He'd been wandering in the market for quite some time. Would the gossip ever find him?

He slowly made his way towards the edge of the square, pausing at a stall to inspect a bolt of cloth.

"That's very fine wool," a woman said from beside him. "It would make a lovely warm overcoat."

"For me or for you?" Hewitt asked. He dropped the cloth and turned to the woman. This must be his busybody. No one other than vendors had spoken to him all day.

She was round and her face was cheerful, but her eyes were

calculating.

"For someone, is all I meant, Master Conjurer," she smiled, but it didn't reach her eyes. "I'm Mistress Bleddyn. I thought a chance meeting over some market goods would be best." She leaned in closer. "The bridge has eyes and ears everywhere."

"I suspected," Hewitt said. "I trust the candle seller has told you what I seek?"

"He did," she replied. "And I do have a thought, though the specific names mentioned are not known to me." She took his arm and led him a few steps away from the cloth vendor. "But there is a family where the lads are always named Collen. I spoke to the current matron of the family—she says it's an old family name, although she doesn't know exactly who the first Collen was. It's her husband's family."

"And is there a current Collen?" It *had* to be the Kellen line. He knew the second daughter had moved to Waglenn Landing—wouldn't the family of a conjurer want to keep that tie?

"There is," she replied. "Two of them. The younger Collen is right here." She waved a hand and a boy of about eight stepped out from behind a cart laden with root vegetables. "Collen, come meet the Master Conjurer."

"Pleased to meet you." The boy bobbed his head but remained a few steps away.

"Likewise, young Collen." The lad had dark hair and eyes, like most of the other townspeople he'd seen. "I dare say you've never met a conjurer before."

"No, Master Conjurer."

"Call me Conjurer Hewitt." He was a good age. Could he convince the lad to apprentice to him? He would have his own Kellen conjurer.

"Yes, Conjurer Hewitt," Collen replied. He took a step closer and reached out a hand.

Hewitt grasped it in his oversized one and the boy studied it.

"Mistress Bleddyn." Hewitt took a coin from his pocket and handed it to her. "You've done me a great service, thank you."

Mistress Bleddyn nodded as she slipped the coin into her purse. She put a hand on the boy's shoulder and started to turn away with him.

"Please," Hewitt said. "I would like a few words in private with the lad."

Mistress Bleddyn hesitated, then nodded and dropped her hand from the boy's shoulder. "Of course. I'll just stand over by the cloth seller's."

Once she was out of hearing, Hewitt leaned down to speak into the boy's ear.

"Can you read?" he asked.

"Some," the boy replied. "I'm to be a cooper like my da, so I don't need much."

"A cooper," Hewitt said. "Do you like making things?"

"Yes, Conjurer Hewitt, very much."

"I make things as well," he replied. "Although they don't have the substance of a barrel or a pail."

"You make magic," Collen said. "That must be great. My ma's mother went to the bridge once, to get a spell made, when my ma was a girl. My aunt was ill and she was looking to buy a spell to heal her. It were Conjurer Sherston who helped. She had to meet him in the dark."

"And did his spell help?" Hewitt asked. Now, he knew that Sherston didn't have a powerful healing spell: all he had was the reputation of saving people.

"Oh yes, it did. My aunt got better right away."

"Excellent," Hewitt said. At least Sherston's charade had given the lad a high opinion of conjurers.

"I must be getting back to the bridge," Hewitt said. "You can visit me there. Anyone can tell you where to find me."

"Yes, Conjurer Hewitt," he said. "I've never been on the bridge. Can I come soon?"

"Certainly. Why don't you come in a few days?" Hewitt replied. "I'm quite busy but I'm sure I can find time for a short visit." He'd need to figure out how to get some Kellen spells, even though the spell books weren't allowed out of Conjurers Hall. "And I ask that you keep our conversation private. Don't tell anyone what we talked about."

"Not even Mistress Bleddyn?"

"Not even her, I'm afraid." Especially not her. Would the Bridgers think to question the busybody? He hoped not, but even if they did and the names got back to Wailes, they would mean nothing to the Head Conjurer.

He left Collen with Mistress Bleddyn and made his way back to the bridge.

The Bridger who let him back through the gates gave him a long look and Hewitt knew his talk with Collen had been noted.

If Wailes asked he'd say the boy had seen Councilman Larwood take Faelin and Aric upriver. That's where they'd gone, he was sure of it. Aric couldn't stay on land and Faelin would stay with him. So Faelin was upriver. He refused to believe that the body was hers.

Chapter Eighteen

Once Fae finished reading the sentence, her eyes slid from the page to the rest of the books. They were all so important, and she'd already lost one journal, they couldn't chance losing the only copies.

"Aric." She waited until he looked up from the book he was reading. "I need to make copies of all of the books."

"I'll have my mother hide the copies somewhere else," he said. "Are you sure you can do it? Sure you *want* to do it? We don't know what side effects magic will have on you."

"There shouldn't be any," she replied. "Not according to Keetley Kellen. Side effects happen when someone not related by blood to the conjurer who created the spell, recites one."

"What should I do?"

"Watch," Fae replied. She set the journal down on the table and lined it up with two of the shaman books. Aric laid the last book down beside them. Fae frowned. Could she copy them all at once or did she have to do it one at a time? One at a time, she decided, in case something went wrong. She'd start with the book she'd already copied.

She moved the journal to one side, placed her hand on the cover and recited the spell.

"*Geedcenne deanboc boc.*" Her hand warmed and then there was a second, identical journal beside the first.

"You did it," Aric said.

"I told you," Fae said. But she couldn't hide her relief. She *had* done it. And she could do it again.

In moments they had two sets of books. Aric picked up an identical pair.

"I can't tell the difference," he said, staring at the books side by side. "Even this tear along the binding is the same."

"I know," Fae said.

"All those years and the bookbinders were the true conjurers," Aric said. "I'll hide a set until my mother comes back." He picked up one of each book and headed towards the small bedchamber.

Fae picked up the journal. Now, where was she? She flipped through few pages then stopped. She'd read this page already, but now there was more writing in the margins. She turned the book to the side. The words wrapped around the page—she had to turn the book to follow the sentence. She went back to the first page of the journal.

There was writing that hadn't been there before.

"Aric," she called. "Aric!"

"What's wrong?" He rushed back into the room. "What is it?"

"What do you see on this page," she asked. "What's the last word you can read?"

He peered over her shoulder and pointed at the last word before the new writing started. "Here. The word *chronicle.*"

Fae looked up at him. "I see more words, more writing, after it."

"What does it say?"

Fae pulled the book closer. "*I write this with hope that someone, someday, will be able to read it,*" she read aloud. "*I, Keetley Kellen, have been witness to the fall of conjurers. I am the last of the blood, though there are those who bear the names of seven of the ten families.*

"*I started this journal when I was in my middle years and knew my brother would be the last Kellen conjurer. I write these words now as an old man, one who hopes, likely in vain, that one day another Kellen conjurer will exist. He is the only one who will be able to read these added words.*"

"That's all it has on this page," Fae said. She was almost afraid to read more.

"You're the Kellen conjurer," Aric said. "Though you're not a he."

"But I couldn't read it an hour ago," Fae said. "Why can I now?"

"You did magic," Aric said. "You copied the books. Perhaps that triggered it?" He shrugged. "Or maybe Keetley Kellen will explain why." He sighed. "I will make us something to eat. You keep reading."

FAE TRACED THE words that ran around the edges of the book. Aric had suggested she move to the bedroom while he made their meal. Now she lay on the bed with her head propped up against the hull of the boat, the journal resting on her chest.

She'd spoken earlier of worlds changing, and how difficult it must be. Now she was experiencing the same thing. Her world had changed—*she* had changed. But at least she had this journal, at least she knew why.

"Fae," Aric opened the door and stuck his head into the room. "Supper is ready." He started to back out but stopped. "Are you all right?"

"Yes. No." Fae slid off the bed. Aric opened the door completely and she walked into his embrace.

"I'm not a Kellen conjurer," she said. "But I will be. Keetley Kellen wrote down everything he knew about conjurers—about *Kellen* conjurers. Including how to become one." She stared into his eyes. "I will be able to create spells," she said. "Spells of power that won't cripple me."

"Then you can help my people," Aric said. "And reverse the Wailes curse."

"Probably," she said.

"It will be a good thing," Aric said.

"Will it?" she asked. She shivered. Keetley Kellen claimed that Kellen conjurers were the most powerful of the ten families. She would be able to defeat Wailes and any other conjurers working with him. But she might have to destroy them completely.

"Yes," he replied. "Because you will *make* it a good thing. Just as I will make being a shaman a good thing." He pulled her through the door. "Time to eat, my conjurer."

Fried fish and a dark green mass of cooked seaweed were on

the table. She sat down. Aric was right. She would make being a conjurer a good thing. Besides, Wailes had ruled the bridge with nothing more than the threat of doing magic. She would be able to actually *do* magic. They'd heed her out of fear, like they did Wailes. Not that she wanted to rule by fear, but she didn't want to rule by hurting people either. And she would rule, she and Aric, whether they wanted to or not.

HEWITT NODDED AT Shiv as he swept past him and into Wailes' study. The head conjurer looked up from a book that lay on the desk in front of him. There was the smell of sulfur in the air. Hewitt assumed another apprentice had met his end.

Wailes motioned to Tymm who, as usual, stood behind him. The big man reached out a hand and closed the book.

Hewitt hid his surprise. Had Wailes' condition deteriorated so much that he no longer had the strength or dexterity to close a book? He wanted to see Shiv's expression but didn't dare turn to look. And the book—it was one bound in the same skin as the journal.

"You have something to report?" Wailes asked.

"Yes, Master Conjurer," Hewitt replied. "I do not believe the girl is dead."

"No?"

"No. She was seen leaving Waglenn Landing in the company of the Riverman Aric Rawley. I cannot imagine him letting her drown."

"No, I suppose not," Wailes said. "And you are right. The body was not Faelin Keetley. The Rivermen finally found it and sent it to us."

Hewitt suppressed a sigh of relief. Faelin was alive—he could still convince her to work with him, become his Kellen conjurer.

"Why is the bookbinder's daughter with this Riverman?" Wailes asked.

"They are friends," Hewitt replied. "Have been since childhood." He wanted to add that his apprentice would have known this, but Thorpe was dead.

"I remember," Wailes said. "He was at the bookbinder's ceremony. Shiv, isn't his mother the shaman? We told both her and their leader to hand him over to us."

"Yes, Master Conjurer." Shiv stepped up beside Hewitt.

"Fetch her," Wailes said. "I want to ask her again, where her son is."

Shiv hesitated for a moment before he turned to leave.

"She won't be able to tell you anything if you bring her here," Hewitt said. He heard the door open but Shiv didn't exit.

"That is true, Master Conjurer," the Bridger said. "She's more . . . affected than most of them. Won't be able to set foot on land. Or the bridge."

"I must question her," Wailes said. "Bring her to the foot of the stairs. Tymm will have to take me down."

Hewitt waited until the door closed after Shiv, before speaking.

"There is more, Master Conjurer."

"Tell me," Wailes said.

"The head councilman of Waglenn Landing helped Faelin and Aric escape. A man by the name of Larwood. I have a report that says he actually stopped Bridgers from taking the girl."

"I was told a townsman intervened," Wailes said. "Do you know why?"

"I'm not sure. He claimed he'd only helped the Riverman, that he took pity on him because he was suffering from the effects of the curse."

"But you think they both went."

"They have been friends since they were children," Hewitt said. "They both went."

"Thank you," Wailes said. "You are being so very . . . useful." His eyes narrowed. "I have to wonder why. Is there anything else in the journal I should know? Anything relevant to conjurers?"

"The writing is difficult to make out, Master Conjurer," Hewitt said. "It takes time to read it. It has the same binding as the book you were looking at." He gestured to the book in front of Wailes. "Perhaps if I can view them together it will make deciphering both of them easier."

Wailes looked from Hewitt to the book and back again. "I see no harm in that," he said finally. "You've seen yourself what happens when the spells are recited improperly."

HEWITT RAN A hand across the journal first and then the spell book. The spell book seemed older—but it would be, since the journal had been started when the last Kellen Conjurer was a mature man.

He opened the older book and traced a finger along the words. The urge to speak them aloud, to try to execute the spell, was almost uncontrollable. Finally, after so many years of pretending to be a conjurer, of reciting his tired spells for petty problems, he held in his hands words with real power.

But the only way he could wield that power was through another. He had to have a Kellen conjurer. If Wailes found Faelin, she was lost to Hewitt. Then his only option would be to ensure she didn't become a weapon for Wailes.

He still had hopes for the boy Collen. But he needed proof that he *was* a Kellen. And how would he get that?

Hewitt sighed. Faelin was the best option. He knew she was a Kellen and her father had done magic for years without any debilitating physical side effects. He just had to find her before Wailes did.

Wailes would concentrate his search efforts upriver, and even though Hewitt was sure Faelin was there, he would try to talk to someone downriver. The fishmonger still had access to the stairs. He'd accompany him next time he went down. Or, when Wailes interrogated the shaman, he might be able to send a message to someone. Surely fishing boats would follow the shaman to try to find out what the bridge wanted with her?

He reached over to the shelf beside the desk and pulled a piece of paper off it.

If he was to succeed he needed more than a Kellen conjurer. He needed Kellen spells. He sat down and dipped his quill into the ink pot. He didn't need the whole book. He'd look for some useful spells. Useful to overthrow Wailes, he hoped.

FAE TOOK A deep breath and let it out through clenched teeth. Another headache—the worst one yet. But now she had a good idea of what caused them.

Magic—Kellen magic. Someone was reciting a Kellen spell. It had to be Wailes—he had the books. Not that Wailes would recite the spell—he'd have someone else do that. And no doubt whoever it was had been afflicted, maybe even to the point where they could barely function, like what had happened to poor Thorpe.

Once the waves of pain had subsided, she flipped back through the journal. There. After the death of his brother, Keetley

Kellen had written that unexpectedly, he missed the feeling of magic being performed. Missed the reminders that his brother was alive.

But he described it as a flash of warmth, not the excruciating pain Fae felt. And he'd also explained that it was only felt by those who had used magic themselves. His daughters, for example, had never done magic and so did not feel it being used.

Fae closed the book. She'd read through the hidden writing twice. Her next step would be to actually begin Keetley Kellen's lessons on how to become a conjurer.

The first lessons were seemingly straightforward exercises to aid her concentration and focus. After that, she would recite existing spells, and then change them. The last lesson taught how to create new spells.

But she only had the copy spell—just the one spell to use for the first lessons. Would it be enough to learn with? She wished she'd taken one of the other books, but it had been difficult enough to keep this book. She would have lost it—*had* lost it— except that she'd been able to make a copy.

She heard the sounds of running and suddenly the boat rocked as someone jumped on board.

She tucked the journal under the bed and joined Aric in the main room. He stood facing the door, an oar in his hands. She touched his shoulder to let him know she was there and he nodded without taking his eyes off the doorway.

"Aric," a voice whispered. "It's me, Rand."

Aric set the oar aside and bare feet descended the stairs. Rand was nervous and breathing heavily.

"They've taken her," Rand said. "The shaman. Your mother. They've taken her."

"Who's taken—" Aric started, but Fae cut him off.

"Wailes has taken Sigrun?" she asked. Rand nodded, and Fae looped her arm around Aric. "When?"

"How?" Aric asked. "Bridgers don't have boats."

Rand scowled. "It were Fiske," he said. "He's been taking the catch over to the bridge for a few weeks now. Seems he's made friends with more than just the fishmonger. Today he went there, as usual, but he came back with three of them Bridgers. Took 'em right to Sigrun. Grabbed her quick and then went back to the bridge."

"Why would Fiske do that?" Aric asked. "Did they threaten him?"

"Didn't look like it to me," Rand said. "When they was here they was all off his boat and on the dock—he coulda stranded them, but didn't. Pulled up nice and close so's they could drag yer ma into his boat."

"They won't take her onto the bridge," Fae said with more confidence than she felt.

"You're right," Aric said. "They'll need her to be able to speak."

"What do they want with her?" Rand asked.

"Me," Aric replied. "They want to ask her about me."

Fae put her hand on his arm and he covered it with his own hand. "They will think we're upriver still," she said.

"That doesn't mean they won't hurt her," Aric replied. He turned to Rand. "Who else knows we're here?"

"Just the shaman and Pax," Rand said. "And Gern, who picked you up after you came past the bridge. Pax told me to come tell you and it surprised me." He paused. "I'm supposed to bring him something of hers. That was the reason to come to her empty boat."

"I'll find something," Fae said. She left the two Rivermen talking in hushed tones and went back to the bedroom.

Aric had not mentioned any tools used by a shaman but that didn't mean the rest of the Rivermen wouldn't expect one. It took her a while to find it. She'd left it here before venturing into Waglenn Landing with Aric but it seemed that Sigrun had moved it. Had she been curious? Or had she felt cursed by it? Fae knew she did. But it was unusual enough to be something the shaman had kept.

She stepped out of the bedroom. "Here." She held it out to him.

"The stinger," Rand said. He took it from her and coiled it around his upper arm. "I'll give it to Pax." He turned and scrambled up the stairs.

Fae led Aric to the bench and forced him to sit down.

"Will he kill her?" Aric asked.

Fae sighed. "You must be prepared for it. Wailes doesn't seem to care who dies."

"As long as it isn't him."

"Yes," she agreed. "As long as it isn't him." They sat in silence for a few moments before she spoke again.

"She'd moved it," she said. "Your mother. She'd moved the stinger."

"Then she knew," Aric said. "She must have had a feeling about it. She couldn't tell me, but she moved it so we would know."

"We'll need a small boat," Fae said. "And I need to dress as a Riverman. We may not be able to save her, but you need to see."

"Yes."

Chapter Nineteen

HEWITT PERCHED ON the stairs, craning his head to see what was happening down on the pier. Someone jostled him from above and he leaned back into the rough stone of the bridge, clutching the rope railing.

"Careful," he muttered, turning to look.

"Sorry." It was the Burrage lad, still alive.

Hewitt nodded. Graylon Burrage looked like he was sorry for a lot of things.

"I saw your mother," Hewitt said softly. "She asked about you." If the lad lived he might be a useful ally. And if not, a kindness for its own sake wouldn't hurt *him*.

"Is she all right?"

"As well as can be expected," Hewitt replied. "She is imprisoned, but is not forced to read from spell books."

"What do you think will happen to her when . . ." Graylon Burrage trailed off.

"When Wailes finally asks you to read?" Hewitt finished. "My guess is something unpleasant."

The man sighed. "At least my death will be quick."

Hewitt had no comforting answer so he nodded at the young man again. It was possible that an apprentice had true conjurer blood—Keetley Kellen's daughter may have been the last with conjurer's blood to leave the bridge and marry a townsman but others would have done it before her. But even with conjurer blood there was only a one in ten chance of reading from the correct family's spell book: and a nine in ten chance of not. They needed the blood of *the* conjurer who had written the spell they read. And Hewitt guessed that if anyone was lucky enough to survive one spell, Wailes, because he didn't know, would make them read from a different book. And that would be the end of that conjurer.

But Hewitt wasn't about to volunteer his information to Wailes; to let the head conjurer know that an apprentice could only read from a single type of book. It would mean giving up an advantage when he had so very few of them.

Hewitt shook his head. If he could get Faelin to trust him they would be able to overcome Wailes with real power. But he had to find her first. He scanned the scene below him with renewed attention. He was certain that someone on one of the Rivermen boats knew where Aric and Faelin were.

Wailes, strapped to Tymm's back, was at the bottom of the stairs. The tide was out and the small pier was exposed. In chest-deep water, Shiv and another half dozen Bridgers ringed the pier.

And a few hundred yards downstream it looked like every fishing boat the Rivermen possessed was out on the water. Men and women sat or stood, silent and watchful, and Hewitt had to wonder what their shaman meant to them, what powers she had.

One boat bobbed in the water beside the pier, a small figure hunched in the prow. Webbed hands pulled back the hood and he could see the shaman's face.

Shiv had spoken the truth—she was more affected by the curse than other Rivermen he'd seen. Far more than her son. He straightened and stared. He'd never thought about Aric's father. Clearly he had been more . . . normal than his mother—was he from one of the towns? It would make sense, bedding a non-Riverman in the hopes that your child was less malformed than you. Could they have bred with conjurers long ago? Would they have a record of paternity? His understanding was that the history was oral—but that they had it.

Excited now, he hoped that Wailes let the woman live. Because Hewitt wanted to question her.

"You are the shaman," Wailes' voice carried up to him. "And mother of Aric Rawley?"

"I am," the woman answered. She stared at Wailes, and Hewitt shivered. Though her face was in shadow, her eyes seemed to have a light of their own. "And you are a conjurer who is not."

Did she know? Hewitt thought. Did she know that conjurers were born? That there were bloodlines?

"I am Head Conjurer Wailes," Wailes said. "I asked before. Where is your son?"

The woman stood up and the lone Riverman in the boat shifted his weight to keep it steady.

"My son is on the river," she said. She looked up and her gaze swept past Hewitt before resting on Wailes. "It is the only place he can live, thanks to a long-ago conjurer not of your line but of your name. The Wailes curse has done as much to you as it has to us, conjurers who are not," she said, her voice loud enough to carry up to the crowd on the stairs. "But the day comes when the curse will be broken."

Wailes laughed. "Broken—it will be completed! Tell me where your son has taken the bookbinder's daughter!"

"The curse will be broken," the woman repeated, more quietly. Abruptly she sat down and pulled her hood over her face. She turned her head and spoke to the Riverman who stood in the boat. Hewitt didn't hear what she said, but the man paled and tried to set an oar into the oarlock, but a Bridger waded over and grabbed the oars and tossed them onto the water.

"I did as you asked," the Riverman said. "I brought the shaman."

"I still do not have the girl," Wailes said. "Put them both on the pier."

The Riverman struggled, but the shaman was eerily calm as Bridgers pulled them from the boat and set them down at the base of the stairs. Tymm, carrying Wailes, shuffled back a few steps.

Hewitt could hear the harsh rasp of the woman's breathing as she sat and stared at Wailes. The Riverman sobbed loudly until one of the Bridgers knocked him down. He lay on the damp stone of the pier, whether dead or unconscious, Hewitt couldn't tell. And it didn't matter. The man would be dead soon anyway. Bridgers would make sure of that.

"Tell me where your son and the bookbinder's daughter are or I will let you die!" Wailes yelled. The shaman's only response was a wide smile. Her breathing became more laboured—the harsh rasping sound was now louder than the river. But still, she continued to smile up at Wailes.

"Conjurer Wailes?" Shiv called softly.

Hewitt's gaze swivelled from Shiv, to Wailes, to the shaman, then back to Wailes. He was going to let her die! He'd lose any chance to discover whether Rivermen carried conjurer blood. But there was no way to help her and no chance to get close enough to her to ask a question.

The shaman had fallen onto her side now, her smile broken by her gasps for breath. Her eyes were fixed on Wailes even as she lay dying. What powers did she have? What did she know? Then she collapsed and her eyes glazed over. There was a cry from one of the fishing boats and then a collective moan, as though the river itself had felt a deep pain.

Hewitt looked out at the boats. For a moment they continued to face the bridge, then suddenly the men and women on-board sprang into action and the boats started moving downriver. One small boat didn't move, not right away. Another boat came alongside it and someone jumped in and manned the oars.

Hewitt turned back to the scene below him. Once their shaman was dead, the Rivermen hadn't waited to see what happened to their compatriot. He'd lasted a few moments longer than the woman he'd betrayed, but then he too gasped and was still.

Hewitt looked back out across the river. The small boat was still heading away, trailing the second boat behind it. Someone had been distraught at the exact moment the shaman had died. His eyes narrowed. Had she left a successor? Someone she'd trained, someone who possessed all the same knowledge? Or . . . was it her son?

He frowned and shook his head. Aric was upriver, all the information he had pointed to that. He himself had talked to witnesses who saw him head that way. Even Councilman Larwood had admitted to taking him upriver. But he was born and raised on the river. Was it possible he'd made it past the bridge? That he was fooling them? Keeping the search focussed upriver while he hid in plain sight downriver?

He turned to leave, only to face Burrage. The young man looked even more miserable than before.

FAE HUDDLED IN the stern with Aric's head on her lap and a sail covering the both of them. The boat lurched forward every few seconds as Rand rowed them towards the village.

Sigrun was dead. She'd known the moment she died because Aric had cried out and collapsed into the bottom of the boat. When she'd knelt beside him, she'd been relieved to find him breathing, although there was a small gash on his left cheek. He had no other injuries she could see, but she hadn't been able to wake him.

Thankfully Rand had been close. He'd jumped in and grabbed the oars and started rowing so they would not be left behind.

"Aric." She wiped his forehead with the sleeve of her borrowed shirt—Sigrun's shirt. His breathing was steadier now, but his skin was clammy. Worried, she leaned her head against his. "Please wake up."

"Almost there," Rand said from the stern. She lifted a corner of the sail. The sun was still shining and a few wispy clouds feathered the blue sky. She nodded at Rand. She could see the Riverman village just past his left shoulder. A few other boats travelled beside them and she dropped the sail. Her and Aric's presence was supposed to be a secret. Was it still?

A few moments later the boat shifted direction and the sounds of the river dulled to soft waves slapping against wood. They would be close to Sigrun's boat now.

"Aric," she said, staring into his eyes. "We're home." The boat bumped into something and Rand slipped the oars out of the oarlocks.

"We're here," he called softly.

Fae carefully pulled the sail off her and Aric. "He's still unconscious," she said. "I'll need help getting him aboard."

Rand nodded and bent to grab Aric under his arms. He dragged him upright and, with balance Fae knew she didn't have, hefted him into his arms and stepped onto the shaman's boat. Fae scrambled after him, hurrying to open the door so Rand could take Aric straight in.

The small bedroom seemed even smaller as Rand lowered Aric onto the bed, Fae crowding in behind. Rand edged past her and she dropped down beside Aric.

"Aric. We're safe now." She touched his forehead. It seemed warmer, and he had some colour in his cheeks. She was aware of Rand leaving the room and the door closing softly.

"Fae."

She dropped the cloth into the small bowl of water, almost spilling it.

"Aric?" She leaned towards him. His eyes fluttered open and he grimaced.

"Yeah," he replied. "What happened?" He started to sit up but she held him down. "My mother." He turned his head away.

"I'm so sorry," Fae said.

"Did Wailes . . . ?"

"No." Fae shook her head. "She was on the pier at the bottom of the stairs."

"I remember," Aric said.

"She didn't make a sound," Fae said. "And then you cried out and fell. I think you hit your head."

Aric reached a hand up to his head. "No," he said. "It was something else." He turned to her. "I knew when she died. Something happened to me when she died."

"Should it?" Fae asked. "I mean, you and your mother never really had a chance to talk much about you becoming a shaman."

"I don't know." Aric slowly pulled himself up until his back was against the hull of the boat. "But we need to leave. We can't be found here." He turned to her and his eyes lost focus. "They will be looking for us. Someone on the bridge believes we're here."

"I won't let Wailes find us," Fae replied.

"Not Wailes," Aric said. He closed his eyes and took a deep breath. When he opened them, she saw exhaustion and pain. "A shaman feeling, stronger than ever."

"Rand will be back soon," she said. "He's gone to fetch Pax. In the meantime, drink some water." She reached for the glass.

It took him more than a few minutes to just stand up and make his way to the door. He could hear the soft rumble of voices. Fae and Rand, he guessed. Or Pax.

He grabbed a fresh shirt from the cupboard at the end of the bed, pausing as his hand brushed an old skirt of his mother's.

A wave of anguish swept over him. He'd had a troubled relationship with his mother, but he'd loved her. And he thought she'd loved him, although she hadn't always shown it. Hadn't known *how* to show it, not to a boy child when she'd only ever expected to bear a girl.

He clamped his teeth together and dragged the shirt on. There was no time to mourn Sigrun Rawley. He and Fae were in danger.

He opened the door and stepped into the small living space.

Rand and Pax stopped talking and turned to stare at him. Fae came over and, with an arm around his waist, helped him sit on the bench at the table.

"I've made tea," she said, reaching across to the small stove. She placed a steaming mug in front of him, and gratefully, he put his hands around it.

"Sigrun told me," Pax said. Shaking his head, he squeezed in across from him. "The first male shaman in memory."

"Yes," Aric replied. "Although she didn't warn me how I would inherit the full powers."

"You mean when she died?" Rand asked. "Is that why you fell?" He looked nervously from Pax to Aric. "We thought it was the shock of it. Seeing your mother die like that."

"She knew she would die," Aric said. "And I think she knew her powers would pass to me when she did. That's why she didn't struggle." He sipped his tea, enjoying how the warmth spread through him. He sighed. "We need to leave."

"That's what Fae said," Pax replied. "But Wailes is looking upriver for you."

"Yes," Aric agreed. "But it's not Wailes we need to worry about. At least not yet. There's someone else."

"Who?" Pax asked. "Wailes is in control of the bridge."

"I don't know," Aric replied. "But we have to leave as soon as possible. And we have to go now, before the tide goes out." He met Rand's eyes. "I'm not yet recovered from whatever has happened to me. Can you help?" Rand nodded, and Aric closed his eyes in relief. "Thank you." He opened his eyes. "Fae, I'll need your help packing everything away for travel. We're taking this boat—my mother's boat—and we're going to the sea. We'll be safe enough. No ships are expected at this time of year. Rand, I'll need you to sail it. Bring your fishing boat so you can get home."

"Won't they miss the boat?" Fae asked. "The Bridgers? They could come back."

"Pax will tell them that the boat has been scuttled," Aric said. "It belonged to the last shaman and after the way she died, everyone believes it's cursed."

"Not far from the truth," Pax said. "Only we four know she wasn't the last shaman."

"I'll get my boat," Rand said. "Let me know when you're ready and I'll tow you out from the docks."

"Thanks," Aric said.

Rand left and Pax stood to go as well.

"You'll come back, won't you, lad?" he asked.

"Yes," Aric said. "I need to recover and try to understand exactly what gifts my mother passed to me." And Fae needed to learn how to create spells, but he didn't tell Pax that.

"Wait," Fae said as Pax was about to leave. She went into the bedroom and returned a few minutes later with the books. The three his mother had given him and the journal.

"Keep these safe." She handed the books to Pax.

Pax nodded, tucked the books under his jacket, and left.

"Good idea," Aric said to Fae. He sighed. "We might want to make another set of them to be safe." He started to stand but she gently pushed him back down.

"I already did," Fae said. "We can give them to Rand. Or I can hide them on land somewhere. But you need to rest. Tell me what to do to get the boat ready."

ARIC SLUMPED ACROSS the table. Even just giving Fae directions had sapped what little strength he had. Fae slipped onto the bench across from him.

"Rand is towing us now," she said. "Tide is going out so he'll have the current with him."

"Good," Aric said. He reached across the table and placed his hands on hers. "I'm sorry I didn't ask you about leaving, but I have such a strong feeling."

"Then we need to go," Fae said.

The boat lurched and tilted slightly. He nodded and Fae stood up and blew out the lamp. If the story of scuttling his mother's boat was going to be believed, it had to look abandoned.

He clutched Fae's hands tighter and smiled when her fingers

tightened on his.

Were Rivermen watching the shaman's boat being towed away from the village? He thought so. He couldn't remember the last time his mother's boat had been away from its mooring, although like all Rivermen boats it was seaworthy.

He and Fae were still silently holding hands in the dark when the jerking motion of being towed by a rowboat ceased. A few minutes later they were gliding smoothly through the water and he knew Rand had put the sail up. They should reach the mouth of the river soon. Then he would have to take them out to sea, away from the pull of the river tide, while Rand returned to the village.

Chapter Twenty

HEWITT LOOKED UP from his desk. He was reading the journal—again—hoping there was some clue he'd missed that revealed another conjurer name. But all he had was what he'd had before. The only certainty was that Faelin was a Kellen.

Wailes had sent men upriver but he was certain Faelin and her friend were downriver. He couldn't ignore what had happened when the shaman died. Someone on the river—downstream—had . . . had what? Had collapsed when the old woman died? It could have been anyone, an old friend—perhaps a sibling.

He shook his head. He had a feeling there was more to it than that.

He wished he knew more about Riverman shamans. Sigrun Rawley had been the only one he knew of, and then only because Aric was her son. All his life he'd lived on the bridge, years and years of eating the fish brought by Rivermen, seeing them out in their boats day after day. And he'd never thought to try to understand them. Now he needed to know their secrets but there was no one left to tell them.

And he was worried that Wailes' actions today would have far reaching consequences.

There was a sharp knock on the door and the Bridger who was guarding him stuck his head in.

"Visitor," he said. He jerked the door open and stepped aside.

Startled, Hewitt got to his feet as Collen, looking afraid and nervous, stepped into the room.

"Wailes has already seen him," the Bridger said. "You have twenty minutes." He closed the door, leaving Collen standing a few steps into the room.

"Collen, my lad," Hewitt said. He edged around the desk and pulled up a chair. "Please, sit." The poor boy looked from him to the chair before staring at the floor.

"Did Conjurer Wailes treat you all right?" Hewitt asked.

"Yes sir," Collen replied.

"But he scared you, didn't he," Hewitt said. "He and Tymm."

"Yes sir."

"Don't worry," Hewitt lied. "Conjurer Hewitt and Tymm aren't as terrible as they seem. It's just that being Head Conjurer is a very important job, and Conjurer Wailes is a very busy man." He went back to the other side of the desk and sat down. "Please, have a seat. I'm very happy you came to visit me."

Collen hesitated for a moment, but then he sat down across from Hewitt.

"Tell me, did Conjurer Wailes ask you any questions?"

"Yes sir," Collen replied. "He asked why I was here. I told him I met you in the village and that you had invited me to visit." He looked up, his eyes wide. "On account of I'd never been on the bridge before. It was all right for me to say that, wasn't it?"

"Of course it was," Hewitt said. If it hadn't been the boy would never have made it to his study. His body would have been found downriver in a day or two. He leaned forward. The boy was scared—which showed good judgment—but he might be too afraid to accept his offer.

"Would you like to stay on the bridge?" he asked. "Live here and learn a trade. One that can help people?"

"Live here?" Collen looked like he wanted to run away. "I'm not sure."

"You would be my apprentice," Hewitt said. "I'd teach you to read, and to do magic. You'd like that, wouldn't you?"

"Magic?" Collen's face lit up. "You can teach me magic?"

"I can," Hewitt said. "If you agree to be my apprentice."

"Would I be taught by Conjurer Wailes?"

"No," Hewitt said. "He has his own apprentices. He will not interfere with mine." At least he hoped he wouldn't. Hewitt had seen little of the rest of the conjurers but Wailes still needed them to be neutral, didn't he? Meddling with another conjurer's apprentice would force them to take sides. He hoped.

"Then yes," Collen said. "I would like to learn magic. Can I tell my ma?"

"Not yet," Hewitt said. "I need you to perform a task before I can officially take you on." He opened the book of spells. A short one, something simple without a lot of words. He flipped through the pages. The boy could not quite read so he would have to sound the words out—out of sequence—before asking him to recite the whole thing. There, that one. He read the spell a few times. Something to do with duplicating a page. Excellent. It was only two words *geanboc tramet*. He had to stop himself from saying the spell out loud.

"Come here, lad," Hewitt said. "I will teach you some words and when you put them together it will tell me if you are able to learn magic. Not everyone can."

"I'll do my best, Master Conjurer."

And he did, Hewitt had to admit that the boy was quick. He glanced at the door. The Bridger would be back soon, ready to escort young Collen off the bridge. He had to know.

"All right, Collen," he said. Just in case, he eased his chair away from the desk.

"Geanboc tram . . ."

The last syllable was drowned out by a soft sucking sound and then the boy was gone, consumed by a burst of flame. There was a smudge of soot on the floor where he'd stood and Hewitt quickly scattered it. Had the Bridger heard anything? He couldn't let Wailes know he had tried to find someone to recite spells.

He settled back in his chair and calmly opened the journal again. He stared at the page in front of him. He'd just killed that boy—sent him to his death—and all he could think about was finding Faelin.

He'd tell the Bridger the boy got scared and left on his own. Let him figure out where and how he'd slipped off the bridge— they wouldn't hear it from Hewitt.

FAE SHUDDERED AND clutched at the table. It wasn't just a headache this time—she'd almost been knocked off her feet.

"What happened?" Aric asked. He sat on the bench, his back against the hull and his feet stretched out in front of him.

She'd thought he was asleep.

"I think someone tried a Kellen spell," she replied. She shuddered. "I think it killed them." She'd been working with her one spell for hours and now there was a small pile of copied items on the table in front of her: a lamp, a broken cup, and a knife. It hadn't been that difficult to adjust the spell to copy things other than books, but working with magic seemed to have made her more sensitive to it.

"How many people does Wailes have to kill before he gives up?" She'd felt the presence of something, someone—in the magic—then they suddenly vanished. But she'd felt their pain just before a wave of power slammed into her.

"Not Wailes," Aric said. "Someone else."

"Could Wailes be dead?" Fae asked.

"I don't think so," Aric said. He closed his eyes and paused. "No, he's still alive." He opened his eyes and fixed them on her. "I think there are two conjurers trying to use the spells."

"Hewitt," Fae said. "It has to be. He knew about my father copying books—he suspected there were more. He must have made some bargain with Wailes to access the old spells."

Aric nodded. "Hewitt. That feels right."

His head drooped and Fae went over and pulled the blanket higher on him. "You need to take it easy," she said.

"What's the use of having new abilities if I'm always too exhausted to use them?" he asked, but he pulled the blanket tighter around his shoulders.

"You just need some rest," Fae said.

"You hope."

"Yes, I hope," she replied. "You've had no chance to rest until now. What with me being totally inept at sailing." He smiled at that, but she knew it was the truth.

Rand had gotten them to the mouth of the river, but then he'd had to turn back or risk being trapped by the low tide. Aric had managed the boat—sailing them far enough away from the mouth of the Aberhayle that the next high tide wouldn't push them back in—before dropping anchor. Then he'd had to take down the sails and pack them, a complicated and time consuming task that had surprised Fae. But he'd said it was necessary, that they had to put the sails away properly or they could rot and become unusable.

In the hours since, he'd dozed at the table while she completed the lessons left by her ancestor. She was almost ready to create a new spell but she wanted to wait until Aric was feeling better. Without any way to know what creating a new spell would do to her, she couldn't risk both of them being weak. They were assuming no one would look for them this far from the bridge, but that didn't mean someone couldn't spot them by chance.

It was rare, but ships travelled across the Dark Sea to Waglenn Landing and Durnham, bringing spices and fine cloth and taking away timber from Durnham and the stone and marble that was mined from the cliffs above Waglenn Landing. If a ship happened to see them, the news would quickly spread from the towns to the bridge. Aric said it wasn't the right time of year for ships, but if he was wrong, it wouldn't take long for Wailes and Hewitt to learn where they were.

She sighed and sat down across from a now sleeping Aric. They hadn't yet talked about what they were getting ready for, but Wailes could not be allowed to finish the curse. She looked at Aric. Even in sleep his face wore a worried frown. His mother was dead and his people were being threatened.

Absently she flipped through the pages of the journal. Aric's premonition was right—if both Hewitt and Wailes were searching for true conjurers, powers on the bridge *were* building. Did they know she was one? Had one or both of them read the journal she'd lost at the Burrages? If they had, neither of them would rest until she was found.

But someone had just died trying to recite a spell. So did Wailes and Hewitt not know? Had they not read the journal? But it *was* a Kellen spell—that was too much of a coincidence for Fae to disregard.

IT WAS EARLY when Shiv burst into Hewitt's room without knocking, a murderous look on his face.

"Is there a problem?" Hewitt asked calmly. He'd done a lot of thinking overnight and had come to a decision. Wailes had powerful spells, but he couldn't use them. Magically, he wasn't any more powerful than the rest of them. He had the Bridgers—

like Shiv—but would he be willing to kill every last conjurer? If so, then who would he hold power over?

After causing Collen's death, Hewitt had realized that he would do anything to restore conjurers to their past glory. And if he couldn't do it, he would rather not live.

Collen hadn't known it but he'd had a chance to be great. Hewitt would rather die trying to be great, than continue to live his pathetic, *trivial* life.

"The boy who was here yesterday," Shiv said. "You lied. He did not leave on his own. His father is at the gate asking about his son."

"Just because he did not make it home does not mean I lied about him leaving," Hewitt replied. Shiv paused, as he'd expected him to. There was no proof the boy hadn't left—but no trace of him remained after reciting the spell.

"Wailes wants to see you," Shiv said. "Now."

"Excellent," Hewitt said. "I would like to see him as well."

He took his time getting ready. He might die in a few minutes so he was in no rush. He followed Shiv through the corridors of Conjurers Hall, his large shoes shuffling on the stone floor and the journal clutched in his oversized hand. He would hand the journal over to Wailes—there was no more information to be gleaned from it anyway—and then he would go back home. Assuming he lived through this little interview.

In Wailes' study, another two new apprentices stood beside Graylon Burrage. Hewitt's brows lifted and he nodded a greeting when he caught the young man's gaze. Burrage had lived far longer than any of Wailes' other apprentices. He obviously hadn't been forced to recite a spell . . . yet.

Hewitt sighed. There were three spells books on the table in front of Wailes, each with a different binding. Was Wailes going to force his apprentices to read spells today? Would he expect Hewitt to read from one?

"You told Shiv that the boy had left," Wailes said. He sat in his chair, hunched sideways, and to Hewitt, it sounded as though he was having trouble speaking.

"So I did," Hewitt said. "Not that who visits me and when they leave is really your concern."

"Everything on the bridge is my concern," Wailes said.

"Not any longer," Hewitt said. "I am going back to my own

quarters. Right now. And you will not send any of your guards to harass me."

"You're not going anywhere," Wailes said.

"I am. Here's your journal. I didn't find anything in to keep these poor, young men alive." He paused. "Nor to keep you alive." He smiled. "Because the others may have forgotten what I have not. This is all about the conjurer quest to reduce or eliminate our afflictions. You've been killing people in the hopes of finding a cure. But you haven't found one—you're not even close—and now you can barely speak."

"Shut up!" Wailes tried to shout, but his voice held little strength.

"Does Shiv know that you have only a few weeks left to live?" Hewitt glanced at Shiv and smiled. The man was staring at the floor, a grim look on his face. His fellow guard looked shocked. "What will he do then? Do you think the other conjurers will look kindly on him when they learn he killed one of their own?"

"Kill him!" Wailes called.

"Your choice," Hewitt said. "But I know you will not risk a spell—even one of your old, weak ones would kill you now. And these three?" He gestured to the apprentices. "They are your prisoners. I doubt they want to help you. Shiv?" Hewitt asked. "It's up to you."

Shiv shook his head and Hewitt relaxed.

"I won't kill the conjurer," Shiv said. "But I'll do whatever you wish to these apprentices."

"Shiv!" Wailes yelled. "Kill him!"

"No, Master Conjurer, I will not," Shiv replied. "I will not risk my people's future. The other conjurers would force us from the bridge when you die. We know nothing else, have nothing else." He paused. "But I will search him before he leaves."

Hewitt kept his eyes on Wailes and a huge smile on his face while Shiv searched him. The Head Conjurer was furious—and it was costing him physically—but he had no power to make Shiv do his bidding in this.

His search complete, Shiv stepped aside.

"Get out," Wailes said, his voice weak. "All of you, get out. Tymm!"

The apprentices hurried out of the room. Hewitt put a hand on Graylon Burrage's arm as he went past.

"I hope you are a survivor, lad," he said softly. "For your mother's sake. If you live through a spell, take note of the book's binding. Reading from a book with a different binding will kill you."

"Shiv, get him out!" Spittle flecked Wailes' mouth and Tymm whimpered as he fussed with Wailes' restraints.

As Shiv manhandled him out of the room and into the hallway, Hewitt wondered if Wailes would live through the day.

"I know the way," he said, shaking the Bridger's hands off him. A few moments later, Shiv still following him, he stepped out of Conjurers Hall and onto the roadway of the bridge.

It was difficult not to run the short distance to his own home, but once inside he closed the door and heaved a huge sigh of relief.

His study was a mess. It had been searched and they hadn't worried about keeping the search a secret. He sat down behind his desk, took off his left shoe and dug out the copied spells. He sat back and giggled. He hadn't really expected to live through his meeting but now that he had, he felt giddy.

He'd contact the rest of the conjurers once he'd settled back in. Then he'd search for Faelin. Starting with making friends with the fishmonger and his Rivermen suppliers.

Aric dropped the fish onto the table and slumped down onto the bench. He was still feeling the effects of whatever had happened to him when his mother died, but his stamina was returning. Not quickly enough, though. Simple tasks that needed to be done to keep them fed and safe took most of his strength, leaving him little energy for the shaman books. He dragged one of the books over and opened it. But he had to; he had to understand what powers he might have.

He looked up when Fae stepped into the small room.

"I'll clean the fish," she said. "And make lunch. You keep reading."

He nodded and returned his gaze to the page in front of him. The quiet sounds of Fae working lulled him as he tried to concentrate on the words in front of him.

He was still reading Zevach's tale—the story of the last male shaman. Similar to Fae's journal, the man who wrote it was trying to preserve his knowledge for the future. Unlike Fae's ancestor,

Zevach had *known* that another male shaman would exist.

"I have spent much time searching the future," he wrote early on. *"Generations will pass but another male shaman will be born. This I have seen. It gives me great hope, and great despair. For with none to teach, how will this man learn what he needs to learn? How will he become what he needs to become?"*

A few pages later, Aric sat up. *"I am certain Osred Wailes' curse affected the conjurers. In the years since, no shaman has had a son and no conjurer has fathered a child. I do not know if I should take credit or blame. Osred's hate was so intense, and his power so great, that his spell was split into two. I sensed that the intent was to do great harm and was able to take hold of the magic of the first half of the spell and redirect some of it back onto the conjurers."*

"Fae," Aric said.

Fae came up beside him, wiping her hands on a towel.

"The curse," he said. "The Wailes curse. Zevach somehow altered it to include the conjurers. He thinks that's the reason why they could no longer have children." He pointed to the page.

"But it didn't affect Keetley Kellen and his descendants," she said. "Maybe it only afflicted those doing a lot of magic." Fae leaned over the page. "And he did something to the spell *while* it was being cast," she said. "Is that a shaman ability?"

"Maybe," Aric said. "My mother never said anything about sensing magic. It could be an ability tied to being male."

"Or maybe there just isn't enough real magic being done to be sensed," Fae said. "I can feel Kellen magic, but the spells being used are old and probably more powerful than anything the conjurers have used in generations." She straightened and frowned down at the book. "My journal doesn't mention being able to manipulate someone else's spell. *That* must be a shaman ability. I wonder if conjurers ever tried to do that—if they ever knew it was possible. Maybe I could do it? I mean, I can feel the spell and the person who's casting it. Maybe Zevach describes *how* he took hold of the magic?"

Aric scanned the rest of the page, and the one after. "I don't see anything here but I'll look for it," he said. "I still have more than half of this book to read, along with the other two."

"All right," Fae nodded. "We knew this would take time." She sighed and stepped away from the table.

Time, Aric repeated to himself. They had so little of it to spare. He bent his head back to the book, staring blankly at the words that scrawled across the page. Answers were here, he could feel it—he just had to find them.

Chapter Twenty-one

HEWITT HAD MUCH to do, but after being under Wailes' thumb for so long, more immediately, he needed to feel in control. So he took a few minutes to straighten his study and have a cup of tea.

He could see Conjurers Hall from his study window if he chose to look out it. He chose not to. Instead, he surveyed his study, taking pleasure in the neat rows of spell books that lined the shelves. They were useless, he knew that, but they had been his life's work up until now. Now he had a new task—a new purpose. And with Wailes' health failing he had a real chance of realizing it.

The question was whether his fellow conjurers would embrace his goal. Would they want to restore conjurers to glory when that glory could never be theirs, or would they simply want to hide with their useless books and be shadows of the men whose names they bore?

It was time to find out.

ROTH SHERSTON CRACKED the door open a sliver. Hewitt knew it was Sherston because he could see dirty bandages covering the man's eyes. Was the man completely blind since seeing Dabel die?

"Sherston, it's me, Hewitt. Let me in."

"Hewitt, we thought you were dead." Sherston sniffed once, loudly, before opening the door wider. "It smells like you. Come in and be quick."

Hewitt slipped into the house and strode down the dark hallway. He heard the door close behind him and the shuffling steps of Sherston as he followed him. The study was on his left and he almost gasped when he walked into it.

If this is what the conjurers who were left were reduced to they might not be of any help to him, he thought as he picked his way through the clutter on the floor to a small chair.

Sherston unerringly walked through the scattered items to sit behind the desk.

"Excuse the mess," he said. "It's my own system. I know exactly where everything is but an intruder would stumble."

"Have you had intruders?" Hewitt asked. He was relieved that Sherston at least seemed interested in surviving.

"Not since poor Dabel died," Sherston said. "Since I can no longer see to read, I am of no use to Wailes."

"Ah, yes," Hewitt replied. "Be thankful for small mercies."

"Mercy! Dabel is dead and the rest of us are living under threat of death," Sherston said. "There is no mercy in Quillan Wailes."

"Then you'll be glad to hear that he is dying," Hewitt said. "He can no longer turn the page of a book and now he is losing his ability to speak. He won't last more than a few weeks."

"Unless he finds a cure in those books he has."

"It's possible, but unlikely," Hewitt said. "You know what happened to Dabel. The same thing has happened to more than a few of Wailes' apprentices."

"Reduced to ash," Sherston said. "I'll never forget it. There was barely even enough of the man left to do a proper ceremony."

"Yes," Hewitt said. The same had happened to the lad he'd thought was a Kellen. Just a small pile of ash. "Wailes kept me locked up at Conjurers Hall. Has he forced any of the rest of them to read?"

"He tried," Sherston said, and he seemed to deflate. "Dabel's apprentice, Gerick? He's dead. He refused to recite a spell and Wailes' Bridger killed him."

"Shiv." Hewitt nodded. "I saw him do the same to one of Wailes' apprentices."

"At least Gerick was included in Dabel's ceremony," Sherston said. "Wailes allowed us that much."

"I see," Hewitt said. Did Wailes want at least some of the conjurers alive? In case Hewitt proved uncooperative?

"Hewitt," a voice said from behind him.

He turned, startled. It was Maykin, and behind him stood Tadlow.

"Another one of my systems," Sherston said. "I left a cloth in my window to alert those I trust that someone was here." The other two entered the room, found chairs, and dragged them forward.

"It's not that we think we can save each other," Maykin said. He sat down facing Hewitt, his large, misshapen head silhouetted against the covered window. "But we want to know *what* has happened if one of us disappears."

Tadlow pushed his chair beside Maykin's, careful not to touch anything. The hand on the chair was scabbed but Hewitt could see patches of raw, red skin.

"Has anyone else been lost?" Hewitt asked. The other three conjurers sat in a half circle with him in the middle.

"Not yet," Maykin said.

"Hewitt claims Wailes is dying," Sherston said.

"Wailes has been dying for years," Tadlow said. "That's what caused this."

"I last saw him this morning," Hewitt said. "He can barely speak anymore. He's dying—and his Bridger knows it. That's why I'm out here." He paused. "Shiv knows he can't afford to kill too many of us. Not and have his people be allowed to live on the bridge once Wailes is dead."

"But he did kill Gerick," Sherston said.

"Wailes killed Gerick," Hewitt said. "And Dabel and Thorpe and probably more than half a dozen others. He is obsessed with using the spells in those books."

"Books?" Maykin asked. "I thought there was only one?"

"There are so many more," Hewitt said. "It was the bookbinder. He was copying our spell books. He and all the bookbinders before him."

It took more than an hour to tell his tale—at least as much of it as he wanted to. He didn't say anything about Faelin being a Kellen conjurer, or his own attempt to find another one.

"So you've been deciphering the spells so that these other poor souls could recite them and die," Sherston said. "How do you live with yourself?"

"We all want to live," Maykin said. "I want to know *why* Wailes let *you* live."

"The same reason he wanted Dabel to read from the book of spells," Hewitt replied calmly. He would not be baited into a discussion over whether he should have refused Wailes' request and died—like Gerick. "I have some familiarity with the archaic forms of the language. And Wailes' eyesight is failing him."

"So he has not read this journal you talk about?" Maykin asked. "He's had to take your word for what was in it?"

"Yes," Hewitt replied. "You know far more of the truth in the journal than Wailes does."

"But not all of it," Maykin said.

He stared at Hewitt and Hewitt met his gaze calmly. Maykin finally looked away and Hewitt hid a smile. Maykin might be far shrewder than expected. He might be the right ally for him.

HEWITT PAUSED IN front of Sherston's door. He took a deep breath, enjoying the sun on his face.

"There is more in the journal." It was Maykin.

Hewitt had thought the man had gone home, but he must have been waiting for him. "Come with me," Hewitt said and led them across the street to his home.

He let Maykin get comfortable as he made tea. When he brought it into his study, the other conjurer was staring at his books.

"In the past you would never have trusted your spell books to another," Maykin said.

"That was before I knew how worthless they are," Hewitt said. He put the tea on the desk and poured two cups. He sat down behind his desk while Maykin took the chair across from him.

"And yet you still keep them," Maykin said.

"They are still spells," Hewitt said. He took a sheaf of papers out of his pocket. "Just not as powerful as these." He tossed the papers on the desk and Maykin stared at them.

"They won't hurt you unless you recite them," Hewitt said.

"Then they are of no use. Unless you mean to force me to say them."

"No," Hewitt said. "And the spells are of use—to one who can recite them and live."

"Which is no one," Maykin replied. "You said yourself that Wailes has killed more than half a dozen people this way."

"He has not found one who can recite them," Hewitt replied. "Because he doesn't know what to look for."

"And you do?"

"Yes."

Maykin leaned forward. "I believe you do," he said. "At least, I believe *you* believe you do. Which is not the same thing." He leaned back in his chair. "Why tell me this?"

"You impressed me today," Hewitt said. "We have not had many dealings in the past and I was struck by your practical grasp of the current circumstances. And my time with Wailes has convinced me that I need an ally."

"What do I get out of it?"

Maykin's question made Hewitt smile. A man who had a price was a man he could bargain with. "You can be part of bringing conjurers back to greatness, of helping real magic return to the bridge."

"How will that help me?"

"Ah, that is the wrong question," Hewitt said. "You need to ask yourself what will happen to you if I can do this without you. Where will your place be when magic is restored? When I control real magic, you can too."

"I don't want to control magic," Maykin said. "I want to be rid of this deformity." He lifted his hand to his lumpy head and frowned. "I was forced into this life by a father who gave me no choice. I haven't done a spell since old Maykin died because I don't want to become any more grotesque than I already am."

"None of us do," Hewitt replied, raising his own oversized hands. "Real magic will allow us to cure ourselves."

"That's what Wailes is trying to do," Maykin said.

"Yes," Hewitt said. "But he doesn't know what I know."

"Tell me," Maykin said.

"Will you help?" Hewitt asked. "Will you keep this information from the others until I have what we need? I cannot trust them all and this cannot get back to Wailes."

"Yes," Maykin agreed. "As long as you promise to help me cure my affliction."

Hewitt considered the other conjurer. He had to chance it. Wailes wasn't dead yet—the man had already lived longer than Hewitt had thought possible. And while he lived, he controlled the Bridgers.

"The bookbinder's daughter," he said. "Faelin Keetley carries the blood of true conjurers. She can recite these spells."

HEWITT SAT IN his study as the day turned to dusk and then to night. Shiv hadn't come looking for him so obviously Maykin hadn't betrayed him to Wailes. Perhaps he wouldn't.

Maykin had been stunned but thoughtful when he'd told him that the ability to do magic was inherited. But once again Maykin surprised him.

The man truly didn't care about restoring conjurers to glory or about using magic to his own gain. All he wanted was to cure his affliction.

He'd agreed to visit the fishmonger and try to talk to the Rivermen—a task that was bound to make Wailes nervous if Hewitt was seen doing it. But Maykin already had a relationship with the fishmonger—they were second cousins—so keeping him company when he went to secure his catch wouldn't be suspicious.

With any luck, Maykin would be able to find out where Faelin was.

ARIC BOLTED AWAKE and shivered, despite the warmth of Fae sleeping beside him. Something was happening—or was about to happen. He dragged a hand through his hair. He wished he could tell which of his shaman abilities had been triggered.

"Fae," he whispered. "Wake up." She turned and snuggled deeper into his shoulder, and he almost let her sleep.

"Fae." He said it louder and slipped his arm out from under her.

"Aric?"

"Something's . . . wrong," he said. He propped himself against the boat hull and concentrated on what he was sensing. "We're not in danger—at least it's not immediate."

"But it's something that will be dangerous?" Fae asked. She sounded awake now.

He drew back the covering from the window. Dawn, it looked

like. Or almost. In the dim light, Fae faced him.

"Yes," he agreed. "Something that will be dangerous."

"What do we do?"

"We wait," Aric said. He pulled her against him. "And hope whatever it is happens in the next few hours and not the next few days."

They only had to wait an hour. Aric was in the middle of an internal debate over whether or not to get up while Fae dozed, her head on his shoulder. He had just enough time to shake her awake before he felt it.

A blast of power washed over him. Fae gasped and then it was gone, leaving a pounding headache.

"A Kellen spell?" he asked.

"No," Fae replied. "At least I don't think so. But they died." She turned sad eyes to him. "The person who recited the spell. They died."

"I felt that too," Aric said. He sighed. "At least they went quick."

"In the end," Fae replied. "We have no idea what torment Wailes put them through to make them recite a spell that will kill them."

"No, we don't." And Aric had to admit that he didn't want to know. "But it wasn't a Kellen spell." Fae nodded. "Yet you felt it." Another nod.

He scrambled across the bed and grabbed the journal. He flipped through to the page he'd been reading last night before Fae had come to bed and distracted him.

"Here." He pointed to a line on the page. "Zevach talks about feeling another spell, but he doesn't distinguish between the names of the casters. I think he could feel *all* spells. At least all spells of a certain power."

"But why did I feel it?" Fae asked. "Keetley Kellen only felt Kellen magic."

"I'm not sure," Aric said. He turned to her. "But I think another spell is going to be recited." Unconsciously, he grabbed her hands and drew in a deep breath. Then the magic hit him. He met Fae's eyes and she nodded, her brows furrowed in concentration. A moment later they were blown apart. Aric flew against the hull and Fae's hands slipped through his. He heard her yelp and he scrambled to his knees. She was sprawled at the foot of the bed.

"What happened?" she asked.

Gently, he helped her sit up.

"You tried to do something," he said, trying to keep any accusation from his voice. "What was it?"

"I tried to do what Zevach did," Fae said. "I tried to take hold of the magic."

"I guess it didn't work," Aric said. He rubbed his head. There would be a lump where he'd hit the hull. "But if you did that, why was I hit with the backlash?"

"I think for the same reason I was able to feel a non-Kellen spell," Fae said. "We were touching."

"What?"

"You grabbed my hands, just before the second spell, you grabbed my hands."

"I did," Aric said. "I didn't even think about it."

"And you got the backlash." Her smile was apologetic. "The backlash I caused."

He wrapped an arm around her. "It was worth it," he said. "Now we know that if we are together, touching, we can combine our talents." He rubbed his head again. "Next time we need to make sure we're ready . . ." His thoughts trailed off as a wave of premonition flowed over him. "Fae." His voice sounded strangled even to him. "This is what we've been waiting for."

He felt Fae lean into his shoulder as power swept over them and then it was gone. He shook his head and met her gaze.

"This was different," he said, and she nodded solemnly.

"Yes," Fae said, and he felt her shiver against him. "This time they lived."

Chapter Twenty-two

HEWITT FROWNED AND leaned out the window. It was Shiv. What did he want so early in the morning? He quickly dressed and shuffled down the stairs, careful not to let his oversized feet slip on a tread.

"What does he want now?" he asked when he opened the door. Then he took a step back in alarm. Shiv's face was white. Was it worry or fear? Hewitt couldn't imagine it would be fear.

"You have to come now," Shiv said. "They're both asking for you." The Bridger took off across the street, not bothering to wait to see if Hewitt was following.

"Both who?" Hewitt mumbled under his breath as he hurried towards Conjurers Hall. There was a single Bridger at the open door. He stepped aside and let Hewitt enter, closing the door after him.

It took a few moments to navigate the narrow halls, but then he was at the open door of Wailes' study. A woman stood just inside the door.

"Oleda Burrage?" Hewitt said. "Is that you?"

She turned to give him a cool glance but when she recognized him, she smiled. Triumphantly, Hewitt thought in surprise.

"Finally, a conjurer who treated me with some respect," Oleda said. She turned to face someone in the room. "Conjurer Hewitt is here."

Hewitt nodded to Oleda and stepped into the room.

"Conjurer Hewitt," Graylon Burrage said. "Thank you for coming." He took a step forward. "I asked Shiv to fetch you. Wailes agreed." He looked over his shoulder and Hewitt followed his gaze to Wailes, who was slumped over in his chair. Tymm crouched beside him, whimpering.

Hewitt stepped forward, taking in the table scattered with three books, the two bodies that lay on the floor, each one exhibiting an extreme conjurer affliction. And the way Shiv's eyes darted from Burrage to Wailes and back to Burrage.

Hewitt smiled at Burrage. "You survived! Well done!"

"See, Mother," Burrage said. "I told you he hoped I would live."

"Of course, my boy," Hewitt said. He would have wanted any of them to live. Only a single, live conjurer was required to control the bridge. Hewitt turned his gaze to Shiv. "Is Wailes conscious enough to understand what this means?"

The Bridger shook his head. "He agreed that I should fetch you but hasn't said a word since."

"*I* don't know what it means," Burrage said. "That's why you're here. You told me not to read from any other book if I survived once. Why?"

"Because reciting spells from a book bound in a different hide will kill you," Hewitt replied. He stepped over to the table and ran his hands across the covers of the three books there. "Which one was it?" And what did the spell do, he wondered?

"The one on the end," Burrage said. "The dark grey one."

"This one?" Hewitt picked the book up. "You're sure? Your life depends upon it." Burrage nodded and Hewitt flipped the book open.

"What are you smiling at?" Shiv asked.

"Am I smiling?" Hewitt replied. "I hadn't noticed." He gently closed the book and ran a hand across the cover before turning and handing the book to Burrage. "The binding is shark skin. You can never recite a spell from a book bound in anything else." He looked past Burrage to Wailes. The man's eyes were open and now Hewitt did smile. "Open it to any page, lad. And be prepared to recite. It seems that you are a true Wailes conjurer. One with real power."

"You mean I can do magic?" Burrage asked. "I can use any spell in this book?"

"Yes, you can do real magic," Hewitt replied. "And there are many more books of spells you can use. Dozens more." He almost clapped his hands together, he was so excited. A true conjurer! And one who valued his advice. He would keep looking for Faelin, of course, he didn't know Graylon Burrage very well, and he thought the mother was rather opportunistic. But it would be better to have two conjurers rather than one.

FAE TRIED TO concentrate on the spell she was creating—on putting words in the correct order to produce the base intent of the spell. When she added a word that fit, she could *feel* the magic build around her. One more word.

She sighed and looked over at Aric. He was bent over his own task of reading the three shaman books. It was slow—he wasn't as good a reader as she was—but at least he didn't have to deal with figuring out the archaic wording. Keetley Kellen's journal listed many of the most common words used in casting spells, but it wasn't complete. She sighed again. What if she simply used current words? At least with them she would be sure of the meaning. And really, the archaic words had been the current language at one time.

"I'm going up on deck," she said to Aric. He looked up and smiled before dropping his eyes to the page in front of him.

Fae climbed the steps and ducked through the doorway. It was afternoon and the sun was high in the sky. A breeze blew in from the south, lifting her hair off her neck. She closed her eyes for a moment, enjoying the coolness on her skin and the soft sway of the boat as it rose and fell with the swells. She opened her eyes and squinted as she looked north, toward land. Trees lined a beach, and off to her left was the wide mouth of the Aberhayle.

If she asked him, Aric would sail them far away. They could leave the bridge and conjurers and Rivermen behind. Let them fight their own wars—she and Aric could start over somewhere else. It was tempting. Aric was the only one she truly cared for, and now that his mother was dead the Rivermen had less of a hold on him.

But it would be wrong. They would be leaving people in

danger—people who had done nothing wrong, people who simply wanted to live their lives. And the Wailes curse hung over not just Aric's head but hers as well. Who knew what would happen to either of them if the curse was completed?

And there was another conjurer. She and Aric had both felt someone live through a spell casting. And they'd felt nothing since. Did the conjurer know enough to not cast a spell from a different line of conjurers? Had Hewitt or Wailes read Keetley Kellen's journal? She had to assume someone had.

She shook her head and sat down with her back against the cabin. They couldn't run—there was no escape from the curse. So they needed to understand their strengths, she and Aric.

And they might need to try to contact Hewitt. She hadn't mentioned it to Aric but Hewitt was the only one who might know what had happened—who might know who the conjurer was. She was hoping that Aric would have some premonition or feeling about it and tell her they needed to talk to Hewitt, but she wasn't sure she could wait that long.

She put everything out of her mind and closed her eyes. A small spell to start, but what? Keetley Kellen suggested fire, but Fae didn't think that was safe on a boat. Or the bridge, for that matter. Water? She looked around—she had all the water she could want. But she could . . .

She jumped to her feet, grabbed a bucket and lowered it to the sea by the rope. When she pulled it back up, she dipped a hand into and licked her finger, tasting the salt.

Now to turn it into drinkable water. She closed her eyes and thought about the words she would use and the placement of those words for a spell that was a *remove* spell. Nothing archaic, just concentrating on normal, everyday words. She felt a small spurt of magic and opened her eyes.

She leaned over the bucket. It was empty. She peered closer. Except for a small dusting of white at the bottom of the bucket. She reached in and dragged a finger through it before holding it up. Tentatively she tasted it. Salt. She'd done a remove spell, but not exactly the way she'd wanted. She sighed and stood up. They could use the salt. But she still had to learn how to create the correct spell.

She went inside to find a container for the salt.

"Fae," Aric called. "I think I found some . . . instructions on how to manipulate magic. See here?" He pointed to a page and she leaned over to read it. "I think it's talking about what you said earlier—a base spell? Although Zevach calls it the intent."

"Once you know the intent of a spell, you can change the focus," she read. She looked up at him. "But how do you figure out the intent of the spell?"

"That's a shaman ability," Aric replied. "Part of the feeling I have about magic." He frowned. "Apparently it's a very difficult skill to master. Only Zevach and one other shaman were ever able to do this."

"Does practice help?" Fae asked. "I mean, can feeling regular spells help you determine the intent of any spell?"

"I suppose so," Aric replied.

"Then you can practice with me. I have a lot of spell casting to learn and you have a lot of spell deciphering to learn." She picked the bucket up off the table and found a bowl to dump the salt into.

"Come on, I am not spending the rest of the afternoon inside."

ARIC STIFLED A yawn and wiped the sweat from his forehead. He and Fae had been at this for hours and they were both improving, but it was slow. He shook his head. To anyone watching it would look like they were simply sitting on deck, staring at different objects. It had been the bucket until Fae had mastered a spell to remove the salt and keep the water. He'd understood the intent of the spell before she'd mastered it—but then, he'd known from the start what she had been trying to do. Now she was doing something else with water and he had to try to figure out what she wanted before she told him. Hopefully before she could actually do it.

Fae waved and he sat up straight, concentrating on the magic. He couldn't see it, not exactly, but he could feel the waves it made in the air around them, rolling and twisting and trying to . . . "Solidify," he said abruptly. "It's a spell to solidify the water—in this case to freeze it."

"Yes," Fae replied not looking at him. "Now all I need to do is complete it."

There was a burst of magical energy and she slumped over. She dragged the bucket towards her and peered inside. She smiled and turned to him. "I did it!" She pushed the bucket onto its side and rolled the opening towards him. "It's frozen."

Aric could see the solid surface of the ice from where he sat. "Can we make something cold to drink with that?"

"Yes." Fae jumped up and disappeared into the cabin. A few moments later she returned with two mugs and a knife. She chopped at the surface of the ice, grabbed a few shards and put them in the mugs. She carried them over to Aric, handed him one, and sat down.

"We had tea left from this morning," she said. "I thought it might be nicer than just water." She took a sip and Aric followed suit.

The cold liquid puckered his mouth but it was refreshing all the same.

"I should catch us something for dinner," he said. "We completely missed lunch."

"All right." Fae sighed and leaned her head against his, and he breathed in her fresh scent. "I'm too tired to do much more anyway. I wouldn't have guessed using magic would be so exhausting."

"I don't think it's the magic," Aric said. "I think it's from concentrating so hard. I felt like this every day when you were teaching me to read."

"You did? You never said anything."

"I was twelve," Aric replied. "And I wanted to impress you. I wasn't about to complain about being tired."

"I was impressed," Fae said.

Aric knew Fae was speaking but he couldn't hear her. His fingers lost their grip on his mug, and it slipped to the deck, spilling the cold tea on his bare foot.

"Aric?" It was Fae, shaking him. He tried to turn to her, tried to answer, but all he could do was moan. And then it was over. He sucked in a breath and time went back to normal.

"I'm all right," he gasped. "I'm all right." He met Fae's eyes. There was worry in them, and fear. "What?"

"You spoke," she said. "Do you remember?"

He shook his head. "I tried to speak. At least that's what it felt like to me. What did I say?"

"The same as before, that powers on the bridge are building," she said. "Then you added that Wailes must be stopped." She paused. "But we already know that."

"Do we?" Aric said. He didn't remember saying those words,

but repeated back to him, they sent a chill down his spine. "Wailes is only a threat if he can find someone to finish the curse."

"You think this new conjurer is a Wailes?" Fae asked.

Aric closed his eyes and tried to sort through his feelings. It was hard to know what was a shaman warning and what was simply a gut reaction. Was there even a difference? It didn't matter—both were screaming that what Fae said was true. The newly discovered conjurer carried Wailes blood. And could complete the curse and change the Rivermen forever.

And that they had to stop.

To Be Concluded in
The Shaman's Son
Coming Summer 2017

About the Author

Jane Glatt loves that along with creating original worlds, writing fantasy allows her to indulge her curiosity about an eclectic group of subjects. So far she's researched synesthesia, medieval guilds, tidal rivers, cities atop bridges, pirates and privateers, plants used for healing and the history of spying. For that last one she blames a visit to the International Spy Museum (yes it's a real place), in Washington D.C.

For news on Jane's future releases visit her website http://janeglatt.com/index.html and sign up for her newsletter.